HALF

ELI LANG

RIPTIDE
PUBLISHING

Riptide Publishing
PO Box 1537
Burnsville, NC 28714
www.riptidepublishing.com

Half

Cover art: G.D. Leigh, blackjazzdesign.com
Editor: Sarah Lyons
Layout: L.C. Chase, lcchase.com/design.htm

ISBN: 978-1-62649-520-3

First edition
February, 2017

Also available in ebook:
ISBN: 978-1-62649-519-7

HALF

ELI LANG

RIPTIDE
PUBLISHING

For MLM—I miss you.

TABLE OF CONTENTS

CHAPTER 1

Sometimes, when the weather was just turning from autumn to winter, and the last of the late fruit was clinging to the trees, we partied in the apple orchard. The stories always talk about fey partying, and mostly those stories are true. The fey love a good revelry. They love the music and the fire and the food and the complete abandon of it all. And the apple orchard was as good a place as any to do it. It belonged to my father, and I'd laid the glamour on it myself. It was hidden, tucked away, the perfect place to get lost, let go.

Most nights when I went to the fey parties, I enjoyed myself. Everyone pretended a bit at those gatherings. I could be someone else there. Or no one. I got a few sideways glances, and most of the fey still kept their distance. But I could be lesser there. Or more. The fey let me pretend for a while that I was a whole thing, not a creature living in two worlds. That I wasn't my father's son. I loved being able to disappear into the fey, become invisible. There was a freedom in it I found almost nowhere else.

But sometimes, I hated them. Sometimes even the sneakiest glances were like weights, levered against me. Sometimes I didn't want to be anywhere near the fey, didn't want to spend my midnight hours in the middle of a cold, damp apple orchard, no matter how beautiful the music was. No matter how much I liked the way the bonfire turned the trees' branches red and gold. Sometimes I just wanted to be home, curled in my bed, warm and alone and safe. But some of the fey found it easier to deliver messages to me here, make requests, and it was my job to listen.

I stood at the edge of the lit area, close enough that I could see the fire in the middle of the little clearing, but deep enough into the dark between the trees that no one tried to pull me forward to dance. I switched from resting on one foot to the other. The ground was frosted over, the weather far colder than it should have been for this time of year, for this place. Even my leather boots couldn't keep the chill from seeping in, not when I was standing still like this, away from the warmth of the fire and the fey, my back against the old tree's gnarled trunk.

A tiny woman appeared at my elbow. Her head barely came up to the middle of my chest, and I was not a tall man. Her hair was a wild puff of blond curls, frizzy and disarrayed but downy. The way it fell over her shoulders, soft and flyaway, made me want to touch it. She wore a thick sweater, holes here and there in the weave of it letting the cold air in. Her feet were bare.

"You should dance," she said, her voice high and breathy. She ran a hand down my arm, her fingers stretching like claws over the leather of my jacket, catching on it the same way the bark at my back did.

I shook my head. "What do you need?"

She turned her face away and watched the dancers. For a long time, she said nothing, but I didn't need to remind myself to be patient. I was used to the way the fey got distracted, lost track of conversations. I waited, letting my body go still so she wouldn't think I was restless.

"Saben wants you," she said at last, her voice rising and falling in strange places. "And I need two copper pocketknives."

I sighed and ran a hand through my hair. "What for?"

The woman turned her head and smiled at me, her eyes just a tiny bit unfocused. "For coring apples."

I didn't get any more out of her after that. Her mind was caught in the music, in the flutes and fiddles and the pulsing beat of the drums. I glanced around for Saben, but either her messenger had mixed up her times, or Saben hadn't bothered to wait for me, because she wasn't there. I admit I didn't search too hard. I wanted to leave.

I didn't go straight home, though. I had to drive through the center of the city to get back to my house, tucked out of the way and far from my father like it was. It was the weekend, and the streets were packed, people walking to and from clubs and bars and restaurants, arms around each other, faces lit up, maybe a bit rosy-cheeked from drinks. It all seemed so far away from me. I was still wrapped up in the fey, their music stuck in my mind, calling to me, just like it'd called to Saben's messenger.

I wanted to get it out of my head, the lot of it. I found a place to park, not far from a few of the clubs. I picked one at random and ducked inside. The room opened onto a bar and a few tables. There was another door off to the side, a bouncer standing in front of it. I paid him the cover, and he opened the door so I could walk down a steep set of stairs, narrow slats that caught at my boots. I stopped halfway down, squashing myself to one side so I wouldn't block anyone, and glanced around the room.

It was darker down there, of course, and warmer. The shadows were highlighted with bright flashes of pink and purple and blue, sparks of light that came and went. They illuminated just enough that I could make out the mass of people, all tangled together on the dance floor. The music was something thumpy and deep and electronic. It pushed at me, made my heart beat faster, but in a way that was totally different from the fey music. This sound, this place, wasn't forcing me into anything. I was being asked.

I wasn't sure that I had the energy to join the crowd, but I wanted to be near them, near all that humanity. I made my way down the rest of the stairs and around the edge of the dancers, dodging people who were too lost in themselves to watch where they were dancing. I found an empty spot against one wall, and I tucked myself into it, pressing my back against the concrete. Blending in so I could watch. So I could lose myself in a completely different way than I usually did with the fey.

I let my gaze drift around the room, stopping whenever I saw someone who caught my attention. There were fey here too. I'd expected it—they loved to party, no matter where the party was taking place, and there were more than a few who had no problem interacting with the human world. No humans would notice if they weren't searching for something out of the ordinary. The fey glamours were good. But my eyes snagged on hair that was too feathery, glittery skin, the soft flutter of wings, all of which could have been a costume or my imagination, but weren't. I ignored them. They didn't really matter anyway. They weren't there to see me, and I wasn't there to see them. And this place, for once, was more my world than theirs.

I swayed back and forth with the music and the flickering lights. The crowd moved in a lazy way, and I watched them in a lazy sort of way. I wasn't looking for anyone in particular, didn't even expect to stay long. I just wanted to be part, even a fringe part, of something different, for a few minutes.

My eyes snagged on a bright-blue shimmer. I turned my head, searching for whatever it was I'd seen, that deep-aqua light. It sparkled again, and I saw the boy, the man, it had come from. He was maybe a bit taller than me, his skin lightly tanned, his hair long and black and straight, loose over his shoulders. The sparkle had come from the flecks of glittery color at the corners of his eyes, across one cheekbone, down the side of his neck. He raised his hands over his head, and I saw splashes of green, shining and catching the lights of the club.

If I hadn't known, if I wasn't always so aware of things that were different, I would have thought the shimmer was makeup or some elaborate jewelry. But I'd spotted the other fey in the crowd, and I knew this man was one too. I wanted to turn away. I'd come to get away from all things otherworldly, not to latch on to it, even in this indirect way. But I couldn't take my eyes off him. He was sleek and graceful and beautiful.

He didn't act like the other fey. Fey don't seem self-conscious, to the outside observer, but they are. They always want to be noticed, want someone to be staring at them, watching them, falling in love with them. Most of the fey I'd spotted in the club were either clustered together, doing their damnedest to attract attention, or they were wooing some poor unsuspecting human. Or both. But this man was solitary. He was dancing with his head thrown back, his eyes closed, his arms lifted. He didn't focus on anyone, and he danced by himself. He was in the middle of the crowd, and it was as if he was absorbing the energy of the music and the people around him through his skin, pulling it in, but he wasn't trying to move closer to anyone.

While I watched, a girl bumped into him. He opened his eyes and looked down at her, laughing and waving away her apology. She smiled back at him, and gestured to the gaggle of young men and women around her. An invitation if I'd ever seen one. But the man with the glitter on his skin smiled again, a little gentler, and shook his head. The girl shrugged and drifted back into the crowd. The man twisted his body, a sinuous flick of movement that pushed him in the opposite direction. While he drifted away, he glanced up, and his eyes met mine.

He didn't smile at me like he'd smiled at the girl. His shoulders went a little straighter, though, and he held my eyes. He was still swaying to the music. He should have had to break our stare sooner. But we watched each other for long seconds. I took him in, the black hair falling in his eyes, the slender line of his throat, the splashes of color across his skin. Scales, I thought. Like fish scales or snake scales, chips of blue and green and purple. He was as beautiful as I'd thought, lithe and elegant. I wondered if he'd keep staring at me. I wondered if he'd come over. Or if I'd go to him. I almost wanted to, wanted to press myself against him, feel the way he moved while he danced. My heart beat harder in my chest, hard enough that I could feel its rhythm over the thump of the music.

A group of people danced between us, blocking him from my view. I looked down, and when I looked back up, he was gone. I could have searched for him, waited until I caught sight of his colors again. But I didn't let myself. I shook my head and inched my way back around the crowd. I was tired and achy, and I'd seen something better than I'd planned. It was time to go.

My sister, Saben, was staying in an apartment near the outskirts of the city, where there was less iron in the air. It was still more iron than she could handle, and she didn't belong there, but she pretended it didn't matter. I didn't know why she was doing it. Maybe so she could prove something to me, or to our father, or to herself in her mind. It was all a guess to me, and it didn't matter much, anyway. She wasn't really any of my business.

When I got to her apartment, the door was ajar, and I pushed it open the rest of the way, letting myself in. Saben was standing in the kitchen. She spun toward me, no surprise on her face, like she'd already known it was me before she even saw me. Her arm lifted.

"What's this?" she asked, holding an object out to me.

I squinted at it. "A kettle." I couldn't blame her for not knowing. It was one of those artsy, modern types, with more angles than any kettle really needed. And the fey didn't really deal in kettles anyway.

She set it back down on the stove and watched me while I took in her apartment. It was small, just a tiny living room and kitchen, and a bedroom I couldn't see. I knew her rooms at our father's house weren't much bigger, but they felt bigger, more opulent and airy, the curtains always thrown open to catch a breeze, the puffed pillows pleasantly chilly when you lay down against them, the carpets thick and stark white. This place was cramped and dingy, gray, and a bit too warm with the afternoon sun coming in through the window. But Saben didn't seem to notice. She considered it with me, and although she didn't smile, her face lit up a little as if she actually liked what she saw.

"Where are the apples?" I asked. She squinted her eyes at me. I shook my head, dismissing the question. "I have the knives for your errand girl," I said, and pulled them from my pocket to put them on the counter.

"She said you wouldn't dance."

I flicked my eyebrows up. "I wouldn't."

"Luca."

"Saben. What do you want?"

She narrowed her eyes, her mouth clamping into a tight line, and I looked away. I remembered when she was small. I remembered when she was milk thistle fuzz I could hold in my hands. She had been soft and agreeable and I'd loved her.

"What?" I repeated.

She straightened her spine, stretching every vertebra, even though, as inadequate as my own height was, she would never quite reach it. The fact of my height didn't stop her from pretending we were eye to eye, though. "Father wants you to do something."

I didn't even need to listen to what it was. "Get one of your girls to do it," I answered right away. "Or one of your boys."

"You have to do it."

"Why?"

"It's not a job." Her voice was flat.

"What is it, then?" It hadn't always been this way between us. I hadn't always been forced to pry information out of her like I was pressing water from stone.

"He wants you to see someone. A witch." She frowned. "Or maybe not a witch. A healer. A person who fixes things."

I just kept myself from laughing. "A doctor?"

She shrugged, a short, sharp rise and fall of her shoulders. Her hand snuck out, and she touched the handle of one of the knives I'd laid on the counter. "No. Yokai."

"What?"

"Fey. From Japan. Father thinks he knows things our healers don't. He wants you to go."

I should have guessed. "Why didn't he tell me himself?"

Saben shrugged again, apparently uninterested in the question or the answer. "Busy."

Sometimes when we talked, when we were together, I thought she would act like a human. Normal. Sometimes I thought she'd take down her walls and smile at me, or touch my hand like she'd done as a child, or complete a sentence in a way that didn't drip with how high-class fey she was, with how different from me she was. But she never gave me an inch. She hadn't for a long time.

I turned my head to the side and coughed into my palm, and from the corner of my eye, I almost, almost thought I saw her face flicker out of its stillness. Her hand folded into her dress and twisted the soft fabric into a knot.

It was bad timing on my part, to cough right then. It meant I couldn't argue. Not when it was obvious that a person who fixed things was exactly what I needed.

I sighed and tried to figure out what to say to get myself out of this. "I told him I wasn't going to do this anymore. That when I came home, I was done." I'd been gone for years, had traveled pretty far, searching for healers, for answers. I hadn't spent all of that time searching, that was true. A lot of it had been spent living, because there wouldn't always be much time for me to do that. I'd spent those years getting lost, pretending I was someone else, someone whole in all the ways I was half. But I'd searched too. It was why I'd gone, and I had wanted an answer.

I hadn't made it to Japan. But I doubted that mattered. I'd come home because there wasn't anyone who could do what I needed. It didn't matter where they were from or what kind of healing they did. And there wasn't anywhere on the planet that could make me someone else, either. So I'd come back.

Saben's lips flattened into a thin line, and she glared at me, but I was used to that too.

"He wants you to go."

"Do you?"

She raised her eyes, too fast. I stared at her, waiting, but she didn't say anything. Didn't shrug or nod or shake her head. She just stared back at me.

"You want me to go," I said, slowly, "so you can tell him you did as he wanted and made me." Her eyes flickered away from mine at that, and I nodded. "You said it wasn't a job. But it is. It's a job for me. Right?"

She didn't answer, but it didn't matter. I would go, because she'd delivered me a message, and my job was to follow those messages, whatever they were. I wasn't her brother. *I* was her errand boy. I found her pocket knives to core apples with. I touched iron when her people couldn't. I told her about kettles. I did as she told me.

CHAPTER 2

S aben didn't know much about the healer at all, except that he was here in the city, that he'd come up from a short ways south, apparently because there was more for him to do here. That he was a yokai and a man. That my father had heard about him through whatever fey grapevine he was tapped into and decided I needed to go. She didn't know where this healer slept, where he lived, who he was aligned with in the fey world. She had set up a meeting through some of her people, the string of young fey who trailed around after her, so she'd never even spoken to him.

I was supposed to meet him in a park. It was a big park, with lots of tucked-away spots to get lost in, and it was neutral territory. Clever, but most fey were interested in taking care of themselves above all else, so it wasn't really surprising. Saben told me to go in the afternoon, didn't even give me a definitive time. That was more annoying than trucking it down to the park to see a fey I didn't even really want to meet, because I knew how fey worked, how they thought of time as this malleable thing they could play with. I knew there was every chance I'd show up, and the yokai wouldn't, and my day would be shot.

But on the other hand, it wasn't as if I had much else to do, either.

Saben had told me to walk to one end of the park, to a tiny pond with an even tinier waterfall. The spot was hidden behind a copse of trees, and it was chilly enough in the early evening that there weren't too many other people around. The pond had a small clearing around it, a flat stretch of grass between the trees and the water. I stood on the edge of the tree line, a glamour pulled around me to hide myself, and looked for the man I was supposed to meet.

I didn't see anything at first, and I figured I'd been right that he would be flighty, like all the other fey I knew, that he'd forget he was supposed to meet me, distracted by something more interesting. But then there was a short splash, a spray of water from the pond, and I realized a man was swimming to shore. He rose a little way out of the water, the sun sparkling off the droplets beading on his skin. His hair was black and slicked back, showing off the long planes of his face. He shook his head, brushed his hands down his arms. Then he stepped to the bank of the pond, out of the water. He stooped and picked up a long piece of cloth and draped it around his waist. It was almost like a skirt, but not quite.

I watched him for a second. There was something familiar about him, about the graceful way he moved. He bent forward again, picking up something else off the ground, and I saw a thick line of blue-green scales running down his back. I'd seen those same scales before—not on his back, but on his face and his wrists. In the club, with the lights bouncing off them and making them shine, while he tipped his head back and gave himself over to the music.

I didn't step out or call to him. I just dropped the minimal glamour I'd been holding, and the minute I did, he turned to where I was standing against the tree. I took a step forward.

Now that I was here, I wasn't sure what should happen next. I'd been planning to brush him off, to do whatever it'd take to make my father believe I'd completed his task, and leave. But now this man was staring at me, and I knew that he recognized me too, remembered me from that brief, sharp stare we'd shared the night before. He didn't make a move toward me, though. Didn't speak. He just stood there, his back straight, his chest bare, water dripping off the ends of his hair, wetting his cheeks and his jaw and the line of his shoulders. He was so regal, so strong and lovely, as lovely as when I first saw him.

I thought of Saben and my father, the icy, excruciatingly polite high-court fey that they were. Sidhe, same as I was. They used formality and manners as weapons, always had them to fall back on, and I could do the same here. I rested my hand, tucked into a fist, against my chest and bowed.

When I rose from it, the man stepped toward me. He faced me, his shoulders back, his hands loose at his sides. He was slender, maybe small by some standards, but standing there, he was like cut glass, like copper wire. It seemed as if he'd draw blood if I touched him. Scales shimmered unevenly over his skin—along his left cheekbone, down the right side of his neck, tapering to nothing over the first two knuckles of his right hand.

He made a small bow, not as deep as mine, in my direction. I waited.

"Did you come from the sidhe court?" His English was so flawless it had to be his first language.

"You're not Japanese." I'd expected him to have a foreign accent, to be from somewhere that wasn't here, but it didn't sound like he'd come from farther than the next county over.

He shook his head once and clicked his tongue. "You're not fey."

"Not completely." There was a part of me that wanted to jerk my chin up, to face him squarely, to beat him back with what I *was*. But I couldn't make myself do it. He was right. I hesitated, then nodded. "I came from the court of the sidhe. My father sent me to see you. He thought . . ." I studied him, this man, tilted my head and ran my eyes from head to toe. He looked like a warrior. Not a healer. But he stayed still and let me stare, let me judge him, and it made me feel . . . better. Safer. "He thought you could help me."

"But you don't," he said, and there wasn't a question behind the words. It was just a statement.

I shook my head. "I've looked. I've been looking a long time."

He nodded again. "Your court told me something about you. Not much."

"Then you know," I said, and right then, with perfect timing again, my breath caught and I coughed.

It wasn't a little cough that I could contain, like it had been at Saben's apartment. It was a thing that tightened and twisted and grew inside me, so that the more I coughed, the worse it was, until I thought I might expel something important. Like a lung. It hurt, deep in my chest, but the pain was a distant thing, because I couldn't breathe, couldn't get any air in, and the panic over that blocked out every other thing in my mind. I clapped a hand over my mouth, trying to stop myself, to get control, but then I had to double over. I reached out with my other hand, blind, searching for the tree I'd been leaning against, for anything I could use to keep myself upright.

A hand cupped my elbow, and an arm wrapped around my waist, steadying me.

"Breathe through your nose." His voice was so deep, so even, right by my ear. He was holding me up, his hands strong on me, and knowing I wasn't about to go down let me calm myself enough that I could try to do as he said.

"Breathe," he repeated. "In. Count." He started counting, then breathed in with me when I did. I coughed again, but he was patient, waited, and then started counting and breathing with me again. His palm skated over my back, soothing. His touch made me want to shiver, made me want to lean into it, but I couldn't think about it, do anything about it, while I was coughing.

It took me a few long minutes, but the coughing subsided. It always did. I knew it would. It was just frightening while it happened. I straightened, and he stepped away from me.

I pulled my hand from my mouth and wiped it on my jeans. My fingers left a rust-red streak on the fabric. I covered the spot with my palm.

"What was that?" he asked, waving his hand as if trying to encompass the coughing fit and the spot I was covering.

"My blood."

His jaw clenched. "I can see that."

But I hadn't meant it quite so literally. I meant that the coughing and the illness and the tiny streak of red under my hand were a product of my blood, my DNA. It was a product of who I was. "It's the fey blood. The glamour, the longevity, the magic, whatever you want to call it. I don't even really know. My fey half. It eats at my human half."

He sighed, and I didn't like how resigned it sounded. "It's poisoning you."

I raised my eyebrows and shrugged. "They didn't tell you much about me, did they?" I was surprised, a bit. My father's court knew about me, the oddity, the half creature that shouldn't exist, and they liked to gossip about me amongst themselves. Maybe not so much with outsiders, though.

"No." He raised a hand and pushed his hair back. It had started to dry, the shorter pieces in front falling into his face. "Just that you were sick." He ran his gaze over my face, and I knew what he was trying to find. The markers, the things that would tell him what I was. The way my hair was a strange reddish-orange—fey. The lavender gray of my eyes—fey. The too-sharp points of my features, my relatively short stature, my pale freckles—all human. "They didn't tell me you were half."

"I'm a secret." He was still staring at me, and there was something in his eyes that I thought was fear. I might have thought he was afraid of me, if my ego was large enough. But my ego wasn't, and even though I didn't know him, it was obvious by the power in his body and the way he held himself that he didn't have anything to fear from me. And I wondered if maybe the fear had lodged in his face when I'd started coughing. If, even though he'd been so calm, I'd scared him by being so breakable.

"You're not really supposed to know. You're not supposed to know that a flawed thing like me was created. That my father made such a huge mistake as to fall in love with a human. No one talks about it. Or they shouldn't." I shrugged, very carefully. Just one small lift of my shoulder so I wouldn't set myself coughing again. I wasn't a very well-kept secret, but I was a secret nonetheless.

He pulled at the top of his skirt thing, and the fabric spread and unfolded, into an attached jacket he could shrug on—a kimono. He stuffed his hands through the arms and tightened the belt around his waist.

"Is it just your lungs?" He reached behind him while he asked, gathering his hair into a ponytail at the base of his neck. He dug into a pocket and came out with a tie to secure it.

I moved my head in something between a nod and a shake. That was a bigger and smaller question than he knew.

He opened his mouth and turned square to face me, like he was getting ready to coerce me into telling him, but then he paused. "What's your name?" he asked instead.

I was surprised, because most fey don't ask and don't offer. A name can be useful, powerful, and it's not something to give away lightly. But I'd grown up in the human world, for the most part, and I liked that he wanted to know. "Luca," I told him.

"Sounds fey."

I shrugged. "My mother picked it."

He nodded. "And your mother is . . .?"

"Human," I finished for him, the word clipped. I wanted to take in a deep breath, steady myself, but I was afraid that would start the coughing all over again. "Was."

His face softened a little. "I'm sorry."

I shrugged, brushing it off. "And your name?"

"Kin."

"Kin," I repeated. I wrapped my arms around myself. The sun was starting to sink, and it seemed like it was getting colder by the second. "I'd like to sit down. In my car. Where it's warm." I probably sounded too abrupt, rude, but the coughing spell had drained me, and I couldn't make myself be more polite. "So if you could . . ." I shrugged, because I wasn't sure what I wanted from him.

The thing is, I'd been to dozens of doctors and healers and witch workers and shamans, human and fey. At first it had just been about trying to figure out what was happening. Then, as my sickness had gotten worse, it'd been about searching for a cure. My parents had been desperate when I was a child, and I hadn't even been that sick yet. After I graduated high school and my mother died, my father sent me away. He couldn't leave the city and his court. But he'd wanted me to keep searching. And for a long time, I'd wanted to keep searching too. I'd kept thinking that there must be someone out there who'd seen what it was I had, who knew someone like me. Who had an answer. Or even just something that would make me feel better. That would mean I didn't have to be sick all the time.

It takes a long time for hope to dissolve. Long after I thought I couldn't feel it anymore, it kept popping up. And every time it did, it made the disappointment that followed worse. I couldn't quite get rid of the hope, though. Even now, even though Kin was standing in front of me, doing his best not to seem shocked at what I was and what that was doing to me, a little bubble swelled inside me that wanted to believe that maybe he'd be the one. That maybe this time, there would be an answer. So I didn't know what I wanted from him. If I wanted him to try. Or if I wanted him to stomp out that bubble before it could grow into something that would shatter me.

He pulled in a deep breath. "Come back with me. I can . . . I can see what I can do."

I should have refused him, stopped him right there. But he didn't sound sure that he really could do anything, and that made me want to go with him. It made me want to trust him, because at least he was being honest with me. And I remembered how solid he'd been, when he'd held me up and stopped me coughing. I remembered how ethereal and lovely and wild he'd been in the club.

I nodded.

CHAPTER 3

Kin said he could ride in my car. I didn't really believe him. I'd never met a fey who would willingly get in a car. There was too much iron, and they'd be trapped in it. The iron wouldn't kill them, but it made them sick when they got too close, spent too much time around it. Saben and I had tried it when she was younger—she'd wanted to celebrate with me after I'd gotten my license. It hadn't gone well. She'd passed out, and I hadn't been able to get her to wake up for the longest time. I'd been so afraid that I'd slapped her. When she'd come to, I'd sworn I would never take her in a car anywhere again.

I'd met fey with different tolerances to iron. Most of the brownies I knew acted like it wasn't there, but even they stayed away from it when it was right in front of them. On the other hand, I'd seen water horses actually shy away from it, like it would attack them.

Kin laughed when I hesitated at the car, though. He swung the passenger-side door open and shook his head. "I'm not like you. Not like the sidhe."

I blinked, but then I nodded, because that was obvious. He didn't act, didn't behave, like any fey I'd ever met. He seemed more human than anything, and if he hadn't had those scales, I'd have thought he was. Maybe.

"Ningyo." He pointed at himself.

I'd gone around to the driver's side, but I leaned over the roof to look at him. "That's what you are?"

He nodded. "Water fey. Except, not fey. I'm yokai. So the iron . . ." He shrugged. "It doesn't bother me."

"So you can ride in my car, no problem," I said, letting a little bit of disbelief leach into my words.

He grinned at me and opened the door. "No problem."

He had me drive to his house. It was an actual house—or maybe a condo, since it was small and smooshed up against the houses on either side—with a lock on the front door, not some abandoned, glamoured, hidden place like most of the fey used. I mean, it seemed like he was probably actually paying rent on the place, and that surprised me. Two in one day—first Saben, then Kin. It was weird for me to see these fey acting like humans. Fey pretended all the time, made out like they wanted to live the way humans did, but they never quite got there, because when it came down to it, humans and fey were different. Different species with different ideas and different ways of living. But Saben was going at it like she meant to really make it work. And here was Kin, actually living like a human, from what I could see.

The house seemed normal on the inside too. Regular furniture, a few potted plants clustered near the door and hanging in the kitchen. I'd been expecting, again, something more fey—a kitchen with all the appliances ripped out, doors and windows thrown open so the wilderness could come crawling in, leaves on the floor, holes in the ceiling. Disrepair and magic marching hand in hand, because that was what you usually got when you went where the fey lived. But this was nothing like that. Beige carpeting, boring but clean. A red couch, and a blue easy chair that didn't match but didn't look too bad, either. There wasn't any art on the walls, not a lot of personal touches at all, except the plants, but the place was homey, like a work in progress. It was warm inside, and it smelled just slightly dusty. Sunlight was pouring through the windows, lighting the place up, making it airy and softening all the edges.

"I just moved in," Kin explained, throwing his keys on the kitchen counter. He glanced back at me. He must have seen the way I was looking around, trying to find something, anything, that would tell me this was a yokai's house and not a human's. He smiled at me, slow and gentle and kind of knowing. "I was raised by a human—my mother, the one who wasn't ningyo." He turned and headed down the hall. "I'm not what you think," he called over his shoulder.

I heard a door click shut. I waited there, in the space between his living room and his kitchen, not really sure what to do with myself. I didn't know if I should sit or if I should give up this whole weird endeavor and sneak away while he was out of the room. But he was only gone for a minute, and before I'd decided what to do with myself, he came back down the hallway.

He'd changed out of his kimono into a pair of tight gray jeans, and he was tugging a black long-sleeved T-shirt over his head while he walked. I caught a glimpse of his flat stomach, the sleek, tan skin of his chest, before he pulled the fabric down over himself. He looked up, and I know he saw me staring, because he smiled that wry little grin again, just the corner of his mouth lifting. Something sparkled in his eyes—amusement or pleasure—and I realized all over again how lovely he was. This magical being. He was, somehow, more and less human now, dressed almost like I was, dressed like any man our age might be, but too long and lean, too beautiful, too perfect.

He watched me watch him, until whatever was building between us got too thick, too heavy, and I cleared my throat. His smile slipped away, and he gestured with a flick of his hand, asking me to follow him. He walked into the kitchen, motioning at the stools lined up at the counter. I pulled one out and sat, a little confused, while he went to the cabinet and brought down two glasses.

"Aren't you going to . . ." I shrugged. "Examine me or something?" Healers might be different in their techniques, but they all wanted to get their hands on you, poke and prod at you, one way or another.

Kin nodded without looking around. He turned on the tap and held one glass under it, filling it. He glanced over his shoulder. "I have tea in the fridge, if you'd rather. Or . . ."

I shook my head. "Water's fine."

He filled the second glass, then set it in front of me. He put his glass down too, across from me, and leaned on the counter. "I can examine you. I'd like to listen to your lungs and your heart. But I'd rather you just tell me what's happening, first. What you think. You know your body. And I'm not a doctor." He smiled at me, gentle, maybe a little sad. "I don't work miracles, Luca. I think your father hopes I will. But I can't promise that."

I liked how blunt he was. I liked how he didn't try to coddle me or tell me everything would be okay, that he would fix everything, when we'd both have known he was lying.

"Where do I start?" I asked him.

He considered. "You said it's the fey bits eating at the human in you."

I lifted a shoulder, let it drop. It wasn't a medically or scientifically sound answer. But it was the best I'd ever come up with. It was what made sense to me. Human doctors thought I had some undefined genetic disease. Fey healers had seen people like me, but few and far between. And always half. Half human and half other.

"Would you believe that?" I asked.

He pursed his lips and tilted his head to the side. "I've seen a lot of things. Haven't seen many half fey, half humans, though. There must be a reason for that."

Because they didn't live long enough. Because they were dirty secrets. Because they weren't supposed to exist, and there was a handy malady that made sure they didn't for long. So convenient.

"Did you grow up with your father?" Kin asked, surprising me. I raised my face, met his eyes. He shrugged. "Your people made it seem . . . You make it seem like you're doing this, seeing me, for him. Not for yourself."

I sighed. When he'd said he wanted me to tell him things, I hadn't thought it would be this kind of thing. I didn't talk about my family. It was a practice I'd had to start as a child, when kids wanted to know where my dad was and I couldn't tell them the truth. Or when the fey taunted me about my mother. I thought about refusing to answer. Just shaking my head, because what did it matter, in the long run, if this man knew who had raised me? But he leaned back a little, as if he'd just realized himself that he'd asked something too personal. He tightened his hands on the tile and opened his mouth, like he was getting ready to say something, to apologize or take the question back.

"Yes," I said, stopping him. "I mostly lived with my mother. But my father took me in the summers. I was . . ." I trailed off, trying to figure out how to say this clearly, simply. "I'm an open secret. He shouldn't have wanted anything to do with me, should have abandoned me. But he never did." Not completely. He hadn't lived with us, he and my mother hadn't been a couple, and he hadn't always been there for me as much as I'd wanted. As much as I'd needed. But he'd been there some. In the summers, I'd gone to live with him in his large, white, wild house in the woods, not that far away, really, but separate from everything I knew. I'd lived with the fey for those months, with my father and Saben, and it had been my home. They had been my home.

Kin nodded. He didn't say anything else, just turned around and pulled a tin from somewhere. He opened it, laid it between us, and gestured at it. Cookies were piled inside, and I took one. The cookie was good, sweet and buttery and spicy. It tasted like some of the cakes I got from the brownies, when they were in the mood to feed me.

"Is this a payment from a fey? For your services?" I asked him.

He laughed and nodded. "You got fey feeding you too?"

I nibbled at the cookie. "I run errands for them." Sometimes they fed me, cakes and pies and preserves. Sometimes they gave me a basket of peaches or a necklace that I could never wear, or a handful of iron keys I could turn in for scrap. Sometimes I got nothing. Sometimes they spilled pennies into my hands, thousands of them, and were pleased that they'd managed to pay me in human currency. It was enough, most days. I had my mother's house, and the food the fey gave me, and their payments left me enough money that I could buy things, now and then, pay the electricity and the water bill. It was more than I'd had for a lot of my life while I was roaming, always moving, living hand to mouth. I was content enough.

We ate in silence for a few seconds, and then Kin wiped his hands on a dishcloth. "Tell me," he said.

So I did. I told him about the coughing and the blood that had started coming up. I told him about the muscle aches, so bad some days that it took effort to get out of bed. The bruising, horrific black and purple splotches that happened when I did the stupidest things, like bumping into a table. The dizzy spells, the occasional fainting. The idea I had, sometimes, that there was something inside me, inside my chest, growing and gnawing away at me, a monster trying to eat its way out. I told him about the iron tablets I swallowed, how, when I was lucky, they seemed to subdue it, subdue the fey inside me, enough that I could get through the day without hurting as much. I tried to be quick while I told him, lay it all out like it was just a string of facts. Like it was something that was happening to someone else.

When I was done, Kin nodded, but he didn't say anything else. He washed his hands, dried them on the towel, then came around the counter and held them out in front of him, like he was asking me something. I wasn't sure what he was going to do, but I nodded and turned where I was sitting, so he could reach me. He touched me, just his fingertips, cool and soft, slightly callused, at my jawline. Then his hands dipped lower, his fingers reaching for my lymph nodes, pressing in just a little. He tilted my head up and stared down at me, searching my eyes, running his gaze over my face, looking for I don't know what. He stepped back and walked away, disappearing into the depths of the house. A minute later, he came back with an honest-to-god, old-fashioned, horn-shaped stethoscope. I almost laughed, because it seemed like such an odd clash of worlds, but I couldn't quite. He gestured with it, asking permission, and I nodded. He leaned closer and moved it around my chest, listening, his ear pressed to the other end.

When he was done, he stepped back. I shivered, even though I wasn't cold. Kin's examination had been like most of the examinations I'd endured in my life. But it had been different too. It was like Kin was seeing me, a person, and not a puzzle or a mystery or a thing that shouldn't be. When he considered me now, contemplating, it seemed like he was considering *me*, and not whatever it was that was wreaking havoc inside me.

"I think you're right," he said at last. "I don't know what it is. But I think your fey pieces—something in your blood, a gland, an enzyme, or the way your body takes in energy and turns it into magic and glamour, something—is working incorrectly and poisoning you. I don't know enough about fey anatomy. No one does. There isn't a study on it. So I wouldn't know what was going wrong. Or how to fix it."

There it was. That disappointment flaring to life. Even though I had tried not to hope at all, had tried not to let that in because the disappointment always followed it so closely. Even though I'd been sure this wouldn't turn out any different. And it was so big and so sharp, and it cut so much deeper than it should have. I'd known Kin wouldn't be the miracle that would fix me, right here at home, in my father's court, when I'd searched the world for a cure. I'd known, and I'd accepted it. But I always got my hopes up anyway. And I always ended up feeling like this.

Kin must have seen something on my face, read something in my expression, because he stepped closer again. He reached out and touched his fingers to the edge of my jaw like he had before. But it was completely different this time, intimate and gentle and sweet. And sorry.

"Let me think about it," he told me. "Let me... ask some questions. Do some research. And then I'll come see you with what I've found."

I nodded, letting the weight of that disappointment settle on me. It was bad, heavy and bitter. But maybe I'd grown used to that sensation, because when I looked up and found Kin looking back at me, it wasn't quite as terrible as it had been before. He was watching me like he was the one who'd been broken, like whatever disappointment, whatever loss of hope I was experiencing was being reflected onto him. Like he wanted to do better for me, and he couldn't.

I liked him, I realized. He was too beautiful and a little abrupt and a lot strange, but he'd been kind and honest. I liked him. And something inside me wanted him to like me back. And as much as I understood the expression on his face, as much as I understood the kindness behind it, I didn't want it. I didn't want him to look at me like I was sad. Like I was a tragedy.

He walked me to the door and opened it for me, but before I could duck out, he caught my wrist, turned me back around to face him. "It doesn't bother me," he said. "Not that you're half. Not that you're sick." His cheeks went pink. "I mean, it bothers me that you're sick. I wish you weren't. But that doesn't... doesn't make me not want to see you again."

"Why? So you can try to fix me?"

"I want to do what I can, yes. But I liked spending the afternoon with you, Luca." He sounded almost angry about it, fierce.

I shrugged, trying not to let him see what his words did to me. How they made my breath catch, made me happy even though everything about this afternoon should have depressed me. I didn't believe he could heal me, though. And I wasn't positive he hadn't said he liked spending time with me as some form of pity. But I didn't want to just . . . end things if I didn't have to. "All right. Maybe I'll see you again, then."

I slipped past him, out the door, and I didn't look back until I was in my car.

CHAPTER 4

I lived in the hills, away from the city. If I wanted to avoid the fey, it would have been wiser for me to live closer to town, where there was more iron and less green. I hadn't chosen the spot, though—I'd inherited the house from my mother. She'd never said it out loud, but I knew she liked the idea that it would be easy for my father to get here, if he wanted to.

I didn't think of it as my mother's house anymore. And it wasn't exactly fey-friendly anymore, either. I'd pounded four iron studs into every threshold. The windows had steel frames. I collected wrought iron artwork—stuff that was meant to decorate gardens and walls and walkways. Some of it I set up in the yard, but I hung even more on the walls. I interspersed the metal with leafy plants, not unlike the ones Kin had in his house. The affect was half wild, half modern. It suited me, this blending of themes. It let me make the house mine. It also meant that a fey would have to be incredibly determined to get in, to step over the iron and breathe it in while they were there. I had gotten lucky, this one time, in the genetics department—the iron didn't bother me at all, and I could use that to my advantage.

The morning after I met Kin in the park, I slept late, and after I woke up, I still couldn't quite work up the energy to get out of bed. I had a fierce headache, and my joints were a bit creaky, but I didn't lie there because I was sick. I was just . . . heart sore. Weary, maybe. Angry at myself, for hoping at all, and even angrier for lying here like an idiot. But it wasn't enough to make me move, make me get up and shower and brush my teeth and pretend I was normal. Instead, I curled toward the window at the side of my bed, toward the chill coming off it. I tilted my head until it hit the glass and I could see straight up, past my postage stamp of a backyard, and see the slope of the hill behind the house and the clouds, puffy and pale blue, over the top of it at the same time.

I sprawled on my bed and kept looking up at the clouds, staring until I couldn't tell if they were moving and expanding or not, and their back-lit edges burned my eyes. I wanted to lie there in a tangle. I wanted to twist my sheets around my ankles and wiggle my head enough that it sank just right into the pillow. I wanted to stay that way until it felt like my joints were disintegrating, melting enough that they didn't hurt anymore. Melodramatic, I told myself. But for a second, staring at those clouds, I was comfortable, and my mind was blank, and I wanted that.

Someone knocked on my door. I turned my head away from the window. My bedroom was oddly located, with the front door nearly right across from it. I could see the window that flanked the door and the front porch beyond. It was convenient for observing visitors before they saw me. Whoever was standing there now was out of my line of vision, though.

I waited, and the knock came again. It wasn't a timid knock. It didn't sound like whoever it was had knocked and skittered back, away from the iron. Something told me that they were still standing right there, waiting. I got up.

It was Kin. He wore a blue V-necked T-shirt and those same jeans. His hair hung in a loose ponytail from the back of his head, and one ear was lined with small black studs. The plain outfit highlighted his body, his sleek legs and long chest and the sharp bones of his face. He looked almost like he had at the club, except that his scales were gone. Glamoured away, I supposed, so all I could see was the fine, smooth tan of his skin.

He leaned forward into the doorway, his hands on the frame, and I jumped. "You can't—" I started. He stopped, confused.

"Can I not?"

I'd been thinking of the scales that were supposed to be on his face, the things that marked him so visibly as fey, as a creature that shouldn't have been able to touch iron. I took a deep breath. "There's iron." I gestured at the threshold, and his feet, the way he was standing just over the metal that irritated all the other fey who came here.

"It doesn't bother me," he said, patient, a tiny smile sliding over his lips.

Right. I knew that. I'd seen him ride in my car, completely without complaint. In fact, just past him, I could see an old truck, paint flaking away from its sides, parked in front of my yard, and I realized Kin must have driven here. But the mantra of "fey can't touch iron" was so deeply imbedded in me, it would take a while to remember that it wasn't always true.

Kin was still watching me, waiting. I moved aside and made a little motion with my hand, some kind of half gesture that wanted him to come in. He stepped over the iron and into my house. He turned when we were level and stared at me. Right into my eyes, steady. It wasn't something most people did. It was unnerving.

He had a leather pack slung over one shoulder, and I pointed at it, hoping to break his stare. "What have you got?"

The half smile on his face changed a little, went uncertain, almost nervous. "I brought you things."

I sighed, because I didn't want to have this conversation. It had seemed to me, the other day, when he'd told me what he thought about my illness, that talk about this was done. Everything that could be said, that was important, already had been. I didn't want to draw it out any more than that. But I liked seeing him, standing here in my house. I liked the way he looked against my cream walls and the vivid green plants and the wrought iron I'd hung all over the place. He still seemed almost too slender, like glass or a sharp blade, but he didn't seem small. His presence was massive. He took up so much of my senses. So much of my concentration and my breath. He was energy and stillness and ink. Ink that splashed everywhere. And I didn't want him to go. Even if that meant letting him tell me what he'd come to say.

"Come have something to drink?" I asked.

He nodded, and his hair flopped forward. Strands hung down around his face, a few long bangs curtaining the corners of his eyes and his cheekbones. He pushed them away with the tips of two fingers. He smiled, the gesture small and almost coy. "Yes, please."

In the kitchen, I got water for Kin and lemonade for me. I pulled out a jar of orange slices soaked in tea. Kin dropped the bag he was carrying on my linoleum table and opened the drawstring. He pulled out folded packets of paper, little cloth pouches, small jugs, and a larger jug, all with black characters written on them that I didn't understand.

I handed him the water and a fork. We sat, and I spilled the orange slices onto a plate in the middle of the table. He pushed his fork into one and ate around the peel, his teeth delicate on the pulp. He swallowed and tapped the tines of the fork against his bottom lip.

"Amazing. What's in that?"

I shrugged. "It was a payment."

His lips slid up at one corner again. "They expect a half human to live on orange slices?"

"Oranges. Blackberries. I get a lot of eggs. The brownies like to make casseroles and things." I loved doing things for brownies. They fed me the best. They were mostly interested in making country foods—roasts and potatoes and turnips and squash, fried chicken, pancakes, pasta with a rich red sauce. And jams and preserves and breads. It wasn't true that the fey don't like bread. "There's a sidhe who loves to bake. She brings me pies and cakes. She makes incredible frosting."

Kin laughed. It was a soft sound, but deep, and so genuinely amused it was startling. "They like you."

I smiled back. "I'm very useful."

He watched me and his laughter slowed, his smile going gentle and then disappearing. His gaze flicked to the little pile of things he'd laid on my table. "I can be useful too."

"I see."

He took a sip of his water. Around his fingers, the glass dripped with condensation, like he was calling the moisture in the air to him. "Ask me what I brought you."

"Kin . . ."

"Ask me."

"Why?"

He took a deep breath, let it out. "Because if you ask, it means you're interested. It means you care about whether any of this can help you or not."

HALF

He'd figured me out so fast. But then, I wasn't exactly trying to hide the way I felt. "I care that you brought it all," I started. "I care that you want to—"

He shook his head sharply. "That's not what I mean, and you know it."

So I closed my eyes and took my own deep breath, tilting my head back, steadying myself. Then I leaned forward and looked him in the eye, like he'd done to me earlier. "What did you bring me?"

He pulled each packet and jar forward, telling me about what they would do, how I should use them. There were herbs to eat, charms to hang around the house, drinks in tiny pots with specific dosages. He'd written everything down, but he explained it all anyway, slow and steady and soothing. He didn't tell me any of it would cure me. When he explained what the things would do, he talked about lessening pain and making my muscles work better, easing my airways, blocking the fey parts of me. They weren't cures. He didn't try to pretend they were. But they were things that might make me more comfortable, that might let me live more normally, and I appreciated that.

As he talked about each item, he pushed it to one side of the table. When there was only the large jar left on the other side, he paused.

I reached out and touched the jug. "And this?"

He straightened, and his jaw clenched. His hand folded into a fist, and he tucked it out of sight in his lap. "Good sake," he said, and I swear his voice was tight. "For when anything else isn't enough."

And there it was. The admission, even if he wasn't exactly saying it, that the things he had brought me would not always be enough. That they might not work at all. The idea that there would be times, many times, when what worked the best, healed me the best, would be something that dissolved me, something that took away the pain or made me forget what I was, or both. I took a deep breath and let it out. My lungs were better today. They could do that without protest.

"We'll try the other stuff first," Kin said. His voice was so soft. "If it doesn't help, we can go in another direction."

I blinked and raised my eyes to his. "Why are you bothering?" He knew I was doomed, as well as I did. This was a waste of his time. "You did your part. My father will be grateful."

29

He focused on the spread of shiny white table in front of us. "Your father is a powerful man. It's in my best interest to do my best for his son." He shrugged and glanced up at me, peeking through his bangs and his eyelashes. "But really . . . I just want to."

My arm was resting on the table. Kin stretched out a finger and ran it along a bruise near my wrist. It was purple, much darker than any normal human or fey would get from bumping against a doorframe, which was what I had done. My breath caught with a click. My arm burned where he touched me.

"You don't even know me."

He nodded and took his finger away. His hand stayed on the table this time, though. "What did you think when you saw me in the club?"

He was looking right at me again in that unnerving way. I shook my head.

"I saw you. In the club. And again, when you were hiding in the trees," he said. His voice was so low I had to sit forward to hear him. "You tucked yourself into the shadows both times, but I saw you. I saw your hair. Copper, but too bright, like autumn but not quite." His hand flicked up and touched his own hair. There was a spot between my shoulder blades that got tighter when he moved. He wasn't looking at me anymore. His eyes were still on me, but he was seeing me that day, against the tree trunk, seeing me while I was watching him get out of the water. "I thought you were very beautiful."

I couldn't get a breath. My lungs were failing for the wrong reason. "Kin."

"I still planned to brush you off, until you coughed." His eyes focused on me again. "Spoiled sidhe. I thought you must be melodramatic. Faking it. I was going to examine you and send you on your way. But then you coughed like that, and you tried to hide the blood from me." He shrugged. "You were all I could think about. Your illness. How to help. But just . . . you, too."

I didn't know what to say. I couldn't think of anything. Then Kin sat back in his chair. "Nothing like the sight of blood to make you fall for someone," he said, his voice flat and dry.

I laughed, right out loud. It sounded awful, like a bark, but it made Kin smile. The tension that had been building around us evaporated.

It wasn't funny, we both knew it, but it was a relief. Kin laughed with me, and it felt good. The way he watched me, a little bit of wryness to his expression, his eyes on me as our laughter wound down, told me he knew what I thought the medicines he'd brought would do. I let my head hang down a little, let the laughter and the tension go from me, sorry and relieved at the same time. It's hard to tell someone that you think you won't live long. But I didn't have to spell it out for him. Didn't have to tell him at all. He already knew.

I looked back up at him. It was as if something had snapped between us, as if the invisible wall that kept two strangers apart had fractured, the masks that we generally gave the rest of the world slipping a little. I stood and got a new glass and had him pour me out some of the liquid he'd said to drink, showing me how much I should take at a time. He handed me the list with all the instructions, and I promised to follow it. I thought I actually would, too. For him, where I might not have done it for anyone else, because he'd tried so hard.

"I'll come back," he said before he left. He reached out and touched my elbow, his fingertips just ghosting over my skin. "I'll need to come see if these things are working, or if we need to switch. So I'll come back." It was meant to be a doctor's order, I was sure, a stern warning to do as he'd instructed. But he sounded almost hopeful while he talked, his eyes trained so carefully on me, watching me. It was personal, more like a promise than anything.

CHAPTER 5

Saben eventually sent one of her girls to check up on me, a day or so after Kin had come by. The girl was there to make sure I'd done as I was told, and to deliver any messages the fey had left me about tasks that needed doing. She didn't even ring my doorbell, just sat outside my house until I came out. The poor thing was miserable. It was obvious that the iron was affecting her, even sitting as far away on my front lawn as she could. She handed me the messages Saben had collected for me, and I told her I'd been to see Kin, and that there wasn't anything else to say about it. She nodded. She might have pressed me harder, to have something more to tell Saben, but it was pretty clear that the only thing she could think about was leaving.

It didn't make any difference to me anyway. Not like I wanted her to hang out. I sorted through the messages, trying to decipher spidery handwriting, ink splotches, and patches gone wrinkly with water damage. Most of the fey, outside the high-court fey like the sidhe, aren't too fantastic at writing coherently. Some things weren't even in English, but someone had carefully translated those notes, attaching the translations with a paper clip. There were other notes in the same handwriting, explaining tasks better than the original message had. I wasn't sure whose handwriting it was, who had bothered to make things easier for me. Saben maybe, although the idea was almost hard to believe.

I picked out the tasks that I'd work on first—the jobs that needed doing the soonest, the fey I liked the most, and the fey I liked the least so I could get those over with. The mer people fell into the last group. I hated going to see them, hated going to the rocky outcropping with the minuscule, gritty beach where they liked to meet, hated getting damp with sea spray when it was this nippy out. And I didn't like the mer, aggressive and cruel as they were, either. They were deceptively beautiful, and appeared almost human, swimming in the shallows, their skin just slightly blue or green, their jaws a bit too narrow. But they were as far from human as any fey I'd ever come across. The mer were violent, bloodthirsty. Monsters.

I decided to do that job first. I'd get it out of the way. And it'd get me out of the house, at least. I hadn't really gone anywhere since Kin had come by. I was letting myself get trapped in my own head, and I knew that was a bad idea.

I drove to the shore and parked. It was deserted, too cold even for the most diehard beach fans. This miserable, rocky stretch of land wasn't very popular, anyway. I got out of the car, and the fog in the air slapped at me, the cold and the salt burning my lungs. It smelled coppery, too alive, too primordial. I shivered and wrapped my arms around myself.

I turned, ready to go and get this over with, and there was Saben, standing a little ways away, her back to the stairs that led down to the beach.

I raised a hand, and her eyes caught the movement. She raised her hand in return and walked to me. I felt underdressed in my jeans and old T-shirt and hoodie, and scruffy when she was standing next to me. She seemed as if she belonged there, perfectly comfortable, completely put together, her too-light dress twisting around her legs. It was yellow, the brightest spot of color in my view. She had blue and yellow bracelets running up one arm to match, and when she met my eyes, I saw that hers were highlighted with sapphire-blue powder and ringed in gold liner.

"I see Elina made it to you," she said, referring, I assumed, to the girl who had dropped off my messages. "I knew you'd come here first."

I ran my hand through my hair, the silver rings I had on three of my fingers slicking against the strands. Saben's own hair tangled around her face, pushed around by the wind. She kept pulling it away from her eyes. "You shouldn't do that to your girls," I said. "All of my iron bothers them."

Saben shrugged. "I told her I would bring the messages to you. But she wanted to do it. So I let her."

I sighed through my nose. "You were never such a spoiled brat when you were a child."

She grabbed her hair at last, in an irritated motion, her hands catching and twisting it into a tight knot. "Maybe you were just in the habit of spoiling me then too." Her words should have stung, and I thought she'd wanted them to, but they came out almost gentle, with no barbs at all. I was surprised by the way she spoke, the directness she was offering me, even if she was trying to wound me with it.

I rubbed my hands up and down my arms, trying to work the chill out of my body. "What do you need, Saben?"

"You didn't tell Elina anything," she said, her face tipped up to me again, her eyes hard and a little cold, like they usually were, but there was something else there too. A nervousness, maybe. Or an energy. "Not really. Just that you went."

"There's nothing to tell." I cocked my head at her. "I thought I told Elina to tell you?"

"She did," Saben said easily.

"So?"

"So I wanted to hear it from you." She leaned toward me, just the tiniest bit, like she could intimidate. It should have been almost laughable with how small she was. But I thought that little tilt of her head, the narrowing of her eyes, the fierceness that was so clear inside her, probably intimidated lots of people. "I wanted to hear the truth."

I took a breath and held it, staring down at my sister. She was very clearly not the small child I'd left six years ago after my mother died and I'd gone traveling. When I'd seen her last, before I'd come back, her head had come just high enough to hit my waist. Now, she had to lift her face back to look me in the eye, but she didn't have to tip it far. Her shoulders were narrow but toned, her cheeks sharp, all the baby softness gone. Her childhood charm had turned into calculating cleverness, an appeal that I had no doubt she wielded like a sleek weapon, using it to her advantage whenever she needed to. I would never have spoken to my sister about this before, any of this. Now, though, we were different people. We didn't know each other, and she'd gone from being a little girl to a grown woman.

"The truth," I said, making sure my voice was steady, nearly flat, "is that I'm sick. The truth is that something has gone wrong inside me and there's no way to fix it. The truth is that I searched and searched, and there isn't anyone on the planet who can make me better. Not human doctors. Not fey healers. Not your yokai. The truth is that I've come back here because this is where I want to die."

She stepped back. It was such a small move, but from her, it was huge. It was like I'd pushed her, reached out and slapped at her. Like I'd hurt her. I was surprised. I honestly hadn't thought she cared. I'd laid it out like that because I hadn't thought it would matter to her.

I wanted to take it back, how blunt I'd been. Everything I'd said, even if it was exactly what she'd asked for. "I'm sorry," I said.

She breathed out and turned away to face toward the ocean. She squinted her eyes against the wind, and for a long moment, she didn't say anything. I thought briefly about walking away, letting us both pretend that none of this had happened.

Then she sighed. "You don't come to see me."

I was nearly glad for the way she'd slipped back into the odd twists of fey conversation, but her words took me by surprise all over again. I didn't think she wanted me around. She never gave any sign she was happy when I was near her. Since I'd come home six months ago, we had only been distant with each other, the gentle ways I'd reached out to her in the beginning rejected. She had let me be around as her errand boy, but never any closer.

I wanted to be closer. I had loved her, dearly, when she was a child. I had considered her mine to care for, even though I wasn't her parent. Even though I was only really around her part of the time. When we'd been together, we had fit. We'd belonged. Now we didn't. I wanted to ask her, really ask, why she was living in that apartment and how she was getting along and who her friends were and how her conversations with our father went, if she still fought with her mother in that passive way I'd been so used to seeing, if she still preferred strawberry sorbet to vanilla ice cream, what she was reading, what songs she'd fallen in love with, everything I'd missed while I was away. But I couldn't. I wanted to tell her how confused I was by all of it, but I couldn't.

It was, when I stood back and examined it all honestly, my fault, what had happened between us. I'd thought I was going to die out there, in some far-flung corner of the world. I hadn't thought I'd come home, one way or another. I'd wanted to leave her and our father and everyone else, let them forget me. I'd pushed them away. And now I was reaping the rewards of what I'd done.

"I was there the other day," I said, instead of anything else, anything that would have been more truthful and harder to explain.

"I had to ask for you."

"You're cold to me," I told her.

She turned to me, but she kept her mouth shut. She leaned forward again, like she wanted to touch me. She did touch me, sometimes, put her hand around my wrist or let me place my palm on her back, so the other fey would know who we were, would know who I belonged to. It was never a warm feeling, though.

I waited, but she didn't come any closer, and she didn't respond to what I'd said. After a while passed in silence, I dropped my eyes and moved around her, walking down to the beach, wanting to get this over with so I could get out of the wind.

I didn't see Kin or Saben for a week. One afternoon I came home and found, waiting for me on my front steps, another bundle of dried herbs and a glass jar of the tart liquid I'd been drinking every morning with my breakfast. A note in a thick, gently slanted hand instructed me to use the herbs as incense, to inhale the vapors they gave off. There was no signature, but I knew it was Kin. I didn't know if I'd missed him while I was out, or if he hadn't wanted to see me again, had left the things while I wasn't watching. I took the herbs and burned some, letting the smoke rise up from the ceramic plate I'd set them on. It smelled earthy and green and smoky. I rolled some into a cigarette and smoked it. It tasted bitter and spicy and the flavor of it made me feel good. I didn't know what it was doing to my insides, didn't think it did anything to loosen the tightness in my lungs or ease the ache in my joints, but I liked the flavor. I liked the way it made me feel warm all the way through.

I was disappointed, I realized. He'd told me he would come back. But I'd been expecting that I would see him when he did. I'd known I liked him well enough, but I didn't think it was until right then, when all that disappointment landed square on my chest, that I realized how much, how good it had felt to just be around him.

I found myself waiting for him, pacing around the house. I kept peeking out the front window, hoping that he'd show up again. It bothered me, that I let myself want that. Want him. I couldn't seem to stop, though. He'd been so . . . honest. So upfront, even when it was obvious that what he had to tell me hurt him, frightened him. I craved that honesty.

I decided I needed to get out of the house. The fey were still throwing their parties in the apple orchard. They'd be partying there until spring, when they'd move to the beach. The orchard was perfect now, though: seasonal and festive. The fey were into that kind of thing. It wasn't that I really wanted to be there, any more than I'd wanted to be there the night the girl had told me Saben needed to see me. But I didn't know where else to go, where else I could get lost, dissolve, disappear. Just for a little while. So I went.

No one says hello at a fey party. There's no small talk. There's only dancing or kissing or strange conversations that go in circles and mean nothing. This night, I walked toward the bonfire, but stopped before I got to the loose crush of people around it. Most of them were dancing, their movements wild, fluid, bodies brushing together, limbs tangling, heads thrown back, the sleek lines of throats drenched in orange from the fire. It was loud, with the music behind me and the fire crackling in front of me. Fey laughed, but I could only see their mouths move, couldn't hear the sound of it.

Someone bumped into me, and I had the brief urge to lean into the contact, the desire to twist myself into those knots of people, but I didn't step forward to join the dance. I looked at the dancers, at their birch-gray, deep-blue, sweet-brown hair colors, at their sharp wrists, at their eyes, too large and too liquid. I was them, and I wasn't. They took me in, and they rejected me. I was part of them, but we both wanted to deny that part. I realized, even though I'd come, I didn't want to dance with them at all.

I felt a warmth against my side. Saben was there, her head leaning onto my shoulder. Her face was soft, relaxed, her body loose, and I figured she'd had something to drink.

"Are you angry with us?"

I wasn't sure if she was perfecting her royal we, or if she meant the fey in general. It didn't matter. The answer was the same either way.

"Sometimes."

Her skin against me wasn't a gesture of closeness. It was something possessive. I hated myself for pretending it meant the same thing it had when she was small.

"I'm still yours." I belonged to her, and I belonged to the fey. It wasn't about blood. It was about where I'd grown up, who I'd spent my life with, who had loved me and hated me and shaped me. No matter how far I'd run or who I'd tried to call home, no matter who I'd pretended to be, I had still always belonged to the fey.

She drew in a breath. I was afraid that she'd try to continue the last conversation we'd been having. That she'd ask me if I'd really come home to die.

"Did you ever figure out your kettle?" I asked, cutting her off before she could say anything.

She snapped her head up, and there it was. A little petulant pout that told me she had a heart, that she was alive and got angry and embarrassed like humans did. She smoothed her face quickly, but I had seen it. That slight pursing of the lips, the frown that had crossed her face for that second. That reminder, that tiny hint at something more inside her, made my night.

"The stove is full of iron. I'll have it taken out."

"Saben."

"Rhian tells me I can get a fire pot and cook on that."

"You can't cook."

"I can make tea," she said, running right over me. "I need you to come place the clay base."

"Saben. You can't start a fire in an apartment. Why are you even staying there? It's ridiculous."

Her bottom lip puffed out, just a fraction. "I like it there."

"You do not." I sighed. "There's so much iron."

"Most of it's gone now. Or covered."

What was the point? No stove, no toaster. She couldn't use the big steel basin sink in the kitchen. She had to cover the taps with silk so she could turn on the water in the bathroom. She put on gloves when she went down the outside stairs, in case she had to reach out and touch the iron railing.

"Just go back and live with Father."

"I will not."

"Saben . . ."

She held up her hand. She had a little lace mitt on that made her long fingers seem miles longer and more delicate. "I'm sorry about the beach," she said, and I was so stunned that she was apologizing that I couldn't remember what I'd been about to say. Before I could think of it, she startled me again, jumping to a different subject in that fey way of hers. "I had you followed to the park. I wanted to make sure you actually saw the healer."

I jerked back. I wasn't sure why that surprised me, really. Maybe it didn't. Maybe it just hurt.

She drew in a deep breath. "Do you like him?"

"Kin?"

She nodded. She was peering up at me, the fire reflecting in her dark eyes, turning her hair gold and bronze. She was beautiful, more beautiful than even a sidhe had any right to be. She had men and women trailing after her, ready to do whatever she asked. I knew she did. I knew she could snap her fingers and everything she needed would be brought to rest at her feet. But her cheeks were flushed, and her hands were knotting themselves together, her fingers tugging at the gloves. And I remembered times when she'd stared up at me like this before. When she'd been young and uncertain and she'd turned to me to tell her what to do, how to act.

I could almost see us, the two of us, like we were back then, a pair, molded around each other, instead of these two planets, carefully orbiting each other, like we'd become now.

"I like him," I told her.

"And you would want to see him again."

I nodded. "I would."

She took a breath. "Guinne says she knows the club he goes to. She says she thinks he'll be there tonight."

I pictured Kin, eyes closed, body twisting, covered in colored light. "Is it the club—" I started to ask, but Saben waved her hand, cutting me off.

"I have no idea of the name of the place. But I would hurry."

I stepped away from her, then turned back to her once more, my jaw opening to speak.

She shook her head. "I will not leave the apartment."

I stopped to ask Guinne about the club, but getting any information from her was an impossible task. When I found myself wanting to shake her, I backed away instead. I left the orchard and got in my car and drove to the club where I'd first seen Kin. By the time I got there, it was past midnight. I felt stupid. Even if it was the right place, there was only a small chance Kin would be there tonight, anyway. The fey often got dates and times wrong. Only when it was important to them did they seem to seriously consider time, and even then it was kind of a gamble. Guinne might have heard that Kin was at the club a week ago, and moved it to tonight in her mind. Saben had sounded so resolute, though. She had sounded like the child who had argued with me about whether she could have any more honey candy, laying out her logic in a way that was so un-fey I knew she'd learned it from me, but perfected it on her own. And I was there, parked on a side street just outside the club, so I suppose some part of me believed her.

I took the stairs down to the dance floor, like I had last time, and like last time, I stopped halfway and looked out over the people. The place was packed, so full it was hard to see where one body ended and another began. I sighed, letting go of the part of me that had hoped. Even if Kin was there, I would never be able to pick him out of that mess.

I liked the sharp, pulsing sound of the music, though. I liked the repetition of the beat and the unpredictability of the melody that ran over it. I liked the glow of focused light on hot, smooth metal, reflecting off tables and bars and the pipes that lined the ceiling and the walls. The electricity and the current and the feel of something modern and smooth attracted me in a way the rough, wild feel of the apple orchard hadn't been able to tonight. I took another step down the stairs.

Kin was in front of me. He glanced up at me, one hand ahead of him on the railing, like he was pulling himself up. His hair was loose, totally loose, hanging over his shoulders. It looked so good like that, so black and shiny, like I could dip my fingers into it and it would feel like silk. Deep-green scales that faded to blue splashed over his cheekbones and up along his right eye. They covered his collarbones and dipped into the neck of his tight tank top. If I hadn't know better, I would have said they were some kind of beautiful makeup, decoration for a night out. I knew better.

"I found you."

His face softened into a wry smile. "Were you hoping to?" The lights sparked off his skin and his earrings.

I touched my chest, my plain black T-shirt. I had only gray jeans and black boots and no jewelry, no eyeliner, no color but my muddy orange hair. I was underdressed and I felt it, then, standing there in front of him. "I was."

"Come dance."

I hesitated, unsure now that I realized how out of place I was there.

He lifted his hand to me. "Come on."

"Why didn't you come see me?" I bit my lip. I didn't like sounding needy, but I wanted to know.

He let his hand drop. He frowned, the expression small and tight, but he didn't let his eyes move from mine. "I was nervous."

"Why?" I noticed that there was a scrap of something sheer attached to his wrist, running down his arm. It caught the lights and shimmered when he moved his hand. A fin. It was a small fin. I could see the fine bones that lined it, like the bones in a bat wing.

He shrugged, a casual gesture, but it was almost uncomfortable, embarrassed. "I didn't know if you wanted to see me again. I don't tell you anything good."

"I do. Want to see you." Awkward, everything about this moment, everything I was saying. But it didn't seem to matter. It seemed, instead, like he was as nervous, as unsure, as I was. Afraid that I would tell him there wasn't anything between us. It made me want to say true things, instead of flirting or playing around like I might have with anyone else. It made me want to reach for him, show him I meant it when I said I wanted him near me.

He held my eyes for another second, and I saw that his were green, deep in color, shimmery, like diving underwater and looking up, past the surface, to see the trees above. He offered his hand to me again.

I took it. His fingers wrapped around mine. It was another reminder that he was fey—he was thin but strong like a willow branch, and his fingers could circle my palm, they were that long. He pulled me deeper into the club. People moved out of his way. They didn't even seem to notice him slipping past, but they stepped aside, and I followed. We reached a spot in the middle, and he turned to me. Our bodies were pressed close by the people around us. The music made me sway. Kin raised his hands over his head, wrists straight, fingers loose. Scales, moss green and chocolate, curved around his arms like bracelets. He tilted his head back and smiled. He was as free as he had been that first time I'd seen him, as glorious and at home, as if he didn't care what anyone thought of him in that moment, or maybe didn't even realize that anyone was watching. Anyone but me.

His body twisted as he danced. One hand came down and rested on my hip. His touch was almost hesitant, his fingers on me light. I moved in to him, pressing against the heat of his palm, and his grip tightened, holding me to him. I was dancing with him. I couldn't stop. He was so comfortable, and I wanted to be in that space with him. He opened his eyes and smiled wide, and it was directed at me this time, not at the place and the atmosphere. All for me. His fingers tucked themselves into my belt loop.

"You're not like my sister." He wasn't like anyone. He didn't behave like the fey I knew. He didn't act like them or speak in circles like them or pretend to be genuine when he was really telling a crooked lie that could be interpreted as the truth.

Kin just shook his head. I didn't know how he'd heard me over the music and the laughter and shouts around us, but I knew he had. He pulled me closer, which seemed impossible. We danced together, and we danced with the people around us. I could feel his body all along mine, the flat planes of his stomach, the points of his hips, the bump of his knee against my leg. He stared down at me, his body still moving effortlessly to the music. He didn't look at me like I was all he could see. It would have been impossible, wrong in a way, to deny everything, everyone, else around us. But he looked at me like I was important. Like maybe in that second, I mattered the most.

I leaned forward and he kissed me. His arms came up and dropped around my neck and his skin was hot, the inside of his wrists pressing against me. I reached up and held my hands to his, held his wrists against my neck, feeling the hard pebbles of his bones, the tiny scales slipping under the pads of my fingers. He pulled me closer, and I went to my toes, making the little difference in our heights disappear. And then I knew there were other people around us, I knew we were in the middle of the club, that we were awkward and unsure, but it didn't matter. None of it did. My mind only thought about him, and him, and him.

CHAPTER 6

When I woke up the next morning, he was beside me. He looked content and warm, loose-limbed, his scales dark against the white sheets. The top sheet twisted over one leg, but otherwise, he was bare. I could see most of the places I'd found scales the night before—along the curve of his thighs, across the muscles at the base of his back, around his kneecaps, down his ankles. And now I knew there were other places too—scales splashed across his chest, along the tops of his hips. In the light, I could see where the blue scales on his face and neck deepened to greens and browns on his hands. I could see how the scales got smaller, becoming minute specks, as they got closer to his fingers and toes. How they were like large chips of glass at the top of his legs. And the fins, visible now that he'd dropped his glamour, opaque and folded to his skin. They ran down his calves to his ankles, down his forearms from his elbows, ending just before his wrists. I'd expected there to be one down the middle of his spine, but there wasn't. Aside from the scales, his back was smooth. His toes were webbed, though.

I didn't know how we'd ended up in my bed. I remembered all of it, I just wasn't sure what had happened, what I'd said or done right, to bring us together. We'd left the club and come here, and he'd been in my arms. We'd kissed, and I'd found his scales and his fins, and he'd touched my knuckles and the bones in my ankles and my shoulder blades and the flat of my stomach and everywhere else he could fit his hands. And after, a long time after, he'd fallen asleep so close to me I'd felt him breathing on me, and now he was still that close. His hair spilled across the sheets, an inky mess. I twisted my fingers in it. It was like I was holding water, liquid and cool.

Kin's eyes flickered open. He reached out and splayed his fingers against my chest, dark on the paleness of my skin, the little fin on his wrist just brushing me. It was soft.

"You're not human."

He laughed and shook his head against the pillow. His arm wrapped around my shoulder and tugged me down next to him, so our eyes were level. I smiled back, but I hadn't meant it as some kind of bawdy joke. His face softened, and he shook his head, serious this time. "I'm not."

The way he'd touched me last night had seemed human. He hadn't touched me like he was superior. He hadn't acted like he was doing me a favor. He'd looked at me like I mattered. Like I wasn't an oddity. Like I wasn't only half of what I should be.

"You don't act fey."

He moved his hand and wiped at his eyes, clearing them. The gesture was sleepy, intimate in how awkward it was. He pulled his hair into a knot and brushed with his palms to smooth the stray pieces. His head flopped back against the pillow and he blinked, still not fully awake. "You know strange fey." His fingers brushed against my cheekbone. "And I told you. We're not all like that. My mothers never wanted me to be mired in the old ways. They wanted me to be able to survive in a human world." He smiled, like he was pleased with himself, and his eyes slid shut. "Make me breakfast?"

I agreed, but instead of sleeping for a while more and waiting for me to come back with breakfast, he got up. He went for the shower, and I thought maybe he needed the water, since he had told me he was a water fey, of a sort. I asked him if the chlorine in the tap supply would bother him, but he shook his head.

I stayed in bed and watched him walk to the bathroom. We had only been together one night, and I was still self-conscious. He, however, walked around the bed without holding the sheet against himself. He walked like he had nothing to be embarrassed about, like he wanted me to see him—the same way he'd held his arms, covered in those green and brown scales, over his head while we danced the night before. When the bathroom door closed behind him, I let my head slip back on the pillow. I ran my hands through my hair and wondered what the hell I had been thinking when I'd rushed to the club to find him, and then brought him home.

I couldn't make myself unhappy that I'd done it, though.

I got up and made waffles, and when Kin came out of the shower, we ate them together at the table. We poured the maple syrup into a dish between us and tore off pieces to dip into it. Our fingers got sticky. I watched Kin lick his clean like he was a cat. My mind wandered, and he laughed when he saw me watching, and I laughed too. I poured him more tea, and orange juice for myself. It was weirdly normal to have him sitting there, dripping syrup on the cracked plastic surface of my table.

"What do you have to do today?" I popped my thumb in my mouth and sucked at the skin, tasting sugar.

Kin shook his head. "I don't have anyone coming around. Nowhere to go."

"I need to work," I told him. "But you can kill your time with me today, if you want." It was odd, asking him. This probably should have been the part of the morning where he left and we were both a bit relieved to get a little time to ourselves. But I didn't want to let go of him just yet. I was afraid that if he left my sight, he might disappear, and I'd go back to a quiet house and a slow wait, with none of Kin's brightness in it.

"I do," he said, and the answer came without any thought or hesitation.

While Kin got a last glass of water, I dug two iron tablets out of the box I kept on the table. They were bright red, like little spots of blood in my hand. I barely glanced at them. I slammed them into my mouth and swallowed them with the last pulpy sips of orange juice in my glass. I must have been having a good day—I thought they started working almost as soon as I took them, shearing the edge off whatever fey thing it was that was eating at me, subduing it the tiniest bit. I had no real proof that the iron stopped the fey parts of me from eating away the healthy parts, or that it wasn't doing more damage, in some other way, than good. When I took it, though, the knot in my chest loosened the smallest fraction. The ache in my bones, the cramping in my stomach if I was having that kind of day, the tiredness in me, all faded, just the slightest bit. It was so slight I might have been imaging it. But it was real enough that I kept doing it.

I glanced up and found Kin watching me. I felt a little guilty, knowing I was using something he hadn't given me to treat symptoms. But he just smiled at me and asked if I was ready to go.

We didn't talk much on the drive over to Saben's apartment, but it wasn't awkward. Not quite. Maybe a bit, in that way silences can be when you don't really know someone, but not much. Like we were already learning each other enough to be quiet together.

When we were sitting in the apartment building's parking lot, though, I did start to feel uncomfortable. Nervous, maybe. I turned the car off, but then I just sat there. Kin saw that I wasn't moving and settled into his seat. His hand had been reaching for the door handle, but now he piled his fingers into his lap. They laced neatly together, the sharp knuckles delicate instead of strange. Last night, he had seemed to flicker sometimes, like he was going in and out of spaces too quickly. His hands had always been on me, though. I could remember those fingers everywhere.

"I need to get my messages, to see who needs a job done." I stared straight ahead, through the windshield. It was late enough that most people were at work, and the apartment complex was mostly empty.

"Okay." I was already starting to realize that Kin wasn't the kind of person who'd think it was strange that we were sitting in front of this worn, dirty building while I talked in circles. "Where do you get them?"

"They get dropped off with my sister."

Kin switched his hands, so his fingers were laced in a different order. "The fey sister, I'm guessing."

"Right. Saben. She's my only sibling."

"Saben?"

I nodded. "The sidhe like pretty sounds."

He smiled at me, lazy and sweet. "That's true."

"She's very *fey*." I met his eyes and made a vague hand motion. I didn't know how to explain what Saben was.

"Luca. I've dealt with your fey before."

"Saben's different."

"You're making her sound terrifying."

"No, I don't mean it like that." I didn't know what I meant. I only wanted him to know what he was walking into, but I couldn't explain what a force Saben was, how she ran over people with her words and her gestures. How she didn't even seem to notice when she'd gone too far, when she hurt someone.

Kin sighed. "Kiss me."

"What?"

"Come over here and kiss me." His hand reached for my hip and pulled me closer, across the tiny space between the seats. We kissed, his mouth soft and open on mine, like he was offering himself, offering whatever I wanted from him. We hadn't kissed since last night. I'd been nervous about it, because sometimes it wasn't the same, the morning after. It was with Kin, though. He was warm and solid, and he tasted like him and me and the waffles, and something sweet and cool underneath. His hand on my hip held me like I was fragile. Like he wanted to span my whole body with those fingers.

"All right," he said when we broke apart, and his words were matter-of-fact, but his eyes looked a little lost. He touched a finger to his lip absently, as if unaware he was doing it. "I like you so much." He seemed far away, and his words were a bit faint, like was surprised by the kiss as much as I was. Then his eyes focused on me. "Let me meet your sister."

He smiled, slowly, the slight embarrassment in his eyes acknowledging whatever had just happened between us, and I smiled back. I couldn't help it.

Saben wasn't exactly as enthused to meet Kin as Kin was to meet her. She eyed him, and then said, her tone flat, "Yokai."

"*Hai, hai,*" Kin replied. Then he laughed at himself, a quiet, derisive sound.

"Invite him in, Saben," I said, softly. I could hear that parent tone in my voice. I forgot sometimes that she wasn't six anymore, and I acted like she was still my responsibility. Acted like she was someone whose behavior reflected on me. Like it was still my job to teach her manners and etiquette and that it wasn't polite to spit on guests her brother brought to visit.

She stepped backward. I took advantage of the little gap between her and the doorframe and stepped inside, gesturing for Kin to follow me. He stood close to me. Not so close that we crowded each other, but close enough that it was almost like he was protecting me, or I was protecting him. Like we were a unit and Saben was the piece opposite us. It was strange. I didn't often feel like a unit with Saben, but until now, I'd always been on her side, even when she wasn't on mine. It was a habit I'd never been able to break, had never seriously tried to get rid of. She eyed Kin, letting her gaze go up and down him. She wasn't embarrassed by her rudeness, didn't think anything of it. Kin didn't seem to either. He flexed his hands, making it obvious that they were empty.

She turned her stare on me. "You reek of iron."

I hesitated, then shrugged. "I'm sorry."

"And you reek of him," she said, softer, her head jerking toward Kin.

I bit my lip. "That's none of your business."

My tone hadn't been harsh, but she ducked her head a fraction, like I'd actually managed to chastise her. Beside me, Kin shifted his weight from one foot to the other. I thought it was possible that I'd never been quite so uncomfortable. I sighed. "I need my messages."

Saben turned her head like she was pondering something. I knew the gesture. It meant she was flustered or embarrassed. I waited it out, another ingrained habit.

"Will you have tea?" she finally asked, her voice stiff, the words coming out like she was forcing them. I knew she didn't feel obligated, though. If she didn't want to make us tea, she wouldn't be asking at all.

I glanced at Kin, and he nodded, his head tilting forward into something that was almost a shallow bow of acceptance. It wasn't a mocking gesture, and Saben seemed to see that. She glanced at me and I nodded, and she walked into the kitchen.

I turned, the movement alone bringing us from the doorway to the main room, and gestured for Kin to take a seat. The living room was made out to look like a normal home. Two love seats sat kitty-corner to each other, taking up most of the space, with a coffee table in the middle. The white plush of the couches, the slightly worn wicker that supported the glass top of the table, the cheapness and oldness of the pieces of furniture, made it seem like they belonged in the apartment. Any human could have bought them to decorate with. There was nothing unique or even very interesting about them.

Saben had strewn silk cloths over everything, though, to make the space hers, and the colors of the fabric were too rich—dark reds and royal purples, greens that seemed deep enough to jump into—the embroidery far too fine, for anything not made with magic. The room smelled like fresh apples, and I couldn't tell where the scent was coming from. On one wall, a huge painting of a lake hung, surrounded by a silver frame. On the coffee table, a beautiful, plain white pitcher and a white clay bowl sat, the bowl just under the pitcher's mouth. Every few moments, a trickle of clear water would pour from the pitcher into the bowl, where it would turn into blue and green and purple swirls before fading. There were no lights in the bowl, no reservoir of water in the pitcher, or a pump to make it work. It was just Saben, having fun.

Kin sat against the silk-covered cushions of the far couch. He ran his fingers over the fabric of the cloths, nodding his head in appreciation, but he didn't seem surprised. He'd seen it all before. He watched the pitcher dribble out its water and smiled when he saw it hit the bowl.

Saben came back with a small silver tray full of slices of fruits, but no tea. I peeked into the kitchen and saw her ugly kettle on the stove.

"Are you actually boiling water?" Then I looked again. "I thought you had the stove taken out?"

She sat next to me, just resting on the edge of the cushion, and flicked her eyes at me. "I decided to keep it."

I laughed. "What for?"

Her eyes narrowed. "To boil water, for one."

I sat back and stared at her. Saben could ask water to boil, and it would. The skills of the fey, the magics they have in them, are not all powerful. Usually, they're not even that practical. But they can be useful in the hands of someone skilled, and Saben was that.

She angled her face away from me. "I'm careful not to touch the iron. I put a cloth over it when I'm not using it, to keep the iron from leaking out into the air." She thought about it for a second. "To keep it from leaking so much," she amended.

"You don't put the cloth on when it's still hot," I said, not asking.

She glared at me. "Do I look like such a fool?"

On the couch opposite me, Kin's shoulders tensed. I realized how awkward it was to have this conversation in front of someone. I realized I'd never properly introduced them.

The fey I've known don't really go in for introductions. It can take months for me to learn someone's name, to give mine. Sometimes it never happens at all. Not because they don't consider names important, but because they're considered so important they shouldn't be trivialized. Kin and Saben would never notice if I didn't introduce them. But growing up human, taught manners by a human mother, made me feel like I had to do it. And I thought it might help to move the conversation, if abruptly.

I cleared my throat. "Kin," I said, "this is Saben." I glanced at Saben. "This is Kin." I gestured toward him, a quick tightening and loosening of my fingers in his direction.

Saben turned to face him, her body swiveling on the cushion. Her chin was lifted up, like she was royalty. She thought she was. There were two spots of pale pink, the deepest blush her skin could manufacture, high on her cheeks. "I'm learning to boil water," she informed him.

He inclined his head to her, the gesture solemn, honestly respectful. His lips tilted at one corner. "That will be a wonderful thing for you to know."

The rest of the visit went a bit smoother than it had started. Not smooth, really, because the fact was, despite the tangled relationships we were starting to weave around each other, none of us really knew the others well. It was all still awkward. Just not unpleasantly so.

"Well," I said when we got back in my car, not asking, but wanting to know what Kin thought. I shifted forward and stuffed the messages Saben had given me into my back pocket.

Kin nodded. "She's something." He turned to me. "She would be formidable if she wasn't in your presence."

I'd had the key near the ignition, but now I dropped my hand. "She'd . . . what?"

"She's beautiful and strong. It's obvious how frightening she could be, or overbearing, or powerful. But you diminish her fierceness."

I didn't understand, not at all. I shook my head, asking him mutely for more of an explanation.

Kin's fingers flicked through the air. "I think there's part of her that wants to be a child around you, and I could see it. It made her less intimidating."

My eyebrows pinched together. Then I laughed. "I think she actually liked you. I really do."

He shook his head, and a rueful smile spread over his face. "I wouldn't go that far."

"Truly. The way she turned to you to talk to you. She wanted your attention."

"She was just siding with me over you because you were badgering her." He tilted his head, and the earrings, the sleek shine of his hair, caught the light. My breath hitched a little. I could see, in my mind's eye, those same flashes of light, muted and private and lovely, in my bedroom when he'd leaned over me, when he'd came close enough to brush his lips over my collarbone, my neck, my mouth.

I shrugged. "Maybe."

Kin turned toward me. His left knee bent and rested on the seat cushion, his hands on either side of it. "Were you close, when she was young?"

I shifted my hands in my lap. I stared at them, at the keys twisted around my fingers. So ordinary, sitting here, ready to drive, with him beside me. "I don't know."

He didn't push, just waited.

"I don't know if I was more her brother, or her friend, or her parent." I looked up at Kin and shrugged. "I thought we were. I thought we were close."

"But not anymore." It wasn't really a question.

I answered it anyway. "No."

"What happened?"

"I went away." Another uncomfortable shrug. "My father and his friend sent me away to try to find a cure. Or maybe . . . maybe they sent me so I wouldn't be so visible. So in the way. I went. I searched. For years. And I . . ." I shook my head. "I didn't think I was going to come back, Kin. So I tried to keep everyone away. I didn't keep in contact, not any more than I absolutely had to. I wanted them to forget me. I was wrong. But I'd already done it. And Saben and I lost each other. When I came back, we weren't the same."

Kin nodded. He was so calm, so steady, so ready to accept whatever I told him. But I could see his fingers tightening on the edge of the seat, his nails digging into the fabric, like he was containing himself. Holding something back.

"Did you like it? The . . . traveling? The being away?"

"Yeah. I liked it." I'd loved it, for a while. I'd loved how separate I'd been, how far away from everything I'd ever known. I'd seen some places I was pretty sure most people never did. Back alleys and dusty markets, rivers that meandered through steep mountains and windy plains, and huge cities and tiny towns. I'd met interesting people and let myself disappear into a few of them, for a handful of nights at a time. I'd pretended I was someone else, someone whole and well and not an accident that was slowly proving how much it should never have existed. I'd liked it.

"Why did you come back here, then?" Kin asked, gently.

Maybe it was the way he asked it. Like he really wanted to know. Like it mattered. Or like he already knew why and he just wanted me to tell him. But my throat closed, went tight and scratchy, and I felt, suddenly, ridiculously, like I might cry, right there, sitting in my car in front of my sister's apartment.

"No one could help me," I told him. I looked up, looked him right in the eye, and he glanced away. "There isn't a cure. And I don't have the stamina to move place to place anymore. I had . . . I came home because I was afraid and I didn't know where else to go."

Kin stared down at his lap, his hands twisting and turning over each other. "Have you given up?" he asked me after a long minute.

I didn't want to say those words. I didn't ever want to give up. But hope was hard. "There isn't anything that will work."

"If there was," Kin said, slowly, "if there was, would you do it?"

"Yes," I said, without hesitation. I tried to make myself smile. The expression was brittle on my face. "I want to get better, Kin. I don't want . . . It hasn't . . . It hasn't been long enough, you know?"

He nodded, but he didn't say anything more. He just smiled back at me and leaned forward to kiss my cheek, soft, lingering, so I could feel his breath against my skin. Then he sat back in his seat, buckled his seat belt. I stuck the key in the ignition, more than ready to get out of there.

CHAPTER 7

'd asked Kin if he wanted to come with me on the job I had to do that day, and he'd said yes, so I drove us up the coast. The landscape didn't change much, but the houses faded away, until all that was left were rambling orchards and misshapen fields meandering their way up hills. Sometimes I caught glimpses of fruit in the branches, but most things were starting to go dormant. The temperature didn't drop very far here, not compared to other areas, but something about how the light fell during these months said the season had changed, and the plants responded to it.

We were headed to a farm in the middle of nowhere, and the last leg of the journey was across fields gone wild, grasses and brambles, some browned, others growing out of control, the long dirt road cutting through the middle of it all. Then we passed what I knew were grapevines and raspberry brambles and blueberry bushes, some still with withered fruit clinging to them. Other areas appeared nearly dead, their leaves dried and curled inward toward their bark, waiting for spring. Even when they were green and lush again, though, I knew the place would still be unruly, the plants growing wherever they pleased. Things were tended, but in a carefree way. Their owner let them sprawl where they would, and he walked through the vines and picked only what he wanted to eat or use. I always thought these fruits and berries, and the vegetables and nuts that were grown here too, were better that way. Like I could taste the earth and the season and the complete lack of restraint in them.

I parked in front of a sturdy wooden house. It was small, but well cared for. The grass around it was cropped neatly. The flower and herb garden was chaotic, filled with sprawling plants, but they didn't spill out on the drive or the walkway. Vines were allowed to climb the side of the house as they wanted, but everything else was gently corralled inside a short brick barrier. The driveway wasn't paved, but the dirt where we parked had been packed down and neatly raked into lines.

"Riyad is different too. Not different like Saben," I told Kin as we unbuckled our seat belts and I pulled the key out of the ignition. "Just . . . very himself."

"Will I like him?" Kin gave me a teasing smile.

"I think so." But then I shook my head. Whatever Kin was expecting, I knew it was wrong.

We stepped out of the car. As I shut my door, a figure appeared at the house. He stepped down off the porch and leaned his body against the side of the house, arms crossed. His shoulder brushed against the house's siding; one ankle hooked around the other. He stood still, staring out at his fields, not paying much attention to us at all. Beside me, Kin took a deep breath. We couldn't see Riyad's face yet, or anything much about him but his silhouette, but it didn't matter. I could feel him. I could feel him in my mind and deep in my heart, and on my skin, all over my skin. And Kin could feel him too.

I pocketed the keys, and we walked to meet him. As we got closer, the sun dipped behind him and let us make out his face. He smiled when he saw me, like he was pleasantly surprised. I hadn't told him when I'd be coming, so if he was anyone other than himself, I might have believed that surprise. But I knew better. He'd known I was coming before I had. Even if he hadn't been able to feel me there, feel me whenever I thought of him, I was one of the few people who came to see him. If he'd heard a car coming up through his fields, he could have guessed who was in it. But I smiled back when I saw his lips curve up around his white, white teeth, because he made me feel good.

I studied him, trying to find a difference from the last time I'd seen him. From the time I'd seen him before that, and before that, all the way back to when I was a toddler and my father had brought me to walk through these fields, to play under this man's table. There was none. He was the same. If he'd been human, he would have appeared to be eighteen, maybe nineteen. His face was smooth and his back was straight. He wore skinny jeans, a white shirt, and black ankle boots, strapped tight, that made his feet seem sharp and delicate. I put my hand on my heart.

At my side, Kin bowed. His body bent to a strict right angle, his arms tight at his sides. His hands curled into fists.

Riyad shook his head and straightened, pulling away from his lean against the house. "Don't do that."

Kin slid out of his bow, his body unbending one vertebra at a time. His face was pale.

One of Riyad's hands flicked away from his elbow, the fingers skimming over the air. The sun caught his skin. Desert skin, I always thought of it. It was dark gold and shimmered, sometimes, when it caught the light just right. It made me think of living in sand and sun. His hair matched, some tangled mess of bronze and black. "I'm not what you think," Riyad said. The smile stayed on his face. It was only the hint of an expression, but it had weight behind it, hundreds of years of weight.

"I think you are," Kin said, his voice rasping.

Riyad blinked, slowly, his eyelashes falling into deep shadows against his face before he opened his eyes again. He could do everything slowly if he wanted to, because he had time. "And what would that be?"

Kin said nothing. Riyad's finger flicked again, a little push to get rid of the question he'd asked. He turned to me. "The glamour's wearing thin around the back acres." He smiled at me, and this time it was softer, still weighty because he couldn't help that, but comforting. This was the smile he'd given me as a child, the smile he'd bestowed on me to praise me or show me how much he cared about me. I smiled back. "I can do it. But you are the best at that particular talent. Do you mind?"

"Of course not. I'd be happy to." It was an easy thing. I'd known whatever Riyad wanted from me would either be simple or interesting or both. I'd known it wasn't urgent, too, but when Saben mentioned there was a note from him in my pile of messages, I knew I wanted to take Kin to see him. *I* wanted to see him.

"Will you come with us?" I asked.

He shook his head. "I have a stew on the stove I need to finish. Come see me afterwards. We can have dinner."

I nodded, but Kin stuttered, starting to say something, maybe to protest.

"You too," Riyad said. "Please."

Kin glanced at me, then back to Riyad, and nodded. "Thank you."

Riyad pushed his hair back, running his fingers through it. It was such a young man's gesture. It was futile too, his bangs back in his eyes almost as soon as his hand dropped. It didn't faze him. His hand slipped back into the crook of his other elbow. He was beautiful. I'd always thought that. He was beautiful and worn. Small-framed and fragile.

I nodded and gestured for Kin to follow me. We stopped at the tool shed so I could get a little shovel, and then we walked through the fields, until we came to the back end of a field, bordered by tall, old trees. The sun came down in crystalline green stripes, and the air was cool with the shade from the trees. A perfect place to set up a glamour. It's not that they have to be done in nature, not at all, but it's just that it makes it easier. Makes the glamour want to stay put.

"How old is he?" Kin leaned against the split-rail fence that marked out the border of Riyad's land. I bent and used the old, somewhat rusty shovel to dig at the fence post's base. Rusty, because it was iron. Riyad was the only fey I'd known, aside from Kin, now, who could stand the metal. He'd told me he'd built up a tolerance to it through practice, over all those years. His tolerance had started to fade, though, and he didn't like handling it so much now.

I wanted to get my hands on the post and the dirt that touched it at the same time, and I wanted to bury the glamour, anchor it, as far down as I could. "Old. He's looked like that for as long as I've been alive," I said, answering while I dug. I'd never really asked how other fey glamoured things. I didn't know if my way was the right way or not. It did seem, though, that once I'd glamoured something, my glamour worked a little more efficiently, stuck better, than most. Especially on objects and places. "He's older than my father. He's older than any fey I've ever known."

"Centuries, probably . . ." Kin sounded awed. I understood. I'd grown up knowing Riyad, knowing he was different than us, and ancient, and I loved him, but part of him still frightened me. Still made me hold him on a pedestal. He never liked that, I knew, but I couldn't help it. He had seen so many things, been so many places, lived. He'd lived so much.

I nodded. "Do the yokai not . . . ?"

Kin shifted, resting his weight on the opposite foot. Underneath him, dry grass crackled. "Ningyo don't live forever. Most yokai . . . don't age much. But we're not immortal."

"Neither are the fey. Neither are what Riyad is. Some kind of desert sidhe, or djinn . . . A mix, probably. I don't know if he really knows what he is, completely. But I know he thinks he's not supposed to live as long as he has." I tried to let my hands feel like they were merging the earth and the post, tried to think of the subtle shield that would make this land suddenly uninteresting to anyone who came too close, and not think about the way I sometimes came upon Riyad, standing out at his door, gazing far away, seeing things I couldn't imagine.

Kin watched me, and when I raised my head, our eyes met. "We live a long time," he said. "Longer than humans, definitely. But not that long. Not like that."

"But close."

His jaw worked. "Yes."

I stood and made to climb over the fence. Kin offered a hand, and when I stepped in his cupped palm, he boosted me over the top rail. I turned around to survey my work. The glamour wouldn't work as well on me, since I'd set it, but I could see it, like a film, a minor discoloration. It looked right.

I stepped back to Kin and held my hands out so he could pull me up and back over. "And you?" he asked.

I turned away from him. I knew he'd meant the fey, and that it was simple curiosity. The question stung me, though. I'd heard something different in it, and I wasn't sure if he'd really meant it to be there or not. "I don't know."

I didn't think, as a half, I'd ever have lived as long as a normal sidhe. Maybe I'd have had a human life span, though. But now, now that I was sick and getting sicker, I had no idea how long it would be. Not long enough.

I could feel him watching, could feel those eyes that had no problem staring, warm as they looked down on my back while I looked down at the fence. I felt like shivering, felt like being sick, and

I couldn't explain why. The remark had just hit me wrong, I'd taken it too far, but now it was in me and my answer was lying dead between us, obvious, and both his question and my answer were singeing me inside.

"I didn't mean it like that," he said. He didn't sound angry or annoyed. He sounded like he regretted it.

"I know," I said, quickly. "I'm sorry." But I kept staring at the fence. I was ashamed. Kin didn't treat me like I was weak or sick. While I'd worked, he hadn't told me to slow down or let him do things. When we'd slept together, he'd acted like I was delicate, important, but not breakable. He knew already, I thought, that I didn't want that. But here I was, angry because my life wouldn't be as long as his. Because there was something inside me that was rotten.

Kin stepped closer. His hand ran down my arm, his fingers twisted together with mine. He pulled, just enough to turn my shoulder so I faced him. His other hand came up to wrap around the back of my neck. He brought our foreheads together, breathed the same air as me. His thumb moved back and forth across my skin. He didn't say anything. I closed my eyes. And then I just breathed as well, until everything that burned in me faded away.

When I finished the glamour, making sure it covered all of the back end of Riyad's property, Kin and I walked back to the house. Saben was there, sitting on the front porch. I didn't know if Riyad had asked her, or if she'd decided to come, even though she knew Kin and I were probably there. I tensed when I saw her, ready to continue our near argument from this morning, or a million others like it, but she only nodded her head at us, chilly but polite.

"Riyad's making stew," I said when we got close enough to talk.

"Are you staying?" Saben asked.

I glanced at Kin, who shrugged. I turned back to her and nodded.

She stood, tapping the arms of the chair with her palms and bouncing a bit on the balls of her feet. Then she turned and made her way into the house. Kin and I followed. As we climbed the porch steps, he took my hand in his. I glanced at him, and he smiled at me.

"We don't have to stay," I said. I'd thought his shrug had meant he didn't mind either way, but I didn't want to get this wrong and make him uncomfortable.

He shook his head. "I want to." His fingers tightened around mine. "I want to hold your hand too. Is that okay?"

I laughed, relieved and, in that moment, happier there with him than I could remember being in a long time. "Yeah. It's okay."

Riyad welcomed us when we got inside, and within a few minutes, we were sitting wherever we found the most comfortable, eating out of large ceramic bowls filled with a rich and spicy stew. Riyad had a table, tucked into one corner of the kitchen, but he almost never used it. Instead, Kin and I sat together on the couch, and Riyad sat adjacent, in one of his chairs. Saben perched on a high stool, her back to the short island that separated the living room from the kitchen, her legs kicking back and forth gently. Her feet didn't touch the floor.

The fey like to be comfortable. They like to have things around them that are beautiful or familiar or both. It wouldn't be strange for a sidhe or an elf or a phouka to stretch out and relax. There was something about this arrangement, though, the way we'd angled ourselves, so that we were all almost facing each other, the way the couch felt velvety soft against my skin, how we all kind of hunched forward over our bowls to inhale the spicy scent of the stew, that struck me as weirdly human. It wasn't that Riyad's house wasn't beautiful—it was—but it was a beauty worn down into comfortable patterns, like a threadbare rug that still warmed your feet. And it wasn't that sitting with Kin and Riyad and Saben in one room wasn't awkward. No one seemed to know what to say. Stilted small talk was the only thing going around, but it was all right. It was all so casual, so nearly comfortable but not quite, so normal. This could have been my mother's house. We could have been any family, broken and careful and then not careful enough around each other, having a meal together, *being* together.

I didn't know what to think of it. I didn't know if it was all right for me to enjoy it, to want more of it.

After we were done eating, Kin and I washed the dishes while Saben and Riyad had coffee in the living room.

"Sorry I dragged you into my strange family outing," I told Kin quietly, sure my voice would be mostly drowned out by the running water, so I wouldn't be heard in the other room.

Kin shook his head. He took a bowl from me and rinsed it. "No. This was good. Good for you, especially, I think. How long since you did something like this? Ate with Riyad and your sister?"

I took a deep breath and let it out in a laugh that was a little bit on the bitter side. "Years. Almost a decade?"

"Needed some time, did you?" Kin asked wryly.

"Riyad knew I did. He's the friend of my father's I mentioned before, the one who told me to go and see if I could find a cure." I thought maybe Riyad had made it possible for me to leave simply so that I could get away from everything for a while. Find myself. He'd seen as much of the world as I had. He had to know that there were places where a person could lose themselves, or find themselves, without the ties of family and duty and tradition to hold them back.

"Good man, then." Kin flicked a soap bubble at me. "Still kinda scares the crap out of me, though."

I laughed, a real laugh this time, and Kin laughed with me, smiling while he watched me. His expression was tender and a tiny bit possessive and happy. It was so strange to see someone look at me, really see me, and wear that expression on his face. To know that something about me had put it there. It was so good.

And then I coughed and ruined it.

At first, it was only one cough, not even that bad, and it seemed like I might be able to control it. I could take in a breath, so I thought it would be fine. But then I coughed again, and again, and then I was leaning against the sink edge, hoping I could hold myself up and get enough air in, wishing so hard that this wasn't happening.

Kin's hands went to either side of my face, pushed at my hair, trying to see me. He hadn't stopped to dry them, and warm water and soap foam trickled down my jaw to my neck. I brought up my own hand, grabbing at his wrist, trying to tell him that I was all right, but I couldn't get the words out. My hold on him became as much a support, him holding me up, as it was a way to keep his attention.

The coughing was just a static beat now, something it almost seemed I had to keep doing in order to draw in any air at all. Something was twisting inside me, stabbing, stinging more than the word could convey. I hurt like someone had lit a match in me, like I inhaled the smoke from it and stoked its little flame with every breath I took.

I pressed against the spot, trying to ease it, and slump against the counter.

"Luca!" Kin's hands were tight around my shoulders, keeping me off the ground. His voice was too loud and shaky. A tremor went through him.

Then Riyad was there. He didn't try to pull me from Kin's hands. Instead, he kind of held on to both of us, one hand on each of us, steadying us as much as he could.

"He needs to sit," Riyad told Kin. I could barely make out his words over the rushing in my head. There was more discussion, a quick back and forth of voices, and Kin and Riyad were shuffling me into the living room, back to the couch I'd been sitting on before.

Kin pushed my back against the cushions and sat beside me. "Here, Luca," he said, even though there wasn't anywhere else to go. He sounded calmer now, but I could still feel the tremble in his limbs, the way his body shook with mine every time I coughed.

I wanted to lie down and curl into myself to stop the pain, but Riyad appeared next to me and forced me to sit up so I could breathe. I brought my knees up against my chest instead. I tried to focus on staying upright, on taking in air, on telling myself that I was all right and this would pass. It frightened me, though. There was a pressure in me, building and building, and I was gasping, afraid that this thing in me would burst, that I would fly apart. Between that and the pain, tears were running down my cheeks, but I couldn't stop crying, couldn't even get a hand up to wipe at them. My world tunneled, time becoming long and slow, while I tried to get myself under control. All I could do was sit there and struggle.

Kin stayed beside me while I tried to breathe, and Riyad hovered over us. Kin soothed his hands over my back. "Breathe, Luca," he whispered. He leaned close and wiped at my face with his thumb. "Just breathe."

I couldn't say anything back. For a moment that felt like it lasted years, I wondered if whatever was happening really would ever stop. Then the pressure peaked and I ground my teeth against it, and instead of tearing me apart, it started to release its hold. The pain receded in tiny fractions. I took in a slightly deeper gulp of air, still shallow, still cautious, but enough to feel like I wouldn't suffocate. I had to clear my throat, then cough, but it wasn't anything like what it had been before. I hurt, but the pain was draining away faster now.

I pushed Kin's hand from my face and used my own, pressing my fingers into my cheekbones while I wiped at tears. I took another breath and got a lungful. It stung like crazy, but it was so sweet.

Kin was still watching me, staring down at me. His hands, on the back of my neck and my shoulder now, were so steady, but his eyes were pinched, the bones of his face standing out in sharp relief. He was all over scales, like he hadn't been able to hold on to his glamour, sparkly in the light of evening coming in through the window, but I could see the dark smudge of a flush on his cheeks. It occurred to me that, for all he was a healer, he probably hadn't had to deal with many people who did the things I did. I could imagine him treating iron burns and the minor curses the fey fling at each other. But I doubted he got many cases like this.

"I'm all right." I coughed again, more a clearing than anything, and felt how scratchy my throat was. Riyad leaned down and pushed a glass of something toward us. Kin took it and steadied my hand on it so I could drink.

I sipped, and then sipped again, taking the time to make sure I was under control before I faced him and Riyad.

And Saben. She was standing just behind Riyad, her spine as straight as it always was, but tense, unyielding, her hands bunched into each other, her fingers twisted together. Her bottom lip was tucked between her teeth, and she was staring at me. She watched me with a wariness, as if any second I was going to explode, right there in front of her, and ruin her dress.

"Is that what happens to you?" She sounded like she was interrogating me, like she wanted to get the answer by force. Kin hunched over me even more. I realized that I had one hand wrapped in his shirt, holding him. I loosened my fingers and splayed them against the curve of his arm instead.

"Sometimes," I answered her, going for an easy tone.

"Often?"

There was something else in her voice, anger or curiosity, something that was just strong enough to find its way through and cut into me. I leaned against Kin. "Saben," I said, trying to ask her to stop.

"I've never seen anything like that," she said, softer now, but I could still hear that thing in her voice.

"You've seen me sick," I argued. I'd been sick for a long time. Maybe she hadn't seen it recently, but I knew she'd seen me coughing and unable to stop when she was a child, seen me sitting curled around myself until a spell of pain passed, knew there'd been times when she'd been unable to get me out of bed on any given day because I was too sore or tired.

She shook her head. Her hands rose, grasped at her elbows. "Not like that. Never like that. That bad."

I lowered my eyes, so all I could see was the place where Kin's arm touched mine, our hands clasped. I didn't remember doing that. I didn't want to talk anymore. It beat in me like a pulse, this desire to never speak about this again. "Well, now you have."

I glanced up at Kin, and then over to Riyad. He gave me a soft look, not quite a smile, nothing like a smile, but his face made the same movements, and he shook his head the tiniest bit.

"I'm sorry," I said. I didn't know who I was talking to. Everyone in the room, probably.

Kin moved his thumb over the pulse in my wrist. He leaned close so he could whisper to me. "Don't be." He sounded relieved, but I had heard the fear in his voice, before.

"I'm sorry."

Kin shook his head. I heard Saben shift from foot to foot. Riyad moved away, back toward the kitchen, giving me a little space. He ran his hand over Saben's shoulder as he passed, and I saw her lean into his touch, but she didn't acknowledge it any more than that.

"What do I do?" she asked, still watching me and Kin. She was pulling her elbows in toward her body, folding in on herself.

I sat up straighter. "Nothing. It's done."

"I couldn't do anything."

For a second, I saw the little girl she used to be, in the worry on her face and the way she was holding herself. The girl who had followed me around everywhere I went. Who had held my hand when we walked together. Who had loved me. I knew she had. "There wasn't anything to do."

"Kin did something," she argued, petulant.

I knew how she felt. I knew what it was like to see someone sick and not be able to do anything. Action made you powerful, it made you feel like you were fighting. When it wasn't available, it took your pride and burned a hole in you. It had been that way when my mother was sick. I'd been useless. Scared. Weakened by something I couldn't even see.

But I had known better too, because I was sick myself. I think it had been a real shock to both myself and my mother, when it became clear to us how bad she was, that she would die before me. Not that she'd ever said it out loud. I think it pleased her, though, in some strange way, to go before me. I knew she had never thought it would happen that way.

"You can't do anything about it," I told Saben. And then I broke our eye contact, and called out to Riyad, and changed the subject, because that was it. That was the answer, and I was done.

After we said goodnight to Riyad and Saben, Kin and I walked through the fields in front of Riyad's house. It was dark by then, but we made our way around the tangled vines on the ground with the light of the moon. Kin held my hand and guided me, and I thought about how well those green eyes of his saw in the darkness. He kept a close hold on me, like he was afraid to let me go. I felt fine, as fine as I ever did, though. I'd be sore tomorrow, probably. Tired tonight. But the coughing had passed almost like it had never happened to begin with.

I wanted to apologize to Kin for what I'd done in the kitchen, even though it wasn't really my fault. I was embarrassed, and I wanted him to take my apology so that I'd feel better. And for that reason, I wanted to say nothing. It wasn't his job to make me feel all right about myself.

His hand squeezed mine, and he stopped and turned toward me. "You're thinking too hard," he said. I couldn't see his face. It was all shadows and angles, but I could hear the amusement in his voice. "Just tell me. Whatever it is. I want to hear it."

I laughed. "You're too honest. You're going to get yourself hurt."

"Luca."

"I want to touch you," I said, suddenly, my voice so low I almost didn't hear my own words. "I want to be wrapped in you. I want you near me." I looked up at him. "Is that too much honesty? Is that what you wanted to know?"

It *was* too much. God, it would scare anyone away. But I hadn't had this in a long time, maybe ever, and I wanted as much of it as I could get.

He pulled me in, his hand on mine, then on my wrist, then my elbow, and then he was wrapped around me, just like I'd asked. He tucked me against him, his arms loose against my shoulders. I set my hands on his hips.

"I didn't want to scare you, in the kitchen," I said, and it was just far enough between an explanation and an apology that I felt okay saying it.

His arms tightened around me. "Did you like how honest I was, then?" he asked, sounding bitter. "I *was* scared. I'm sorry. I should have been more in control of that, shouldn't have let it be so visible, and I . . . wasn't. I couldn't hide it."

I took a deep breath. "You grounded me." I slid my hands to the small of his back. "You held me there."

Kin sighed and pulled away. His hand came up to brush against my cheek and cup my face. "Luca. I thought of something."

He sounded . . . nervous. Afraid again. My heart thumped, heavy and tense, in my chest, because I thought this was the moment where he'd tell me that this was too much for him. That he couldn't tie himself, even a little bit, to someone who was so sick. I was surprised at how very much I didn't want that to happen. Even though I'd been half expecting it. Even though I knew it would be fair. I didn't want to lose him, not so soon.

"What?" I asked.

"Remember this morning, when I asked you, if there was a cure, would you take it?"

I blinked. Not what I'd been expecting. "Of course."

He was still standing close enough that I could feel it when he took a deep breath. "There's a legend. About the ningyo."

"Ningyo . . ." I said. "That's what you are, right?"

He nodded. "I'm at least half ningyo." I wanted to ask about that, but he kept talking before I could. "In Japan, they say that if you eat a ningyo, you'll live forever. If you eat part. Immortality." His words came out too fast, tripping and tumbling over themselves. "Fishermen used to try to catch us. That's where the legend came from."

"That's disgusting," I said, because it was the first thing that came to mind, and it was. Completely disgusting.

"I know." His hand came up, and he ran his palm down my arm. "It is. But . . . Luca, you should have seen them. Riyad and Saben. They were scared. I don't want them to . . . I don't want to lose you." He swallowed. "Not if there's something that might work."

"Do you know if it'll work?" I asked, and I couldn't believe I was doing it. I didn't want to know. It was disturbing, everything Kin had just told me. And it was beyond difficult to believe. But there was a part of me, that part that always hoped, that needed to know. That wanted to grab on to this and run with it. That wanted to reach with both hands and cling to anything that might be a cure. "Or is it just a legend?"

He shook his head slowly. He hadn't stepped back, and neither had I, but we were, somehow, farther apart now. "I've never tried it. I've never known anyone who has. Never heard anything but the legend." His hands closed over my arms. "But it could work. You could try it. I . . . I have scales. It would be easy."

I shuddered again, and this time he laughed. "Not like that," he explained. "They fall off, like a snake shedding."

I nodded, absorbing what he was saying. It was still gross, but less disturbing than I'd imagined. But . . . "Immortality." I met his eyes. "Would it make me better? Would I . . ." I swallowed. "Would I not be sick anymore?" The words were tight in my throat, difficult to say because I wanted the answer to be yes so badly, and it seemed so impossible.

"You wouldn't." His voice was firm. "Well. If the legend is true. But that's what I've heard. Good health, and a life that doesn't end. No more illnesses. I think . . . I think it would cure you. If it's true."

I didn't know what to say. His words were bouncing around in my head, and I couldn't pin any of it down enough to actually think about it. But then I had another thought. An embarrassing, awkward thought that made my heart jump with remembered heat nonetheless.

"Kin . . . You said *eat*. I . . . Last night . . . You came in my mouth," I finally blurted out, putting it bluntly because I didn't know how else to say it. I'd been pretty pleased about it at the time, but saying it out loud, now, during a conversation like this, had me blushing. And worried. "Does that . . . I mean, I swallowed." I didn't know what to think about anything that he'd told me, but I knew that, whatever happened, I wanted to have a say in it. If there was even a tiny chance this legend was true, I didn't want it affecting me in such a giant way, just because of what we did in bed. I didn't want it to have happened without my even knowing about it.

He shook his head, and his hands squeezed my arms, soothing me. "No. If it worked like that, anyone who ever slept with a ningyo would be immortal. And I know for sure that doesn't happen. It didn't happen like that for my parents. I don't think bodily fluids work. I know they don't. I think . . . Honestly, I think it's just the scales. They're the most fey part of us. I think that's where the magic is."

I nodded again, a little bit relieved. But I still couldn't really grasp everything that he was offering me. It was huge, a massive thing. It made me hopeful and excited and afraid. So terribly afraid. Afraid that, if we tried it, it wouldn't work. Afraid that it would. Terrified.

I couldn't decide whether I wanted to push away from him, or if I wanted to fall forward into him. I chose the latter, stepping forward. His arms came up, circled me, held me to him.

"I have to think," I mumbled into his shoulder. It was the only thing I could come up with, and I wasn't even sure if he'd hear me. He must have, though, because he said, "Okay," and held me tighter against him.

CHAPTER 8

"How long are you going to sleep?"

I blinked my eyes open. Saben was standing over me, her fists resting on her hips. Her dark-blond hair drifted across her face, only half of it constrained by the knot she'd tied it in. It caught the dim light coming in from her window and turned gold and cinnamon and cocoa. Old nicknames I'd once had for her came to mind, nicknames that played on her coloring and her size and the sweet, demanding way she had asserted her authority as a child. I clamped my mouth down on them. I didn't dare say any of them to her face now.

"How long was I out?" I thought about sitting up, getting off the floor, but my whole body ached. Using the length of the conversation to keep lying down seemed like the most genius idea I'd ever had. There was a pillow shoved under my head. It was almost comfortable, compared to moving.

"Twenty minutes or so," she said. Her voice was sharp, her shoulders squared to me. She bit her lip when she wasn't talking. The corners of her eyes were pinched.

I smiled at her. "Maybe I have the flu." I'd felt bad on the way over to her place. I'd knocked on her door and come inside, and that was it. I didn't remember the floor coming toward me, or falling at all. I remembered the sound I made when I hit, though. A big *thump*. Hearing is the last to go when you pass out.

Saben huffed through her nose. "It's not the flu." She squatted down beside me, her elbows resting on her knees.

I pushed my hand against my forehead, through my hair, trying to ease the pain in my head. I felt like a balloon that had been popped. "I know."

She ran her fingers over my arm, pushing up my sleeve when she got to the shoulder. "Your boyfriend will think I've been abusing you."

I started to say that he probably wouldn't notice, since I hadn't seen or heard from him in four days, since we'd had that awkward, terrible conversation amongst the dead grapevines, and that I couldn't predict when I'd see him again. I realized how bitter that sounded, though, and kept my mouth shut, even though I wanted to complain, if only so Saben would reassure me. She wasn't exactly the reassuring type, anyway, when it came down to it.

I raised the arm she was pointing to and sighed when I saw it. Bruises were forming down the length of it, right to my wrist. "From the fall? Already?"

She nodded. "I think so. I can almost see them coming up. Right in front of my eyes."

I cocked my head at her direct answer. There was no play in her words, no teasing that made me guess at what she meant, no coy reply. Nothing fey-like in her speech. Just . . . the truth. An answer to a question asked. I'd known she was capable of it, but she hadn't shown me that side of her in a long time.

I watched her watching me, her lip going bright red and raw while she gnawed on it and stared at my arm. I glanced back down at myself. The bruises weren't that bad yet, but the splotches were already going from shadowy to purple. I'd have them down my side too, then, and my leg. Wherever I'd hit hard enough. I flopped my arm back down, not even caring anymore that it hurt. Saben knelt beside me. I studied her a bit more. She was wearing a sky-blue linen shirt and jeans that might have been artfully ripped but were probably just worn through. The shirt was too thin for the season, made of fine cotton, threadbare and supple with too many washings, and elegant. And she was holding a dishcloth. A dirty one. It looked like she'd been cleaning.

"Do you usually bruise like that?"

"It's new," I answered dismissively. "What were you doing? What's that?" I pointed to the cloth.

She shrugged. "I was dusting."

"Oh my god, Saben. Since when do you dust?"

She stood, angry. "Since now. I should slap you."

I laughed and risked sitting up. "What are you doing here? You should go back to the fey." I swayed for a second, trying to figure out how my balance was behaving, and then stood.

Saben didn't step back again. Her arms folded across her chest. The cloth hung from her fist. "Why can't I belong here like you?"

"Because you don't!" I flung my hands up in the air. "I was born here. You weren't. You're not half like me. You should be *grateful.*"

Her hand flashed out, and I flinched, but it stopped just before it collided with my cheek. She touched her fingertips to my skin, just enough for me to feel her against me. I wanted to lean into her. I stayed perfectly still instead. She touched me for a short second, and then pulled her hand away. "We all want what we can't have, then, don't we?"

I swallowed hard. "What do you mean?"

She shook her head. The softness that had been there left, and I saw her whole body tighten, her eyes going steely and focused again. "Never mind. Why are you here?"

I sighed. "I was passing by. Wanted to come and check that you hadn't burned the place down."

"Don't say things like that," she scolded, but I was teasing this time, and she recognized it. She gave her cloth a little shake and moved around the couch so she could sit. I hesitated, then came and sat next to her. She leaned forward so she could study me. Her fingers twisted around each other. It was such a blatant sign of agitation it frightened me. She glanced up at me and asked, "Why do you do things for me when you get nothing in return?"

I looked at her, really looked. I pretended I was Kin and I could stare forever, for as long as I wanted. I took in how incongruous she was here, and how beautiful. Her sugar skin was pale and washed out against the white of the couch and the bright colors of the cloths that draped the cushions. Her lips were too pink. She seemed so sure of herself, though, perched there beside me, her head up, her shoulders slumped just slightly, her hair wild around her face. Like she sat here all the time. Like she was completely familiar with the couch, because she was. It was *her* couch. Her room. Her apartment. She'd made it all hers.

I tried to make her the same person as the little girl I'd known. It was hard.

I sighed. "Because I used to love you, and I'm trapped by the memory of that. Because maybe I still love you, somewhere in me, and I just can't figure out how to be with you anymore." I rubbed at the corner of my eye, over my cheekbone. "I can't get away from you."

"You could if you wanted to." Her eyes flicked up to mine. Hers were too large, too liquid, too brown. Inhuman and gorgeous and terrifying. "You did it well enough for a long time, Luca."

I thought of what Kin had said that night, when he'd told me Saben had been scared. She had been. I'd seen it myself. But I hadn't been sure then that that was what I was seeing. I hadn't believed it. I hadn't thought she would actually be afraid for me.

I reached out and flipped one of her hands over. I ran my fingers over hers, feeling the rough spots where her skin was peeling away, the tender areas she flinched at. Iron burns. "Why are you doing this? It must be making you sick. What's worth this?"

She snatched her hand away. "I don't know yet."

"So what's the point?"

She laughed. "*That's* the point."

There wasn't much else to say after that. I wanted her to do one thing, and she wanted to do another. And I wasn't really in any position to tell Saben what to do, anyway. I kept trying, like it was some habit ingrained so deeply in me I couldn't make it stop if I wanted to. But in reality, I'd given that right up when I'd left, when I'd, for all intents and purposes, abandoned her. Like she'd said. I'd tried to get away. I only had myself to blame if I wanted to come back, and she didn't want me there.

I went home. My house was quiet and secluded, away from the city like it was. Quiet enough that my own thoughts started to pile up in my mind. I thought about what Kin had said, what he'd suggested. Of course I did. I'd been thinking about it almost nonstop since he'd mentioned it that night. Part of the reason I'd gone to Saben's was just to get away from the thoughts for a little while.

My first instinct had been not to believe. To recognize that this was just another way to get my hopes up, only to have them come crashing back down. But I wanted to believe. I wanted it so badly. A cure. An answer. A stop to all of this pain, all of the struggle. A way to be normal.

But that was the thing. That was the reason why, over the last four days, I'd thanked my inner doubt, over and over again, for stopping me from jumping at the chance. Because if it worked, if it cured me, Kin's remedy wouldn't leave me normal. Not at all.

Immortality. Not something I'd ever seriously considered. I suppose everyone thinks about it, at least once—a childhood imagining, maybe. What it would be like to live forever. The abundance of time. Maybe I'd even thought about it more than most, because I lived so closely with the fey, with their inhumanly long life spans. Because mine would be so very different than theirs.

And maybe it was because I had thought about it, even in the most fantastical, abstract way, that instead of leaping for that chance, instead of reaching for all that time, I held myself back. The thought of being immortal, of living forever, frightened me. It chilled me in a way that told me it was an idea that would never sit comfortably. I could imagine it, the good parts, where I would be well and whole and my illness would vanish like smoke. Where an endless string of days stretched before me, to do with as I pleased. But I could imagine the bad things, the terrible things, too. My friends, my family dying before me. The press of time. The days, so far in the future I couldn't even imagine it, when nothing would be familiar, when everything would be foreign, a world, lifetimes away from what and who I'd known.

It was almost laughable to consider it seriously. To honestly attempt to accept that immortality might be a possibility. I'd never heard of anyone being immortal, never. I didn't even think Riyad actually was. He just had, for whatever reason, an unnaturally long life span, even amongst the fey. I didn't think that this cure of Kin's could actually produce the results he imagined. But if it could, if there was any chance it was true, a magic kept secret and safe, then it was worth considering seriously. I wasn't willing to take the chance, the risk, without consideration.

Kin finally came to me before I could come up with anything close to an answer. I'd left my front door unlocked—there were enough iron and wards and glamour to keep both fey and humans away—and he just came walking in. I had my headphones on—I suppose he must have knocked first. He was polite like that. But when I didn't answer, he opened the door and found me sprawled on my bed, listening to an album by an old band who had broken up years ago.

I saw him come through the door. The movement made me jump, until I realized who it was. Then my eyes tracked him, following his movements as he stepped across the living room, into my room, to the side of the bed, and took the headphones off my ears. His fingers were gentle against my skin.

"You're here," I said.

One corner of his mouth lifted in that lopsided smile. The skin around his eyes looked too thin. "I am."

"Are you all right?"

Kin crawled in beside me. We faced each other, our elbows touching. He ran the palm of his hand over the bruises on my arm. "Are you?"

I closed my eyes. "I'm sorry."

He laughed, a real laugh. "Don't be sorry."

I opened my eyes. There he was, staring at me. He'd glamoured away all but a few scales at the corners of his eyes.

He reached up and brushed a hand over my cheekbone, through my hair. His fingers circled my ear. "Don't be sorry," he said again, his voice lower, quieter.

I hadn't seen him in days, hadn't heard from him, hadn't known when I would again, and now he was beside me. There next to me on the pillow, his river stone skin soft on my mine, his eyes circled with tiny scales, he was horribly beautiful. I wanted to be with him, to stay with him, so much my bones ached with it. I pushed closer to him, pressed myself along him. The sheets bunched between us. My mouth was on his, and he was cool and sweet. He pulled me closer, his forearms like steel against my back, pushing into me, holding me to him, holding me in place. His hands flattened against the back of my neck. He kissed me like he wanted it as much as I did.

Our lips moved apart, but he kept me against him. My hands were pressed against the cotton of his shirt, and I could feel the thin weave of it, and underneath, him.

"Saben talked to me."

I took a deep breath. As suddenly as I'd wanted to be close, I wanted to move away. His arms tightened nervously around me. "How'd she do that?"

He shrugged against the mattress. "She had her nymphs find me. But she came to see me herself."

"And what did she say?" My voice was tight and stiff.

His fingers circled around my shoulder blades. "She said you were tired. That you passed out on her floor."

I rolled away onto my back, and he let me go. I brought my hand up and rubbed my fingers between my eyes, hard. "And you're here ... why? To report back?" I kept my eyes closed. I sounded bitter, and the bitterness in my voice made me angry and sad and embarrassed. "To do your healer thing and tell her you checked me over?"

"No. Luca." He tugged on my wrist, pulling it away from my face. "Luca." I opened my eyes and turned my head so I could see him. "That's not why I'm here."

"Then why?" I was confused. I liked him. He seemed to like me back, more than I'd expected. But when I added everything up, it didn't seem to amount to much. He'd tried to help me. He came back because I was part of his job, and he had promised. I'd found him in the club and we'd slept together, and I'd taken him to see Saben and Riyad. And then he'd offered what he'd offered. But I didn't know what any of it meant when it came to the two of us. I didn't know where we stood, and I didn't know what he wanted of me.

"Because I was worried," he said. His voice dropped low and soft, like he was embarrassed, like he didn't really want me to hear. "Mostly because I missed you. I wanted a reason to come see you. She gave me one." His fingers wrapped around my wrist, pulling it down between us. He used his touch on my skin like a reminder that he was connected to me, that he had me.

I sat up and looked back at him. He was lying on the pillow, tilted against it so he could see me. His hair was back in its ponytail. It was impossibly black against the white pillowcase. Between us, his hand had slipped down, his fingers twisting through mine. Our palms slid together, a rough glide of skin over skin.

"I'm glad." I couldn't keep holding his eyes. I looked away and saw his skinny gray jeans and his bare feet. His toes were long, and his feet were narrow and strong. Everything about him screamed fey, but he seemed so human when we talked. When we held each other. His heart seemed so warm. "You're so ..." I trailed off, waved my hand back and forth over him, taking in every single beautiful, perfect, impossible thing about him. "You make me nervous."

He sat up next to me. He leaned against me, his chin touching my shoulder, so we were tucked together. "I want to be with you. I like it." His words folded into the space between us, private, quiet, and weighty. "If I didn't, I wouldn't have come back that time with the medicines. I'd have sent them with one of Saben's runners. And I wouldn't have stayed at the club. I wouldn't have let you take me home afterwards."

"It was a stupid choice."

"I know." There wasn't any irony or humor in his voice.

"All right."

We moved forward at the same time, with the same idea, and kissed again. It was sweeter. Not as frantic. Just a brush of his lips, slightly chapped, over mine.

"Have you thought . . ." He took a deep breath, held it, let it go. "Have you thought about what I said?"

I nodded. But even though I knew he wanted an answer, I didn't say anything.

He sighed. "I don't have another solution, Luca. That's . . . the best I can do."

"I know. It's . . ." I laughed, even though there wasn't anything funny. "It's more than anyone else's given me. Way more." I looked down at my hands.

"But you won't do it." His voice was just shy of flat. Like he was disappointed but he didn't want me to know it.

I turned to look at him, to take in how human and unhuman he was. I reached out to touch, wanting to run my hands over all his colors, the dark and light spaces of him. I skimmed the pad of my thumb against a patch of scales. They were velvety, just slightly raised on his skin. I traced the places where the scales met skin, where he sometimes hid them under his glamour. He'd dropped most of that glamour, though, for me. His eyes were brighter, the corners more pronounced. His fingers came up to wrap around my wrists, and they were longer than they had been with his glamour on, the nails perfect ovals, the fins on his wrists spread by the delicate bones that gave them support. He was wild and lovely, untamed, lithe and elegant. Something that shouldn't have been real.

I was just me. I had no second skin that I hid, or that I could hide behind. I could change my appearance like humans did, or use a little glamour, but there was only ever one me, no secret self. I had nothing different to fall back on or conceal. I looked human, my eyes a bit too light, maybe, too gray to be truly un-fey, my bones long and my body slender. And my hair was that odd color that I'd gotten from my father. But I never had to lie away that different half of my blood, because unless I told, no one ever guessed it was there at all.

But I *did* have that. I had that humanity. I wasn't sure I could just give it away.

I moved my hands up, pushed them into his hair, tugged it out of its tie, spread it so it fell over his face and my wrists.

"I can't answer yet," I said, because that was the truth. I didn't know what to do. I didn't know what to think. His proposition was such a huge thing, so massive, so unimaginable, that my mind wanted to block it out, so that I'd never have to deal with it. So I'd never have to come up with a definitive yes or no.

"Is it too much to ask?" I said. "Is it too hard to stay with me, when I won't answer?"

He leaned his head against my hand. "No."

"But it will be."

He turned and kissed my palm. "I don't know."

I breathed in slowly. That seemed fair.

"It's foolish to want to stay," I told him. "Even for a little while. No matter what answer I give. You don't know if it'll work. You only know for sure that, right now, I'm on my way out."

His head moved back and forth in a no. His fingers twisted around mine, curling our hands so they were tucked together. "I just want you, Luca."

We let the conversation go. We had dinner together, and after, we sat on my back deck and read and watched the sun set behind the hill, like we were some old married couple, used to each other's company. I couldn't remember the last time I had just sat with someone, just wanted to be next to them. The last time someone had simply wanted my company. But it was that way with Kin. Easy. Simple. Just being near him made me content. Kind of like I'd searched the whole world for something that would make things make sense, like there was a reason for all the things that were right or wrong in my life. And I'd had to come back home to find that sense, that comfort, in the form of this man. He didn't make everything clear, and he didn't give me a reason for who I was and why. But the reality of him was so much better than whatever fantastical, life-altering thing I'd been searching for.

When it got dark enough that we couldn't see the words on the page anymore, we went inside. I brought him to my bedroom. I didn't turn on a light, just let the moonlight, coming down the hill and in through the window, illuminate us. Kin shed his clothes without any trace of embarrassment and without any vanity. He was still more fey looking than human, his glamour gone, his beauty and strength prominent in the way he moved and the way the silver light shone on him and the way he was never ashamed. I wanted to feel inferior to him—it only seemed to make sense, my pale, bruised body against his—but the way he touched me didn't allow it. He held me to him like I was valuable, like I mattered and I was fragile not in how I was made, but in the fact that I was important to him, in the way I made *him* fragile. It made me want to cry.

After, he lay beside me, and I wrapped myself around him. He fell asleep against me, his body going heavy. I wanted to stay there and watch him, keep him in my sight. There was something in me that was afraid he would disappear if I stopped looking at him, stopped touching him.

But I was restless and couldn't sleep. I got up, moving slow, not wanting to jostle the bed. The bedroom door shut behind me with a soft *click*, and I made my way to the kitchen.

The moon was bright in the kitchen too, so I left the lights off. It was enough for me to find my cigarettes. Like I'd been doing for more than a week, I rolled my own, making it mostly out of the herbs Kin had brought me. I lit it and leaned against the counter.

I stared at the backyard and took a long drag on the cigarette. Outside, nothing moved. The little patio and its few square feet of plants were still. It was boring but beautiful, the moon silvering every leaf, making shadows where there should be nothing but complete darkness. I leaned back and flicked ash into the sink. I was tired. I could feel it in my back, in my legs and my neck. It was a good weight, an accumulation of the whole day instead of the ache of sickness, and I wanted to stay here and feel it, instead of sleeping and letting it all go. I wanted to hold on to the sensation for a little while longer.

"No wonder your lungs are rotting."

I turned my head to see behind me. Kin stepped to me and raised my hand above my shoulder, his lips closing over the cigarette between my fingers.

"They were going before I started smoking. It doesn't make a difference."

"But you think it does, right?" He rested his chin on my shoulder. His arms wrapped around my waist. His bare skin against mine made me shiver. "You think it tamps down on the fey."

I shrugged with my free shoulder. "You're the doctor. What's your professional opinion?" I waved the hand holding the cigarette. "It's your herbs in here," I added.

He huffed out a soft laugh. "My professional opinion is that's definitely not how I told you to use those."

"Does it matter?" I asked. I took another breath of the cigarette and held it out for him. He sucked on it, then took it from between my fingers. He twisted it back and forth in his, peering over my shoulder. When he spotted my ash in the sink, he leaned over and ground out the remains of the cigarette against the steel side. He pushed against my shoulders, turning me so I faced him.

"Does it make you feel better?" he asked in return.

"It makes me feel warm."

He shook his head slowly. There was a strange expression on his face, like he wanted to say something but he wasn't letting himself. Or like I'd said something that had burrowed into him and taken hold in a secret space in his heart or his mind. "I don't think it matters." He pulled me closer, until we touched, and my hands on the counter behind me were the only thing keeping my balance. "I stayed away because I was afraid, Luca. That night, at Riyad's, when you couldn't stop coughing . . . It was different. It was like I could see how bad it could get, and I didn't want to."

I shook my head. I didn't know what to say. I felt like I'd swallowed a stone, and it had lodged in my chest, heavy and cold, choking me.

"Don't let me do it again. Don't let me run because I'm afraid. Let me claim you." He pushed his hair away from his face. He wasn't meeting my eyes. It was so strange, so unlike him. I couldn't see his eyes. "Claim me." His voice was a whisper, but it sounded desperate. It broke me down. I crumbled under how much I wanted him, how much I wanted to touch him and talk to him and hold him against me. It was like a weight on me, the wanting. It would crush me. I knew it and I wanted it.

I brushed my hand against his cheek, into his hair. His skin was warm against my palm, just slightly rough, the scales slipping against my skin. "I can't promise you anything."

He did meet my eyes now. His fingers skimmed slowly over my skin. He was nervous. "I don't care."

My hand moved around to the back of his neck, slipped into his hair. His fingers were at my sides, against my rib cage. They held me in place. I pressed back against the counter with my other hand, holding us up, my knuckles going numb.

"You can't be sure of that," I pushed him, because I knew I needed to. This was important. I didn't want him to promise me anything, promise himself anything, and then have to take it back. I didn't want promises at all.

He didn't promise. He just shook his head, his fingers going tight against me. "Please."

I couldn't say no to that, even though I thought we'd both regret it, regret this thing we were letting play out between us. I twisted my hand into his hair, pulled a little. He moved into the tug. I let my other hand leave the counter, and we slid down a few inches, leaning in to each other. I brought my hand up to his face, so that I held him between my palms. "I claim you."

CHAPTER 9

K in left in the morning. I followed a little while later, took care of some tasks the fey wanted me to do. Nothing too difficult. Routine things, mostly. Things that let my hands work while my mind raced. I couldn't stop my thoughts from tumbling around and into each other, crashing together at a million miles an hour.

When I got home, the house was quiet and empty around me. It was so strange. Kin had only been there a couple of times, but I was already used to his presence. His voice filling up all the silent corners. His laugh and the nearness of him making the house seem occupied and alive and awake. Now it was sleeping around me.

I crawled into bed with a book, but I didn't read it. I had the window cracked open, and a cool breeze came through and touched my skin. The chill of it felt so good. I wanted to lie there until my cheek, the back of my hand, my neck, were all goose bumped with the cold, my nerve endings on edge, alert, ready, my hair cool and slippery when I ran my fingers over it, from the ice in the air.

My eyes burned and my joints hurt. I'd been all right this morning, but the fatigue had hit, and now my body had decided to give it up for the moment, and I was aching. One part would go tender for an hour or so, and then the pain would migrate to another area. My jaw. My shoulders. The backs of my knees. One finger had been stiff and hurting for a few days, and now I could feel the sting of it traveling up the back of my hand into my wrist. It wasn't the intense pain of the attacks I sometimes had, but I couldn't get comfortable no matter how I twisted in the bed, and it seemed like too much work to get up. I just tried to be as still as possible, to let my joints freeze into place and go numb so I wouldn't be able to feel whatever was going on inside them.

Everything from the past months was crashing into me. Being sick, coming home. Realizing that I didn't really know Saben anymore, that we would never be what we once were. Meeting Kin, how sweet and kind and honest he was. His offer. How I didn't know, simply couldn't know, what to do. All of it tangled into some giant, impossible knot in my mind. I thought maybe it would grow and grow until I couldn't contain it anymore. Until it exploded.

I stared out into the backyard, up the hill. My eyes were running a little, like I had an allergy, but I kept them open. The light was fading, and I liked the way it made everything all hazy and mellow. Like the yard and the corner of the house and everything I could see was ringed in sunlight and gold dust. The sight of it made a tightness in my chest that was different than the pain in my body. I hurt, and that light was so lovely. It made me feel open and fragile, made me want to cry. I thought I might feel better if I *did* let myself cry, kind of like a lancing effect, but I couldn't quite bring myself to do it.

While I lay there thinking about light and crying, someone climbed into my bed. For just a second, I was nervous. I thought I'd left the door open again, and someone was here to rob me. But I'd locked the door, I knew I had. So not a human, most likely. Not any random fey, either, if they had gotten past the iron. And whoever it was was touching my back with their fingertips and breathing soft against my neck in a way that was hesitant and oddly concerned. It didn't seem like the kind of thing a thief would do.

There was only one person who would climb into my bed. I reached around and grabbed a hand, pulling it across my body. But I froze when I saw the fingers. Slender and small and salt-crystal white.

My brow crinkled. "Wrong color for Kin," I said out loud.

A high laugh, dry and not entirely amused, came from behind me. "Maybe because I'm not Kin."

I rolled over. Saben. She wasn't in her usual dress. She was wearing old jeans, artfully frayed over her knees. Her shirt was loose and long and sheer. She glared at me, her hands still stretched out, her eyes serious and ringed with dark-blue eyeliner and black mascara.

"I didn't expect you," I said stupidly. I frowned. "How did you get past the iron?" The lock wouldn't have been a problem, not for her. But the iron would have.

"I took a deep breath," she said tartly, which explained nothing. No fey overcame iron with a good lungful of air. I stared at her, throwing her own expression back at her, and she sighed. Her face softened. "I know how much it hurts. It makes it less frightening." She tucked her fingers back in, pulling them against her palm and toward her chest.

"Why bother, though?" Her jaw was a little too stiff, and a tiny, delicate bead of sweat ran down her forehead while I watched. The iron was affecting her, no matter how unafraid of it she was.

"I was worried. Your entrance into my apartment the other day left such an impression."

I shrugged, moving my shoulders against the bedspread. The movement reminded me of all the muscles that were strained and bunched in my body. "I'm fine."

I was uncomfortable, though. Not just physically, either. Saben didn't worry, especially not about me. She'd said it in a joking, nearly bitter way, like it had been a hassle to her, but the fact that she had said it at all was beyond strange.

Her teeth clicked together, and her expression went hard.

I sighed. "Saben." So odd. This was so odd.

"I was afraid," she said. Just three words. But her voice was a whisper and it was tense. It brought me back to the times she'd had nightmares as a child, when I'd held her and she'd told me what she'd seen. It was a child's voice, a voice that had lost control and knew it and couldn't fake it anymore. It frightened me.

"Do I really look so much worse?" I asked, and I wanted a straight answer because I thought, right now, in the middle of whatever this was, she'd give me one if she could.

But she couldn't. "I don't know," she said. Her words rose and fell on a little moan. "I haven't been paying attention for so long. I never noticed how bad it had gotten. Not until the other day at Riyad's. Father told me, a while ago. He said it was bad. But I didn't see it, not really."

I nodded. My throat was tight. She'd been afraid that day, so nervous, her fingers clutching against each other, and I'd pushed her away. I hadn't known what she was thinking, hadn't bothered to stop and wonder.

"I thought you were going to die." Her voice went neutral, almost thoughtful. "You curled up on yourself, and you were so small. Breakable. Spun glass. You couldn't even stand."

I shook my head. "But then it was over."

"But you all treated it like it was an everyday occurrence." Her voice rose into a wail. "Like it happens all the time."

I bit my lip.

"Because it does," she said, her words nearly a whisper again. "And I didn't notice."

I didn't know what to say to comfort her. "It's not your job to notice."

She flexed her fingers. "What happened to us?"

I took a deep breath. I brushed at my eyes, hoping she knew they were running because they were inflamed, and not because I was emotional. I didn't want to have this conversation with her. Not right now, while I felt awful and out of control and tired. Maybe not ever. I didn't know if it was worth it. "I left. You grew up, and we grew apart. And when I got back, we were different people and it was over."

It was amazing that was all it had taken, but I knew it was. A few years apart, a few years in which we didn't speak a word, didn't send a letter or share a phone call, a few years to let our thoughts diverge, a few years, maybe, of the other fey telling her how little they thought of me, and we couldn't be together anymore. And I didn't know where my place was with her.

She nodded, agreeing, and her face scrunched up a little. I drew back. I couldn't remember ever seeing her cry, or come close to it. I didn't really think she would now, but the possibility of it was distinctly uncomfortable.

"I was . . ." She stopped and stared at me. "Look, can we do something about this?" She waved her hand in front of my face. "I can't really talk to you like this."

"Sorry," I said, not sorry at all. "They're itchy today."

"All right." She sat up, and tugged on the strap of my tank top to pull me upright with her. Then she crawled off the bed and disappeared into the bathroom. I heard the water run, and when she came back, she had a damp washcloth in her hand. She leaned toward me and held the cloth near my eyes, then hesitated. The cloth moved back and forth. She bit her lip and kind of flung it at my face, smushing it with her palm against my eyes.

"Ow. Saben." I tried to pull her hand away. She was rough like a little kid would be, rough without meaning it.

"Keep it there," she demanded. I held the cloth in place over one eye, but peeked above it with the other. She was kneeling in front of me, her hand out, like she'd catch the cloth if I dropped it. She looked absolutely serious. "Is it better?"

I pressed the cloth back to my eyes and considered. The coolness was definitely nice. I nodded.

"Good." I heard her shuffling around, and when I looked again, she had settled on the floor at my feet. "Where's Kin? I doubt you'd be moping around like this if he was here."

"Gone for the day." I switched the cloth to the other eye. "He went out to see people who need his . . ." What would you call that, if he wasn't a doctor? "His healing talents."

She nodded. Then she clasped her hands in front of her and sighed sharply. She cast her eyes around the room again, her hands tugging at each other in her lap while she did. I just sat and waited. Finally she turned back to face me and said, "I don't know what else to say to you. I don't know how to have a conversation with you."

"Oh. Well, that's okay." Water trickled down my arm from the cloth. I brushed it away and took the opportunity to break her gaze. She sounded lost, but no one could be truly confused and still stare at another person like that.

"How do you do it?"

I jerked my head back up. "Do what?"

"Make conversation."

I rubbed at my forehead with my free hand. "I don't know, Saben. I'm the quiet kid who sits in the back and listens. I'm the wrong person to ask."

"You must talk about something with Kin," she argued.

What did Kin and I talk about? Whatever came to mind. "It's usually better not to force it. Silence is perfectly acceptable."

"If it's comfortable?" She sounded so damn curious. She sounded like she was reciting a line or a rule from somewhere.

"What have you been reading?"

"Never mind," she said curtly. She stood and then turned back to face me. "Can I make you tea?"

"All right." I decided not to mention her weird fixation with hot drinks, because this was something I could agree to. Tea was easy.

I got up and dumped the wet cloth in my laundry basket and followed Saben into the kitchen. Everything was steel and iron and anti-fey in my house. Despite the way she'd put it, I assumed I would be the one making the tea. She shooed me away when I stepped up next to her, though. She pointed at the table, not even really bothering to watch me while she did, like she had no doubt I'd do as she suggested. I went. I was bemused. I was nearly proud. And I was glad to sit down.

I watched Saben from the table, sure she would burn herself or scald her fingers on my stainless steel spoons. She was too clever for that, though. She took what looked like a little packet of cloth from her pocket. It sat comfortably in her palm, the outside a shiny scrap of silk, the fabric curving around what I assumed was some kind of rubber grip in the middle. Like maybe one of those things people use to twist off tight lids. It must mute the effect of the metal she held it over. She used it deftly, grasping the wrought iron drawer pull with it, using it to grab a spoon, slapping it over the handle of the kettle, just in case.

She was confident. Her movements were still all snap and quickness, careful not to touch any of the metal for too long, even through the fabric, but they were sure. All she was doing was filling a kettle and setting it to boil, retrieving the tea leaves Kin had left and measuring them out. But she did it with grace, and she did it well. Making tea was a simple task, but it wasn't simple for sidhe to work, to make something tangible. They weren't used to it. They'd never really been taught, had never had much use for it. I realized how much Saben must have been practicing, how difficult it must have been for her to learn. And I had teased her and told her not to.

She turned around while the water boiled. The cups were already set out, honey and spoons at the ready. I smiled at her. She didn't smile, she almost never smiled, but the hard, sharp angles of her face smoothed and softened. She leaned back against the counter, the silk grip loose in her hand.

"I'm sorry I made fun of you." My voice was soft, unsure. My sister was in front of me, and I could see the pieces of the little girl I'd known in her, but she was older and better and more now, and I didn't really know who she was.

"I appreciate that."

"How are you dealing with the iron?" I waved my hand around, trying to demonstrate how much of it must be seeping into the air. Saben didn't look sick, but she still seemed uncomfortably warm and pale.

"I went to Riyad. He gave me some herbs to eat." She brushed her hair back from her face. It stayed where she put it, a mess, but elegant. "He also said practice is best. That I could build a tolerance."

"It won't ever be perfect."

She shrugged. "Close is good enough."

I opened my mouth to say more, but I heard a *click* and *thump*. I turned, leaning forward over the table enough to see around the kitchen doorjamb, enough to see Kin coming in through the front door. He caught my eye and smiled that small grin. He kicked off his shoes as he shut the door. He was making himself at home, in my house. I liked that he wanted to do that.

"You left it unlocked again," he said, walking toward me. "Don't you think—" He stepped into the kitchen and stopped speaking and walking when he saw Saben. "Oh. Hello."

"*Okaeri*," she said, her voice light and easy. I didn't know what the word meant, but she made it sound welcoming.

Kin smiled at her and shook his head. "My Japanese is rusty."

"I seriously doubt that." She cocked her head and smiled at him, a tiny smile, but a real one. Then she turned back to the stove. I almost wanted to call her out on it, it was so unexpected, so rare. But I didn't have any idea of what to say.

Kin distracted me. He stepped to me and pushed his hand into my hair, his thumb skimming over my cheek. His touch was soothing, taking the burn out of my skin. I wanted to lean into it. "I don't know whether or not to kiss you in front of your sister."

It was a joke, but his voice was almost a whisper. His eyes were running over me like he was checking to make sure I was still all together. I glanced at Saben and then back just as quickly. I didn't know what she would think of it, but I wanted to feel him. He hadn't been gone very long, but this thing we had, this *us*, was new. I wanted to feel it run between the two of us to be sure of how strong it was.

"Please kiss me."

He bent and put his lips against mine, and I sighed, which was ridiculous and romantically stupid. He laughed against my mouth. We kissed again, slower, and then he straightened. He ducked his head at Saben, a small bow but a very polite one. She ducked back, then waved her hand at him, waving away the formality. She pulled out a third mug. Kin sat down beside me.

And then Saben served us tea. We all sat at the same table and drank the tea and made small talk, and Kin and Saben smiled shyly at each other, and at me. It was bizarre. It was strange and warm and right. I liked it, and it was almost surprising, because I had never even imagined anything like this at all. I had certainly never imagined wanting it again and again. And in the back of my mind was the idea that I could make that happen, that I could make this last, if I took what Kin had offered me.

CHAPTER 10

It was an early night for me. I was aching, although not as badly as I had been before Saben showed up. Kin crawled into bed behind me and rested his palm, flat and warm, between my shoulder blades. He trailed it down my spine, his fingers pushing against my bones. It made me arch my back, it felt so good. The pressure of his hand was solid, undemanding, but I was intensely aware of every place he pressed. I reached behind me to touch him, but he lifted my hand away. I heard him shift and rise up on an elbow. His mouth fell close to my ear.

"Can I kiss you?"

My breath caught. I nodded. He lowered back, and then his lips, instead of meeting mine, followed where his touch had been. His hands shifted over my skin, pushing aside clothing, touching where it hurt and where it didn't, soothing and making me jump. He kissed my shoulder blades, my side, the spot where my hip met my waist, the inside of my elbow. His arms slid around me and held me against him. His body aligned with mine, long and loose, the space between us gone. His lips moved to the back of my neck, kissing hard, and his hands were everywhere, on me and around me. It was so much and so gentle at the same time, a sweet attack. All of the sensations, all of his touches and kisses and the way they lit me up, crept over me, rising and swelling, a wave inside me. And then I was crying out, a desperate mess in his arms, my fingers tight over his. He pushed against me, and I heard him moan, and I knew he didn't even realize he was making the sound. His voice hit me in my bones, in the pit of my stomach. It went all the way through me.

Kin got up and cleaned us both, his touch still as careful as it had been, as attentive. Then he lay down beside me and wrapped himself around me. I nestled against his chest, his chin resting on my head, his arm draped over me. I didn't like feeling small. When I spoke to people, fey or not, I made my spine as straight as it would go. I liked the way I fit into Kin, though, the slight difference in our sizes that made me feel, when I wanted it to, like he could tuck me away inside him. Like he could keep me safe just by putting his arms around me.

Our fingers twined together. I hadn't done it consciously, and I didn't think he had either. It had just happened because it felt better when our hands were together like that. He always seemed to know where I needed him. He'd known how to touch me a few minutes before, known where I hurt, where I could only stand the lightest touch, and where I wanted his fingers to press. He knew how to hold me when I was weak, when I was sick, like he'd been doing it for a long time. He knew how to look at me to make me want him, to make me understand him, to tell me what he needed to tell me. He'd known, already, that second time he came out to see me, how to lay out all the medicines on the table between us, how to get me to accept them. I could still see him doing it in my mind, his fingers lingering on each packet, glancing up at me as he explained what they were. I could see him, sitting there across the table from me, the way he'd looked at me then, not demanding, not pleading, just hoping that I would take the things he'd brought. And that they would work.

I curved my spine into him. He was heavy against me, like he was already asleep, or almost there. I wanted it to always be like this between us. Easy. Good. I wanted it to last. I didn't want to think about how the question of whether or not I'd take the cure he'd offered was still hanging over us. I just wanted, for right now, for as long as I could keep it, this. I closed my eyes and let myself drift to sleep.

I was back up just after midnight moved into the morning. I didn't hurt like I had that evening. I was pleasantly light, my joints loose, my bones and muscles working like they were supposed to. But I couldn't sleep and I needed a cigarette. I got up from the bed, careful not to wake Kin, and went to the kitchen to roll myself one.

I cracked the back door in the kitchen and leaned against the doorjamb, breathing so the smoke moved outside. It twisted through the air, a shimmery, grayish purple at first, and then nothing, going cold and sinking, until I couldn't follow the trail of it anymore. The brisk air felt good on my skin, sweet in how it raised goose bumps and made me shiver. I flicked my wrist, bumped my thumb against the cigarette, releasing the ash.

I looked around the garden. Frost had settled sometime in the night. It lined all the spiky plants, the side of the hill, in dusty silver. When the clouds moved just right and the moon shone through, everything sparkled. Pure magic, but not like fey magic. This was a different kind of magic, created by something so explainable, but so beautiful it didn't seem like it could be real. My feet were cold, my hands starting to chill, and the cold air was working its way inside me, but I stayed where I was. I didn't want to be somewhere warmer. I wanted to see this, be part of it for a second. Because in the morning, it would all be gone.

I tilted my head to the sky, at the few stars I could see through the light of the city, and brought my cigarette to my lips. I breathed in, and the night air and the smoke caught wrong in my lungs. I coughed once, feeling that choke like a thing lodged in me, and then more coughing bubbled up and I couldn't stop it. It really did feel like bubbles. Wet, thick clumps of air that forced their way out of me. I fell back against the door. I couldn't breathe, I couldn't get any air in, my body was heaving with the struggle of it, my back sliding down the doorframe, my hand going out, blind, to catch myself on the counter. I was dimly afraid that I'd fall, or that I'd drop the cigarette and start a fire, but I was more afraid that I'd suffocate right there, that I wouldn't be able to stop, that I'd never be able to get enough air to fill my lungs.

Kin was there, his arms around me, holding me up while I coughed. He crouched over me, protective, like he could shield me from the sickness. He pulled the cigarette from my fingers and flung it into the sink. One arm was around my chest, supporting me. His other hand was on my back, soothing. His body shook with me every time I coughed.

He ushered me into one of the kitchen chairs. He disappeared from my sight, and then came back with a glass. It had an inch of milk-white, watery liquid in it. He knelt in front of me and thrust the glass into my hand. His other hand pushed against my shoulder, making me sit back. My body wanted to curve forward whenever I gasped for air, but he forced me straight. He guided the glass to my lips, his hand tight around mine, and urged me to drink.

"Slow," he said, voice calm and gentle. "Sip it and breathe." I did as he said. The liquid tasted starchy and sharp and it burned with alcohol. It took several sips, long minutes, before my coughing subsided, then finally stopped. Kin's hands stayed on me, one wrapped around the glass with mine, the other on my knee, steadying us.

"What is that?" I coughed again, but it was smaller, more controlled. I moved the glass a little. The last of the liquid swished back and forth. The white part seemed to be separate from the rest, swirling through it in tendrils.

"Sake." He squeezed my hand and unwrapped his from the glass. I cradled the last of the drink against my chest. "Can you breathe?" He looked up at me, his eyes going from mine to the circles under them, to my lips, to the hand against my chest. His gaze never settled, a franticness to the way he studied me, despite how easy his words were, how composed he sounded. He didn't have any clothes on. He'd come running from the bedroom in a panic.

I nodded. "I'm okay." My voice sounded thick, like my throat was filled with liquid, but I didn't cough again.

He took a deep breath and used the heel of his hand to rub sleep from his eyes. He stared up at me again, and I stared back. I was shaky and worn, just from that fit. Kin looked absolutely wrecked, his hair a tangled mess, his scales washed out. The blues and greens near his eyes were pale, muted. I reached down and ran my thumb along his cheekbone, trying to bring color back into them. He leaned into my touch, just a bit.

He watched my face while I touched his. "Did you think about what I said? The scales? Did you think about it?"

I sat back, let my hand fall. I turned away and busied myself with setting the glass on the table. "I thought about it."

His hand clenched around my knee, asking for my attention. "And?"

"I'm sorry," I said. It was a whisper, but it was just us in a quiet kitchen in the middle of the night, and it sounded too loud. I wasn't sure why I was apologizing. Just that I still didn't know.

I heard Kin shift. I glanced down and saw that he'd moved from his heels to sitting on the floor. He combed through his hair, smoothing it and worrying it at the same time. The color had come back into his skin and his scales. His cheekbones were a riot of violets and deep blues now, the skin underneath flushed.

"Is that a no?" he asked. Those deep eyes, black in the dark, watched me.

I sighed. "I don't know what to do." I'd thought about it, that morning. I'd thought about how everything would be so much simpler. How I could be normal and things like having tea with Kin and Saben wouldn't have such a weight on them. How I wouldn't have to think, every time something good like that happened, that it might be the last. How all of the pains I felt, all the coughing and bruising and aches, would be gone. It would be like a miracle. It would be the exact thing I'd been searching for, for so long.

But even while I wanted to say yes, even while I thought that might be what came out of my mouth, something held me back. I thought, right now, that maybe it was the frost. All those plants, the edges of stones, blades of grass, limned in silver. So beautiful, and something I rarely saw, because it melted with the sun. But that impermanence was, I thought, part of what made it so special. If everything looked like that all the time, I wouldn't even notice it anymore. It would be a beauty that was commonplace, usual, boring. I didn't want life to be like that. *I* didn't want to be like that. I wanted every minute I had to mean something. To be bright and amazing, even when it was sad, or filled with anger, or hurt. I wanted all that weight, all that splendor. And if I did as Kin asked, as he seemed to want, I couldn't help but think that I wouldn't have any of that anymore. That infinite days would be infinitely less beautiful.

I couldn't quite make myself say no, either, though. I couldn't take away the option. And I was still afraid, so afraid, that if I said no, Kin would leave. I didn't know how much time I had, months or years, but I thought it was likely I might never again have what Kin and I seemed to be building. I didn't know yet what, exactly, would come of this thing between us, but I knew it was something special. Something rare. I knew that Kin might be the bright spark at the end of my life.

And I didn't want the spark to go out so soon. So I just shook my head again.

Kin sighed, but he seemed to accept that. He pushed himself to his feet, jamming his fists into his knees for leverage. He leaned down and kissed me. It was soft. I could feel his breath between my lips. His thumb brushed my cheek, his fingers moved light and slow through my hair. Then he sat back, took my hands, and pulled me to my feet.

"Come back to bed." His voice was gentle and strong, but his hands were almost too tight around mine. They trembled, just a little.

"All right."

CHAPTER 11

"*Tadaima*."

I turned around and kissed him, which was difficult, because I was holding a sauté pan and a wooden spoon, and he had me tight around the waist. He stepped back, and I set the cooking things down and twisted so we could kiss properly. I gestured, rolling my shoulders in a shrug at the pan of mushrooms and snap peas and tofu and red Thai chilies, and he nodded approvingly. We had both gone out today, him to his tengu and me to my cait sith, and I'd wanted to surprise him like he had me last night. I wanted to make up for what I'd done last night too, or, if not make up for it, create a situation that would be comfortable and simple and undemanding. I was ridiculously glad it still seemed easy between us, with him walking through the door and eager to find me.

"What does that mean?"

He stepped back and let me stir the food in the pan. He slumped against the counter to watch me finish cooking. One hand stayed on my waist. "'I'm back.'" He paused, and I glanced over my shoulder at him. "Or, 'I'm home.'" His skin darkened, going dusky with a blush. I watched it spread, his scales going almost black. "I suspect that's what your sister wanted it to mean, the other day."

I set the spoon down. "When she said that word?"

He nodded. "*Okaeri*. 'Welcome home.' It's traditional Japanese." He ducked his head.

I took a deep breath. "You don't need to say it because she thinks you should." I wanted him to mean it. I wanted to say, *Welcome home*, and have him feel like that was where he was. Like he belonged next to me, or I belonged with him.

He shook his head. "I couldn't say it then. Not yet. Not the way she wanted it. It scared me."

I nodded. He smiled.

"I want to say it now. My choice."

I had to turn away. I didn't want him to know how important this was to me. But I know he saw me smile. Knew he felt me lean into his hand.

"Where on earth did she learn that?" Saben surprised me all the time these days. She'd always known a lot about other fey—it was her duty to know. That didn't mean she needed to learn Japanese, though.

Kin shrugged. "Who knows?" He grinned at me. "Kids these days."

"Do you want me to say it? That other word?" He'd said it fast, and it had flowed out of his mouth, so that I hadn't been able to catch all the sounds in it. I didn't want to say it yet, sure I would embarrass myself with the pronunciation.

But Kin shook his head. "I'm only a Japanese descendant. I was born here. 'Welcome home' works just fine for me."

It worked for me too—well enough that it made a little shiver run up my spine when Kin said it. But I was still curious about where Saben had learned it.

When I saw her the next afternoon, I asked her about it. "Where did you learn Japanese?"

Saben frowned at me. "I don't know Japanese."

I shook my finger at her, taunting. "Oh, but Kin tells me you do."

"Oh. That." She set down a plate in front of me. A salad of mangos and onions and crumbled, salty cheese, which seemed like it shouldn't have worked, but did. She shrugged as she sat down across the table from me. "I read manga."

"You . . . what?"

"Manga. It's a Japanese graphic novel—"

I waved my fork at her. "I know what manga is. I just didn't expect that you'd be interested in anything like that."

She took a bite of her salad and swallowed. "I wasn't. But it's important that I know who I'm dealing with when new fey come into our territory. While I was researching the yokai and whatnot, I found manga."

"Oh." I scooped up a bit of everything on my fork and popped it in my mouth. It was good. It was beyond good. It tasted salty sweet and free of magic, distinctly human, organic—not necessarily in how it was grown, but in how it was made. It had none of the cloying sugariness or false richness that magic and glamour created in food. It felt warm, although the fruit was cold against my tongue. "And why did you feel the need to bully Kin into saying something like that?"

She glanced up. "It wasn't bullying. It was nudging."

"Either way." I rolled my eyes at her.

Her fork clinked against the plate. The dishes were thin, fine china, painted with blue flowers. They were too delicate for the apartment, like she'd brought them from some period ballroom where women would eat from them wearing enormous, tight dresses and men would smoke pipes and laugh softly together while they used their forks to push peas around the patterns on the plates. The truth probably wasn't so far off. They'd come from the fey. They could have come from anywhere, before that.

"Why are we talking about this?"

Because I was annoyed and confused and my heart hurt a little. It stung when I thought of her trying to get Kin to say that, both because I was angry, and because I thought it meant she cared, in her own strange way, and I didn't understand.

"Why am I sitting in your kitchen, eating a salad that I'm pretty sure you made with just a regular knife and cutting board?"

"And a peeler," she added. "I peeled the mango."

"Saben." I set my fork down. I leaned forward so I could look at her. "You've got to tell me what's going on. This isn't about me, not all of it. I know it. What are you doing?"

"It was a ceramic knife," she said. She wasn't looking at me.

"Don't brush me off."

She pushed her plate away and leaned back in her chair, away from me. "How long were you gone?"

I took a deep breath. "Six years. Just about." She knew that, though.

"Why were you gone so long? What were you searching for while you were gone?" She tilted her head, studying me. "It can't have just been a cure. A place to belong? A place where you could disappear?"

Yes and yes. I had wanted to leave them behind. My mother's death and the house she'd left me that I couldn't deal with, my father with his regality, my sister who was all fey where I was only half, the fey and the humans who flowed around me but never fully accepted me. I had wanted to leave myself behind, leave my memories and the knowledge of what I was. I had wanted to be someone different.

It was impossible, though. No matter where I went, I was still me. I still wore the same clothes, because they were comfortable. I ate new foods and liked them, but never forgot the old, familiar flavors I relished. And the fey side of me was always there. It was there when I slipped into a shadow to avoid a pickpocket. It was there in the way my joints hurt if it was a damp morning. It was the color of my hair. And my mother and the human side were the color of my skin, my height. Her eyes in my face, the way I struck up conversations easily, so I could get to know a place.

Saben was watching me. Watching me remember being free, but not really free. That trip had changed a lot of things for me. But it had also made it clear what things would never change. I looked up at Saben and said nothing.

"I don't want it. The fey. The life they live. I don't want it," she said, the words tumbling out of her mouth in an ungainly rush. "I have this long life before me. It's so long. Why should I trap myself in one place forever? Why should I always belong to them? Why can't I try something new? Live how I want? I have so much time." She bit her lip. "Or what if my life is short," she continued, slow now, her words measured. "What if something happens, and I die, and I haven't lived the way I wanted, tried the things I wanted?"

I shook my head. "You can't change who you are."

She sucked in a breath. "Life is malleable."

I started to sit back, to draw away from her in disagreement, but her hand snapped out and caught my wrist. "Listen to me. You think you're the same person as you were when you were a child because you're still sick and you're still half."

I tried to keep my face still, tried not to show how much it surprised me that she could say that so confidently, know it was true. Tried not to show her how it made me want to clench my teeth and turn away from her.

HALF

"You're not, though," she continued. "You were a timid little boy and then a nervous, beautiful teenager, and I worshipped you." She blinked, and I did look away then, and she did too, before she glanced back up at me. I felt her eyes on me and made myself face her. "I don't know if it was because you left, or because of your mother, or just because you had time, but when I saw you again after you came back, you weren't the same. You were stronger. Fierce. You made me nervous. You scared me, and I didn't know how to be around you, because you weren't *you* anymore. That's what I thought."

She took a breath, slowing her rapid speech. "Before, you had a wall around yourself to keep people out, but now you don't need one. They know not to mess with you. Now it's as if you project all that energy out, instead of holding it in. You have some kind of confidence, some kind of massive presence, that radiates from you, and I don't know where it came from, but it was never there when we were children."

Her words stunned me. They cut me down. I was smaller and larger at the same time, a tiny thing in her hand that she believed was great. "And you don't worship me anymore," I said. I was trying for a joke, to dissipate this heavy atmosphere between us, but it came out flat, a question that was really a bitter statement.

She shook her head. Her hand still held my wrist, soft and smooth against my skin. "My heart of hearts always worships you." Her lips rose at the corner, like Kin's did when he was sad. "But you left. You left me there with the fey, alone. You took all that time we could have had together. All that time we'll never get back now. I'll always hold that against you." She smiled then, a full smile that showed me how lonely she had been.

I couldn't look at her while she was smiling like that. "I'm sorry."

She shook her head slowly, her eyes down, and sat back. Her hand slid away. "It's a foolish thing for me to be angry about. Unfair. But I was. I hated you. And I couldn't stop."

"So why this, now?" These meals together, the tea she brewed, the things she said to Kin for my benefit. This tenuous thing between us.

She brushed at her bangs with her hand. "It's easy to hate someone you can't see, can't talk to. So easy to be bitter. But when you're here, always around . . . It's too hard to hold on to that. When you're

101

kind to me, even when I exasperate you. When you run me favors. When I remember how you cared for me before. Every time I see you I remember what we had before." She wasn't meeting my eyes. She laughed, a harsh little sound, and smiled at nothing. "You make me nervous, but I want to be with you. I finally figured out that you're the same person. You're just even more than you had been before. Like you've been distilled. And I can't stay as angry when I see now how difficult everything was for you. I never really understood that as a child."

"Saben," I started.

Her eyes came back up to mine. "Besides," she said, the slight, callous tone sneaking back into her voice, "I realized you might die." Her words were so harsh. But when she said them, her face crumpled in on itself, just for a second, like the words had been toxic. Like they'd burned her.

"That's a terrible reason to forgive someone," I said. I stared at the table. I didn't want to see her face.

She laughed. "I know. But I didn't have a very good reason for being angry to begin with."

"Do you want to go to the beach?"

Kin raised his eyebrows, but his eyes didn't leave the book he was reading. I opened the refrigerator door again. I didn't want anything to eat. I just wanted to feel the cold on my face.

"No. Do you?"

I swung the door a little and looked at him over it. "No. I hate the beach."

He put the book down this time, his expression questioning. He was sitting at the kitchen table, his legs stretched out in front of him, his feet crossed, his shoulders low against the back of the chair. I could see the webbing between his toes, the thin, silky fins that trailed down the backs of his ankles. There were green scales on the tops of his feet, and they shimmered in the sun coming through the window. He looked as good there, in my kitchen, as I'd thought he would the first time I'd seen him in my house.

"There are mer there," I explained. He smiled, his mouth widening slowly. I realized what I'd said. "I didn't mean like . . ."

He waved his hand at me, still grinning. "I get it."

I shut the fridge door and slumped against it. "I thought you might want to go, though."

He cocked his head at me. "Do you know where I was born?"

I shook my head.

"A lake."

"But I thought . . ."

He shook his head. He was still smiling, like the whole thing was entirely amusing. "I'm not a fish, Luca. There's no reason I have to live in salt water." He moved his hand over the table, taking it and the kitchen in with the sweep. "Or in water at all."

I bit my lip, thoughtful. "Isn't it more comfortable, though?" I knew it had to be. He was a man, just like I was a man, but he was also something else. I might not have known much about yokai or ningyo, but I knew fey. I knew that elementals and spirits and fey that came from the sea or the forest or the desert or the snow were better in those places. That the nature was easier on them.

Kin's fingers skimmed over the spine of the book. "Maybe I'm contrary," he said, "but I'm more comfortable where I prefer to be. Not where my genes dictate I live. If I go to the sea, it'll be because I'm craving sun and salt like any other beach lover. Not because I need it to survive. I don't."

He was watching me, his eyes staring into me. It was unnerving. He looked at me because he wanted to look. He wanted me to hear everything behind his words. He wanted me to know he wanted me, wanted me to know him. I'd never had anyone look at me like that before. It made me self-conscious. My hand moved by itself and rubbed the back of my neck, touched the short hair there, and I wondered why he didn't mind the color. Why he didn't mind the way I was too pale, the way my nose and my jaw were a little too sharp, slightly too long. He could have had anyone. He was lovely, even among the fey, and he could have had someone who matched how amazing he was in a second. But he had picked me.

I turned back toward the fridge.

"Luca." His voice was light, like he was giddy on whatever he was thinking, a laugh behind it.

"Hmm?" I had the door open again. I was staring into the fridge but not seeing anything. All I could feel was his eyes on me.

"You're better than water."

I laughed, startled, and shut the door. "Don't say that."

"You are." He held his hands out. "You really are."

I went to him, and he put his arms around my waist and laid his head against my side. "Are you coming with me to see Riyad?"

Kin pushed his forehead against me. "He makes me nervous."

"Oh. Don't be, though. He's . . . he's one of the best people I know."

He sighed. "Yeah. But you know what I mean."

I nodded and ran my fingers through Kin's hair. I knew. Riyad had seen so much, and it was all right there, in him and around him. Sometimes when I was with him it was like I could feel all that time pouring out of him, swirling around him, and sometimes it seemed like it would reach out and grab me too. It was overwhelming.

"Come with me," I said anyway. "I want to be with you."

He pushed his fingers against my spine, making me bend in to him. "All right."

Riyad didn't remark on Kin's presence. He invited us inside like he'd been expecting both of us, instead of just me. Maybe he had.

I liked being in Riyad's house. I'd spent a good deal of time in it as a child. It was welcoming because it was familiar, but I thought it would have felt that way regardless of how often I'd been there. The floors, the table and chairs, the molding around the ceiling were all rich, dark wood. In the living room, he'd spread thick rugs, and his couch and the chairs all had blankets thrown over them, each a bright red or yellow or sky blue, all inviting and comforting, softening any sharp angles, waiting for someone to sit down and relax. There were no pictures, but tucked into corners, along window ledges, hanging from the pull of a cabinet door, were small items that were obviously personal. A bunch of old flowers, gone gray with age, tied with a silk ribbon, sat next to a small ceramic cat. A trio of minute green glass bottles were displayed near the window, so the light could pass through them. An abstract piece of silverwork was propped up by his books on a shelf. Over them hung a drawing of my father's house that

I'd done years ago. It was all so personal, the collection of a long life, a life that Riyad had molded into something supple and comfortable and warm.

In the kitchen, the counter was butcher block squares with blunt edges. The wood was worn smooth like velvet. The room was small, but neat, and we crowded into the little space. On the red tile floor, Riyad had laid out three baskets. I glanced at him, and his eyes softened. I nodded, to thank him, or just acknowledge that he was right about so many things. He handed one basket to me, another to Kin, and took the third for himself. Then he opened the back door, and we followed him out into the yard.

Unlike the rest of his land, which was mostly filled with vines and bushes, Riyad had trees in his backyard. They weren't planted in any kind of rows. Some were clustered near the house, a few too close, in danger of scraping tiles off his roof. Others spread from the house for a long way, meandering up a hill, until they were far enough away that I couldn't tell one's leaves from the next's.

"I planted them as I pleased," Riyad explained to Kin. He had his hand against the nearest tree. I swear I saw it lean into him, just a little, like it knew who he was. His fingers rubbed against the bark idly. "So the varieties are quite mixed."

Kin nodded. He didn't seem ruffled in the least, his back perfectly straight, the basket dangling easily from one hand. He held himself a bit too still, though, and I knew he was nervous.

"The apples are done for the year," Riyad said, turning to look out at the trees. He glanced around, and I thought he probably knew where each type of tree was, exactly. "Some of the pears are coming in. But I think the persimmons are ready now."

Kin laughed. "Persimmons?" His hand jerked, like he wanted to raise it and cover his mouth.

Riyad gave him a small smile. "I have always enjoyed them."

Kin's face smoothed, but some of the tension left him. He nodded and stared at Riyad in the way he did with me that made my heart race with nerves because it was so direct. Riyad's smile widened.

"You know what to look for, then?"

"It would be helpful if you reminded me." Kin's words were formal, but he was smiling.

Riyad led us around a small garden. Half of it was dry and dead now, but at the other end, I saw pumpkins growing on their vines, and cauliflower and winter squash. I hadn't been in the backyard for years, and for the first time, it occurred to me that Riyad lived here off what he grew. I knew my father brought him things sometimes, like I did, and as I assumed Saben and others sometimes did. But Riyad was basically alone in this house, on this plot of land. That was the way he wanted it. If he'd needed more companionship, he would live closer to my father and the other fey. I knew that my father wanted him near. But Riyad stayed out here by himself, and if it came to it, if, for some reason, no one came to visit him, he could still take care of himself perfectly well.

Riyad led us to a tallish, spindly kind of tree. Despite how slender its trunk and branches were, it was robust. Its leaves were thin but glossy, and on each branch, even the smallest ones, hung fruit. They looked almost like oranges, although that would have made it the most oranges I'd ever seen on one tree. The branches were weighty with them, fruit packed into what seemed like every available space. They weren't quite the right neon color for oranges, either. Their color was more organic, ranging from pale yellow to gold to nearly red. They were beautiful. In the shade from the other trees, with the late-afternoon sunlight hitting them only occasionally, the fruit looked like miniature lanterns strung through the tree, their dull skins glowing. When the breeze blew through, they swayed a little. I reached up to brush one with my fingers, and it bumped against my hand, cool and smooth.

"If the color is rich, pick them," Riyad said. He stuck his hand into his basket and pulled out a small knife. He reached with it over his head, taking a fruit in one hand and cutting at the top, leaving a few dried leaves at the head of it. He held it out to me. "If they're soft—very soft—they're ripe. If they're hard, they'll be bitter. They'll ripen indoors, but no sense in picking too many too early when we don't need them all at once."

I took the fruit he offered. "Don't squeeze," Kin said, and I loosened my fingers. The fruit fit neat in my palm, and was liquid-like under the tight skin. I brought it to my nose and sniffed. It didn't smell like much of anything except freshness and cold nights.

Kin took the persimmon from me and brought out his own knife from the basket. I glanced at Riyad and saw that he was watching us, a faraway smile on his face. I looked back at Kin. On one side of the fruit, he made two intersecting cuts, like an X, then handed it back with the cut piece up.

"You can probably just squeeze it out," he said, gesturing to me to bring the fruit to my mouth. "It's very ripe."

I did as he said, raising it to my lips and giving the back a push with my fingers. Velvety, smooth fruit, almost a pulp, slipped into my mouth. The flavor was mild and pumpkin-like, sweeter than I'd expected, with a hint of bitterness underneath. It was exotic and delicious, not quite like anything I'd ever had before.

Kin and Riyad were watching me. "I love it," I told them.

Kin grinned at me. Riyad nodded. "You've never had one? In all your travels?"

I shook my head. I'd eaten a lot of strange things, but I thought I would have remembered this. How beautiful the fruit was, like a drop of light that fit perfectly in my hand. I'd never had one here at Riyad's, either—I'd always visited in the summers with my father. Maybe they had never been quite ripe then, and I'd missed the chance.

"You finish that," Riyad said. "Kin will help me set up the stepladders. We'll do this tree first. There's one more farther back."

While I ate the rest, Kin and Riyad set up short stepladders, just under the branches, so that we could reach the fruit. We took turns standing on them and cutting, passing the fruit down to whoever was on the ground, to be laid in the soft cloth lining the baskets, until our arms got tired and we switched. The work was undemanding and the weather was cool but fine. When I stood on the ladder, I could see the blue sky through the tree branches. The fruit around me smelled earthy. The back garden was at the start of a gentle slope, and when I looked out, I could see the house and the fields and farther, the city a gray smudge against the horizon. All of it was a bit blurred with the elevation, like the city and its surroundings weren't quite real. And when I leaned down to pass the fruit to Kin, when I focused on only where I was and not what was beyond the farm, it seemed that we were tucked away back here, like the rest of the world had stopped and didn't matter. As a child, I'd never been able to imagine myself in a fairy-tale land like other kids had. I'd known that place and I'd known it to be as real and as challenging as the world humans lived in. But here in Riyad's back garden, I thought maybe I understood what those kids were searching for. An escape, for a moment. A place that made them feel safe and at peace and a little dazzled.

We filled the baskets and brought the fruit inside. We lined the persimmons up on the counter and went back out to Riyad's second tree, much farther up the hill, in the back acres where we couldn't see the house. This tree was taller, and we couldn't reach the top fruit, even with the short ladders. Riyad said that was fine. He told us to leave it for the birds.

When we finished harvesting everything we could, the three of us sat around the base of the tree and Riyad selected three ripe fruits. He passed one to each of us, and we ate them. It was messy, and I had to lick my fingers clean, but I didn't mind. I was even more part of a fantasy world here, farther back. The air was loud with the noises of the breeze and the birds and small creatures rustling through the grass, but it was devoid of cars and the hum machines make and any kind of human voice, until we spoke. I bumped my shoulder against Kin's, and he ran his fingers through the hair at my temple, his fingertips lingering on my skin.

Riyad was smiling at us, lazy in the flickering shade. He glanced away and sorted through the fruit in his basket, his fingers careful so as not to bruise the persimmons.

"Did you have persimmons as a child?" I asked.

He glanced up, then leaned back against the tree trunk. "No. We had dates. Figs. Grapes. Things like that." His eyes opened. "Although the trade routes brought many things through."

Kin leaned around me to see Riyad. "You used the trade routes?" His question was still a little formal, his words precise and neat, but somewhere during the afternoon, I thought he'd lost some of the hesitation he had around Riyad.

Riyad nodded. "Even fey can't make oranges fall from the sky. We can't make milk from thin air, can't weave without silk thread. We used the trade routes and the bazaars as much as the humans. With the humans. We had to."

Kin's fingers played idly on my knee. "I don't know that the yokai would do that. Not most of them."

Riyad nodded again, amiable. "Perhaps not as openly," he said, which was not really an agreement.

"Do you miss it?" I asked Riyad. I wasn't sure, exactly, where the question had come from. It was just that, with all the time I'd spent with Riyad, I'd never asked him very much about his past. Not that far back. I guess all kids think that adults only exist within a child's time frame. And Riyad's time frame was so vast as to be unimaginable. But I wanted to know, I realized. About how he'd grown up. What he'd seen. About his life.

He held my eyes and nodded. "I do. Sometimes."

"Do you . . . do you ever want to go back?" I'd gone, instead. He'd sent me to his homeland, a starting place to journey out from. But now I wondered if he'd done it as a way to send himself back, at least in some fashion.

He gave me a soft smile, made strong and lovely by all those years. But it was worn too. A little bit sad. "Not anymore. I must keep moving forward, now."

His words arrowed into me. He didn't know, I was sure, about what Kin had offered me. I didn't fool myself into thinking it. But what he'd said nudged something inside me. I'd always been going forward too. Looking, seeking, moving on to the next place, the next person, the next language. It was only since I'd come home that I'd been in any kind of stasis. And I was enjoying that respite well enough. It was a choice I'd made. But I didn't want to stay still forever. I wanted to always keep moving forward too.

Maybe Riyad saw something of what I was thinking on my face. He reached out and gripped my hand, squeezing my fingers in his. Then he leaned forward, to see Kin. "What fruit did you have as a child?" he asked him.

Kin tilted his head back, going right along with the subject change. I decided to go with it too, and let my thoughts sit until I could poke at them by myself. He hummed, thinking. "Persimmons. Oranges. Pomegranates. Plums, although the yokai complained that they weren't right. My mother grew melons. Some sweet and some not. The yokai always came for those."

"Did you live with the yokai?" I asked. It occurred to me that I didn't know where he'd come from. He'd told me this morning that he'd been born in a lake, but I didn't know where the lake was, or who had lived there with him.

He shook his head. "The yokai were around, often. But I lived in a regular house with my parents." His fingers went still against me, and he looked down into my face. "We always lived at the lake because the yokai were afraid of Catherine. My human mother. They shunned us, but my mother, Midori, wouldn't give her up. So the lake was outside the yokai's territory, but close enough that we could be near them." He gave me his tiny grin. "So I never lived in the ocean."

I swallowed. Riyad was watching us and listening, but this felt private, now. "What happened to her?" I'd noted the way he used the past tense.

He shrugged, but his eyes went far away. "She grew old. She got sick. She died. It was about a year ago."

"I'm sorry, Kin."

He shook his head.

I swallowed. "And your . . . Midori?"

"She lives at the lake still. The yokai won't have her. They think Catherine tainted her with her humanness." He shrugged. "She doesn't want to leave, anyway."

I bit my lip. I wanted to ask him a million things, about his past, about his life and his family. But this wasn't the place. All of that would need to wait, so instead, I stared up at him, and he smiled. He moved his hand and brushed it against mine, so our fingers slid together. Riyad didn't make a sound. I could still feel him there, behind me, but he would give as long as we wanted, even though we were having what should have been a private moment in front of him.

Kin seemed to understood that there were things I wanted to say but couldn't, and I could see that he felt the same. We looked away from each other, content to let it go for now, and Riyad started a different conversation up, smooth, like there had been no break.

I half listened to Riyad and Kin talk. I tipped my head against the tree, let the bark catch in my hair, and gazed out, down the slope. Down onto the fields and the vineyard and the tree line where the forest started, and beyond that, to where I could see the vast, deep blue stretch of sky. The breeze was cool on my skin, just enough to remind me that we were outside and it was autumn, the turn of seasons. That life was moving around us.

I felt terrible about Kin's human mother. I knew what it was like to lose a parent. I knew the space it left, the hole that never went away. There's a fullness that you never realize is there, because it's so much a piece of you. A space made just for that person, a place for all that love to go. That safety, like a net tucked inside your heart, to always catch you. When my mother had died, I'd found that space empty, and it had frightened me terribly. I hadn't known what to do with myself, how to keep going without anything there. If my father and Riyad hadn't given me somewhere else to go, something else to focus on, I wasn't sure what would have happened.

I thought again about the impermanence of things. Kin's mother, my mother, their lives so short, compared to the fey. Too short, even, for humans. But they'd been so bright. They'd left such a mark on us, on Kin's mother and my father and who knows how many other people. Now they were gone, and we mourned them, and it was terrible. A terrible thing. But I remembered, too, my mother smiling up at me from her hospital bed. She hadn't wanted to die. I knew that. But she wouldn't have wanted forever, either. At least, I didn't think so. I thought, at some point, she would have looked forward to a change. To whatever came next. To the mystery of it.

We sat for a while longer, and then we stood and started to gather the baskets so we could head back. I was laughing at something Riyad had said. I bent to grab the basket handle. As my head dipped, my vision went black. My balance went from me, but I couldn't tell where I was because I couldn't see, and my body felt like paper, like it had no substance. And then I heard myself smack into the ground.

When I woke up, I was on Riyad's couch, and he was crouched in front of me. His hand was on my forehead, his fingers brushing over the short fringe of hair that would have been bangs if I'd let it grow.

"I've not been frightened like that in quite a long time," he said, his voice utterly calm.

"I'm sorry."

He pulled his hand away. He touched my cheek as he drew it back, soft, a tiny caress. It reminded me of the way he'd stroked my hair when I was small. When I was only tall enough to come up to his hip, and his hand could rest perfectly on my head.

"Do you know what happened?"

I shook my head.

"You fainted. Your body went rigid," he said, his words blunt, his tone still calm and quiet. "I believe you had a small seizure. When you went limp, Kin carried you here."

"How long was I out?"

"Maybe half an hour."

"Where's Kin?"

Riyad sighed. "Outside, drinking a glass of water." His hand went back to my hair, like he couldn't help touching me. "He was so worried, Luca. He wouldn't leave you alone. I had to send him away. I thought he would make himself sick."

I tried to picture Kin working himself into a frenzy. All I could picture was his face, tight with worry, the way he looked at me whenever I grimaced or touched a sore spot when I thought he wasn't watching.

I drew in a few breaths, trying to decide whether I was awake. I wasn't dizzy or even disoriented. I felt, instead, like I'd had a nap and just woken up from it. The pulsing ache that radiated out from my spine and my back and my arms was the only thing that told me I'd passed out.

"Have you ever seen anyone like me?" I asked Riyad. There were a lot of things I could have said in that minute, but this was what I wanted to know. Needed to know, right then. And I knew Riyad had been all over the world. He'd met more people than I ever would.

But he shook his head. His thumb moved over my forehead in a pattern, like he was anointing me. His eyes were too far away to pay attention to what he was doing though. "It's so good," he said, not quite meeting my eyes. "The magic. The fey blood. And the human part too. When your father told me you would be born, I never imagined that anything would go wrong. I thought it would be wonderful." His eyes focused on me. "It was. You are. But . . ."

I tried to smile. "But I'm flawed."

He shook his head. "I love you. Like you were mine, I love you. I don't know what fey feel for their children, or humans, for that matter, but I imagine it's like this. I wouldn't change you. In my mind, you're perfect. But I would make you well. If there was anything I could give, I would give it for that."

It was odd to hear those words come from a face that seemed younger than mine. I knew he meant it, though, and when I looked into his eyes, they were honest and pained and not young at all. He would never pass for human again. No matter how much glamour he used, people would know, deep in their bones, that he was different. That he was not one of them. His eyes were too deep. I could get lost in how far down they went. It was frightening, but now the weight of that behind what he'd said made me feel strong. It made me feel like I could never brush off his words. His love was a part of me because he'd planted it in me.

I closed my eyes and concentrated on his touch. I was trying not to cry. Riyad let me be. His fingers moved through my hair, along my ear, soothing. He said nothing, made no sound. His touch, his presence, the words he'd said, sent me into a kind of cocoon. I was safe here, with his hand on me and my eyes closed, and I wanted to stay like that and not think.

"Kin made something for you to drink," Riyad said after a long minute. I opened my eyes and came back to earth. He was watching me. His eyes said to let the conversation, the things he'd said, go, to return to normalcy. I nodded.

He turned and reached behind himself for a glass. I sat up. My body protested against the movement. I was sore all over, like I'd worked out too hard, or someone had beaten me with a stick, or both. I took the glass. It was cool in my hands. The drink inside it seemed to be giving off something that wasn't exactly heat. It was more of a sensation, a tingling in my fingers like static electricity, rather than a warmth. Riyad nodded at me, urging me to drink. The liquid was greenish and dark, an unappealing color. It smelled good, though, like fresh grass and herbs and something citrusy. I sipped at it. It tasted almost smoky. The flavor was rich, not raw and sharp like vegetable drinks I'd had in the past. It coated my throat with something thin and silky. It moved down toward my stomach, leaving a little of itself as it went. It felt good, like a salve on everything that was raw inside me.

When I was done, Riyad took the glass from me. As he was turning to place it on the table, he said, "I'm sorry I asked you to work."

"No," I protested. "It wasn't that. I can guarantee it had nothing to do with that." I hadn't been tired. I wasn't worn out by picking the fruit. I'd passed out the other day just walking through Saben's door. I leaned forward and caught his eye. "I loved being out there in the trees. I don't want that taken away because of what's happening inside me." My hand curled into a fist on my knee. "I don't want to live a half life. I don't want to be cautious." I heard my voice getting louder, but I couldn't stop it.

Riyad took my shoulders in his hands. "All right. I'm sorry. I understand."

I took a deep breath. I was so on edge, like I was one emotion one second, and another the next. I couldn't control myself. I couldn't predict what I would do next. "I'm sorry."

He shook his head. "You have every right. You can live however you want. It was wrong of me to imply otherwise. And I do understand that. I understand all of it."

I was near tears again. "I know you do." I breathed in, trying to calm myself, to steady my nerves. "I love you too," I blurted out, negating any calming I'd done. My voice cracked. I'd reverted back to being a little kid in front of him. "I feel the same."

He pulled me toward him, gathering me in and holding me against him. "That means a great deal to me," he said against my ear. His voice wasn't much more than a whisper, and it sounded no steadier than mine.

Kin took me home. We'd taken my car, but he stuffed me into the passenger seat, and I was happy to let him drive. My hands were still shaking enough that I wouldn't have wanted to drive unless I had to. I sat back instead, and watched him while he steered us home.

"I'm sorry." Kin was looking straight ahead. His fingers were almost white around the wheel.

I turned to him. "Isn't that what I'm supposed to say?"

"I mean, I should have been paying more attention. I didn't know you weren't feeling well."

I looked away. "I felt fine."

"Still," he pushed. "That's my job, to notice. I should have seen—"

I realized the brief argument I'd had with Riyad must have come from a discussion he and Kin had had together while I was out. I sliced my hand through the air, cutting him off. "Don't do this. Don't coddle me." My gesture, my voice, were harsher than they should have been. I was tired in a bone-deep way, like whatever had happened to me had beaten the shit out of me. I didn't have any patience left, and I didn't want to have this conversation over again, when I'd just finished having it with Riyad.

"Luca..."

"Do I look like I can't handle myself? Like I don't know my own fucking body?" I was raising my voice. I was sitting straighter and straighter in the seat, my shoulders going tight, my body pitching forward and angling toward him. "Is that what you think?"

Kin's hands gripped the wheel harder. His body was as tight as mine, his face going red. I didn't think about stopping, about closing my mouth. Kin never tiptoed around me, never even came close to suggesting that I couldn't or shouldn't do some things. I hadn't realized it before, but I loved that. I needed it. The idea that he was playing cautious now infuriated me.

"You think I can't take care of myself?" I saw Kin's jaw clench, his hands go impossibly tighter, clamping down. "You think I need you and Riyad and Saben and my father to always keep me in line because I can't do it myself?"

He slammed his hands down on the wheel. "I think you passed out on your fucking face! I think you went down like a ton of fucking bricks! I think you had a seizure that scared the hell out of me! I thought you were dead! When you went still, I thought you had died!"

He shrank back against the seat, as if, once the outburst was over, he had nothing left to keep him upright. I wanted to shrink into my seat too. I'd never seen Kin yell like that. I'd never seen him look like such a wreck. His hands were sweaty, no longer tight, but too damp to hold the wheel, sliding on the leather, and when he reached up to push his hair out of his face, I could see that his fingers were shaking. He was shaking all over. His breath came in gasps.

The fight ran out of me like a physical thing, like water running off my skin. "Pull over," I said, keeping my voice quiet. I reached for his wrist. "Just pull over for a second." Inside, I was a mess at what he'd said, but I just wanted to be calm right then, just wanted him to get off the road.

He nodded, even that movement unsteady. There was no one behind us, the road never very busy here, but he flicked his blinker on, then off right away. He pulled onto a dirt patch by the side of the road. As soon as he set the car in park, he folded forward, crushing his hands to the steering wheel with his forehead.

"Kin." I didn't know how to apologize for something I wasn't really sorry for, for something that had hurt me just as much as it had hurt him, if in a completely different way. I reached out to him, but I wasn't sure whether I should touch him or not. My hand hovered, uncertain, over his back.

"I don't want to coddle you," he said after a long, tense moment. His voice came out muffled by his arms and the dash. "I know you're not weak. I know you'll always want to do things for yourself. Even if you don't have the strength to lift a piece of paper."

I laughed, startled.

He rocked his head to the side so he could see me. "And I'll let you."

I pressed my lips together. "Thank you."

"It's not my call. It's yours. It'll always be yours to decide."

I pushed my fingers through my hair. My hands felt like they didn't belong to me, unsteady and numb. "I stuck you with me. You get a say."

"You didn't trap me." His voice was soft now, calm and no longer angry. He just sounded hurt. Wounded. His eyes were too dark, too shiny. His body was limp, like it wanted to stay draped over that steering wheel for as long as it could. "I chose."

I shook my head a little. "I should have left you alone."

"Don't say that. Please don't."

I bit my lip. Both of us were right, in ways, and I didn't want to point out what idiots that made us.

"I don't think I'll just drop dead," I said after a minute. I rolled my eyes to the roof of the car. I was going for a light tone, but I couldn't look at him while I said it. I was all wobbly like I had been at Riyad's, on the couch. Like I was going in too many different directions and I would break apart.

Kin sighed. "What if you'd stopped breathing? What if your body just couldn't take it?" He laughed, but it was a hard sound that hurt when it hit me. "What if you'd smacked your head when you fell? You could have died up there in those trees, Luca. Don't baby me if I can't do the same with you."

I couldn't meet his eyes. I knew he was staring at me like he always did, his gaze so calm, just watching, and I couldn't meet it. I looked at his hands, loose on the wheel now, his wrists just flexed, his fingers still a little tense. I wanted to grab him, to get those hands to touch me. I wanted his arms around me so that we'd be connected by something tangible and this awkwardness between us would disappear. But I didn't want this to be glossed over and forgotten. I wanted to get through this conversation so that it would be a part of us, instead of something we'd pushed aside. This was important.

"Are you angry with me?" I asked, because I had to, because it was gnawing at my bones to know.

He sat up quickly. "Of course not. How could I be mad at you for being sick?" He leaned toward me. "I was scared, Luca. Riyad thought I was going to lose it, and I thought I might too. I was just so . . ." He raised a hand, dropped it. "You scared me." He inhaled, and it sounded shaky too.

His words took all the breath out of me, until I wanted to gasp for air. "Is it too much?" I asked, before I could decide not to ask it. I had to offer him an out. It had to be done, but I had to do it now, fast, or I'd never be able to. "I don't want you to have to feel that. You don't have to stay. If it's too much."

He was shaking his head before I even finished. "I can't leave. Not now."

My chest was too tight. "No?"

"No." He caught my eye, reached up, and brushed his hair back from his face. "I don't want to go."

"Ah." I was so afraid it wasn't true, that this would wear Kin down until he couldn't take it anymore. But I wanted to believe him. I wanted to believe so much that he would stay. I wanted all of this to be fixed, all the questioning and the wondering and the hurting. I wanted it to stop, and I couldn't make it. And here was Kin, saying these lovely, wonderful things that cut right into the deepest parts of me. It all built up inside of me, and when he said he didn't want to go, it walloped into me and broke the dam, and I started to cry.

"I'm really tired," I said, wiping at my eyes. "I'm sorry."

He pushed himself across the seat and pulled me to him. He drew me in and held me, like Riyad had, and I knew he didn't care if I cried all over him, if that was what I needed. I decided I would believe in that, for right now. I would hold on to that and let the rest go.

CHAPTER 12

I woke up with Kin close, his knee pressed against the small of my back. We'd gone back to my place and had dinner, and we hadn't talked about what had happened at Riyad's, or what had happened to us after, in the car. We hadn't talked about whether Kin would stay the night or not, either. We'd just pretended that everything was the same as usual, two people getting used to being together. Maybe falling a little in love with that feeling. I was. I knew I was. Falling in love with being with someone who wanted me. Someone who was kind and gentle and nervous and sweet. And I didn't want to talk about things that might break any of that.

We'd gone to bed. Kin had laid me down, spread me out on the cotton sheets gone soft and threadbare with age. He'd taken his time over me, like I was special, like I was actually worth looking at. He'd taken my clothes off a piece at a time, slowly, kissing each new piece of skin he bared. When I was naked in front of him, he sat back on his heels and just . . . stared. Ran his gaze up and down my body, until I shivered with it, like I could feel it on my skin, a tangible thing. Until my hands reached up over my head and twisted in the pillow and I tilted my head back and closed my eyes, because I couldn't handle it, couldn't watch him watch me anymore. It was almost more intimate than all the kisses he'd placed on me, all the ways he'd run his lips and his tongue over me. It was as if he was flaying me open, peeking into all the private, guarded places inside me.

When I got right to the edge, right to where I thought I'd fly apart if he didn't touch me, he spread himself over me, pressed me down, and I wrapped myself around him. Let him into me. And he held me and took me until I couldn't remember anything but the two of us together, the strength in him, the ways he wanted me, the ways I wanted him back.

And now it was the next morning and he was sprawled out with his knee pinning me to the bed.

I tried to be annoyed. Another time, when I was aching or in a bad mood or if it was just one of those mornings, I would have been. But I couldn't really be now. It made me want to laugh. I turned my head and saw all his limbs splayed over the bed, his face relaxed, his eyelashes making heavy shadows on his skin, and I smiled to myself. His knee was a warm weight on me—his knee dug into my spine a little, and his foot rested on the back of my thigh, like he'd balanced his leg perfectly against me. I had to squeeze my lips together to keep from laughing.

I wiggled a little, back and forth, and he groaned in his sleep and scooted closer, curving toward me. I let myself sink into the pillow, my chin slipping off my crossed arms. He was so close. I didn't know how anyone, unless they've experienced it, understood the closeness that comes from lying next to another person. Even if we were fully clothed, I'd be able to feel him breathing, to feel every twitch he made, and it would be the same for him. I could smell him, even—the sweet, herbal smell that was always on his skin, the tang of salt, a slight, earthy scent underneath. If he spoke or moaned or snored in his sleep, I would hear it. If he thrashed in the night, it would be me he landed on. If his heart sped up, I would know, and he'd know if mine did.

I reached over and brushed long strands of hair from his face. I ran my fingers over the gentle curve of his nose, around his ear, down his shoulder and his arm, barely touching him. I wanted to stare at him for longer. I wanted to crush myself against him, into him.

Instead, I rolled, dislodging his leg, and sat up at the edge of the bed. He didn't move when I stood. I pulled on my jeans and made my way to the kitchen.

As soon as I stepped past the doorframe of the bedroom, I felt it. Someone was outside. I walked to the front door and pulled aside the blind, remembering to glamour myself, just a little, to be less noticeable before I did. It wasn't that I didn't want to talk to anyone. It was just that . . . I didn't want to talk to anyone.

Saben was sitting on the short step that was my front porch. She had her knees bent, her hands hanging loose between them, keeping her skirt tucked down. She leaned back a bit, so that her hair almost touched the concrete. She was perfectly at ease, like she was planning to sit there all day.

I unlatched the door and swung it open. I leaned against the doorframe, and she tilted her head farther so she could see me, and did something with her lips that was almost the hint of a grin.

"I'm not used to that," I muttered.

"What?"

"The smile."

Her face smoothed over. "Is that better?"

I shook my head. "No, Saben. The smile's a good thing." I tapped my fingers against the doorknob. The metal was cold from the morning air that had seeped in around the doorframe. "Are you coming in?"

"Are you asking me?"

"You'll make yourself sick, sitting out here with all this iron." There was iron in the house, but there was a *lot* of iron in the yard and the doorframe and on the steps.

She tilted her head forward. "It does send a chill through the bones."

I sighed. "I'm asking. Come inside."

She stood and I held the door for her. We stepped into the living room. When I turned back into the house, I could see Kin's legs, still stretched out on the bed. I'd never noticed before how awkward the position of the bedroom door was until Saben was there, staring at Kin's bare feet.

I stepped to the bedroom and reached for the doorknob. Kin looked up at me, bleary, a question on his face. I shook my head. "It's Saben. Go back to sleep." He flopped into the pillow again, and I closed the door.

"I didn't know his ankles were like that," Saben said when I turned to her. I raised an eyebrow, and she moved her hand in a wave, mimicking the curve of the fins on Kin's legs.

I nodded. "Yeah."

I pointed Saben toward the table and went to make coffee. Then I wondered if she drank coffee. I hadn't been around for that time when teenagers decide whether they'll drink coffee or tea, or both, or neither, whether they'll have it every morning or with sugar or milk, or flavored. I turned and held up the bag.

"Do you have cream?"

I nodded, and she nodded back. I set the coffee going and sat down across from her at the table.

"We could sit in the living room," I offered.

She turned her face into the sun coming in through the back door. "This kitchen is obviously the best room in the house. Your living room is dark."

I couldn't really argue with that. I never liked to sit in there, either.

"You look tired," she said. She seemed a little distracted by the sunlight. She kept her face tilted toward it, like she was absorbing it. Maybe she was, I thought. Maybe she was using it to focus, to counteract the iron, as best she could.

"Thanks a bunch."

"Riyad told me to come get persimmons yesterday."

I tipped my head forward and rubbed my hand through my hair. "And you came over here to berate me for passing out?"

"Not to berate—" she started, her voice rising a notch.

I raised my own and spoke over her. "I'm done talking about this."

"Riyad said—"

"Saben, just—"

"Morning, Saben."

We both snapped our heads around to where Kin stood at the entrance to the kitchen. He'd pulled jeans on, like me, but his hair was down and rumpled around his shoulders. He brushed it back with his hands and smiled at Saben.

"Bit early for this, isn't it?" He hadn't bothered to do anything about his scales. They were dark, purple and blue and green, trailing over his face and down his neck. They were silky and too glossy, flushed with blood, like he'd spent the night doing exactly what we'd been doing. His skin glowed, his muscles were loose and liquid. Our evening showed all over him. My face started to burn just seeing him standing there.

Saben slumped, the tiniest bit. "I just wanted to know what happened."

Kin stepped into the kitchen. "He fainted. He woke up. I've already given him hell, Saben, and he didn't really deserve it. Leave it alone." He trailed his fingers over my shoulder as he walked toward the coffeepot.

"I thought you weren't getting out of bed," I said.

He grinned at me. He still looked sleepy, his eyes and his mouth soft, his face more open than it would be after he had coffee. "Decided to get up."

He poured coffee into cups for the three of us, and I got up to get the cream and sugar. I added skim milk to Kin's before he went back to the table, and he leaned into me while we stood at the counter. Our hips bumped and some of the stress went out of me. When we sat back down, I apologized to Saben.

She tapped her fingernail once against the tabletop. "It's nothing."

"I've been living with it for all this time," I said. "And there's nothing I can do about it. So it's like there's nothing more to talk about." I glanced up at them. "But you haven't been living with it like me. I forget that."

Saben dipped her head. "Is it getting worse? Just tell me that, Luca. Because I was there for a long time, and I don't remember it being like this. I don't remember this at all." It was startlingly direct, her words all so straightforward I should have been shocked, but I wasn't. It had been coming, over the last few weeks we'd spent together, this return to the way we'd sometimes conversed when we were younger—more human than fey in our speech. And now it was here.

I stared down at my coffee, at the spoon I'd stuck in it. I started stirring again, just to have something to do. "It's gotten worse, over the years." I couldn't look at her. "That seems logical."

"Was it this bad when you came home?" she pressed.

I bit my lip. "It's not here that's doing it."

"That's not what I was asking. Was it this bad six months ago?"

Kin's body tightened, his muscles bunching, beside me.

"Saben," I said, my tone warning.

"Was it?"

I sucked in air through my nose, my mouth clamped shut. On the table, Kin's hand was making a fist, his knuckles contracting until his skin was white and his scales were almost lime.

"Was it?"

"No." The spoon clinked against the side of the mug when I let go. I sat back in the chair. "It wasn't this bad."

My jaw was tight, like it was screwed shut with bolts, and my mouth could only eject painful words before snapping closed. I was angry again, angry at something that didn't even know what anger was. I had nowhere to direct it. I had nowhere to put it except into the words I said.

"Saben—" Kin started to say, maybe to give some kind of explanation, but I raised my hand, stopping him. Maybe I *should* have let him explain. He was the healer. He could probably lay it all out, a handful of facts, better than I could. Make more sense of it. But this was my sister. And it was a conversation I'd been putting off having with her for her entire life. He nodded and sat back.

"I don't know why." I bit the words off as they came out, so they sounded sharp and clipped. "I think it's just progressing. It could be worse because . . ." I shrugged. "Because of the season. Or a cold I had last month." I glanced at Kin, wanting, at least, to make sure I was more or less saying stuff that was true. He shrugged back, then nodded. A close-enough guess, then. Maybe for both of us. I turned back to Saben. "It could get better next month. Or it might not. I don't know how this thing works. I can't predict it."

I could feel it sitting in me. I could feel the pressure in my lungs and the ache in my joints that never went away. And I could feel that the thing in my lungs was bigger, and that the ache, when it came, was worse, and that when I was tired, I was too tired. But I didn't know whether I would be better, like I was on good days, for longer stretches, or whether the thing in me would take over and tear me apart. I knew that it used to have a bit of a pattern, something I could follow, where A equaled B and an attack was likely, but now it didn't. Now it happened whenever, so randomly, and that made me think that there was something else, something new or bigger or just worse, going on inside me.

"I don't know what it's doing to me," I said.

"You can't do anything?" Saben asked, and although she wore that stiff, upright expression that hid everything, she sounded like she was pleading.

And there it was. The question I couldn't possibly answer. Not to her. Not with Kin sitting next to me.

But this morning, maybe that answer wasn't quite as far away. Maybe it was closer, so much closer than I wanted. I thought about the frost in my garden. I thought about Riyad, about all his days and years and decades, stretched out in front of him and behind him, nearly limitless. Nearly. I thought about how he wanted to move forward.

I almost wanted to say no. Sometime over the last few days, the answer had been forming steadily inside me, growing, swelling. I'd been getting used to the idea of turning down Kin's idea.

But I couldn't bring myself to say it. Not out loud. Not yet. Maybe not ever. I still wanted the cure. Who wouldn't? I still wanted to find something inside myself that would let me reach out and take it, because if the cure worked, it would solve everything.

I didn't want to tell Saben any of that, though. And I didn't want to give her false hope, either. "I don't think so," I said instead.

Saben looked away. Kin's hand flexed, going rigid, and then flattened on the table, like he was forcing it to be still. I wanted to reach for him, but I couldn't.

"I'm sorry," I said. "I'm . . . sorry." I didn't know what else to say. It was, at once, ridiculous to apologize, but at the same time, like my apology wasn't enough. Would never be enough.

Kin took a deep breath. "Don't be." He reached out and snagged my hand, wrapped it in his, tangled our fingers together. He smiled. It was a wobbly expression, and he still seemed a bit far away, like he was lost in his own thoughts. But it was more than I'd expected, and I was grateful.

I glanced at Saben. She was staring down at her coffee. Her hands rested on the edge of the table, her fingers curved around the plastic surface, like she could dig them in if she just pressed hard enough.

"Saben," I said. She jerked her head up and met my eyes. Hers were too brown, too liquid, too deep. And they showed too much, far too much, of what she was feeling.

"Don't be sorry," she said, echoing Kin. "Don't be. This isn't your fault."

I swallowed, surprised and touched and afraid, because I couldn't remember it ever being like this between us. There'd been love and affection, and a certain easiness, but I couldn't remember anything quite like this honesty. Anything like the idea that she respected me, and I respected her, as adults, as equals.

I reached out, touched my fingertip to the back of her hand. I didn't leave it there, or try to hold her hand. We weren't there yet. We might never be like that together, and that was fine.

"I'm okay," I told her. "Right now, I'm okay."

She nodded once. Then she moved her hands, wrapping them around her coffee cup. It was like she was visibly trying to pull herself together, away from whatever was going on in her mind.

"All right." She nodded again, like she was convincing herself. "I'm glad I'm here, then. I'm glad . . . I'm glad you came home, Luca."

It was like she'd lit a flame inside me, a good one this time. A tiny flicker that filled me with so much light and warmth I thought I might burst from how wonderful it felt. "Me too."

We had breakfast together. I had to force the mood around, switch it to something better. I didn't want my life to be about being sick. When I looked back, I didn't want to remember only ever talking about how I was falling apart. So I got up and made toast and forced a smile on my face and into my voice, until Kin got up to help me, and then I really was smiling. It was easy between us, as if we were already figuring out each other's patterns, how to move together, even with something simple like making breakfast. We joked and touched and I handed him pieces of bread to spread jam on and together we made some silent agreement that that conversation was over for now. It took Saben longer. She needed time for it to sink into her body, into her mind. She needed to absorb it and work it over. I remembered that, from when she was small. She did it eventually, though. By the time Kin and I came back to the table, she'd let it go enough that the air around her wasn't so thick with tension. I was grateful.

Saben handed me my messages. There weren't many. Mostly fey who needed tools or items I could get easily in the human world. A shopping trip. It might even be fun. A group of water sprites were upset because someone had dumped a sheet of corrugated steel in their stream. That would have to be dealt with before anything else. It wouldn't be difficult, though. And they liked to pay in gold flakes, which weren't too hard to turn into cash.

"I have to do this one," I told Kin, tapping my finger on the scrawled message about the iron in the stream. "The others can wait until tomorrow."

"I don't have any patients right now. I'll go with you if you want."

"Do you want to do anything else today?" I wanted to be with him. I was sore, like I'd overextended myself, and I was sure it probably had something to do with what had happened yesterday—the fall to the ground alone probably hadn't done me any favors—but otherwise, I felt good. It might be a good day for me, and I didn't really want to spend it inside, if we could do something more interesting.

He ran his hand through his hair, and glanced at the clock. "We could go see my mother. If we left soon, we could make it there and back by tonight. As long as that—" he pointed at the message "—doesn't take long."

"Oh."

He gave me a flicker of a smile. "Do you not want to?"

I shook my head. "No, I want to. I just . . . I don't know why I didn't think of meeting her before."

He leaned toward me. "I didn't know . . . what we were. I didn't know how you felt. I didn't want to have you meet her if . . ." He trailed off, and I held up a hand.

"I know. It's okay." I dropped my fingers. "It'd be good now, though, right?"

He nodded. Then he turned to Saben. "Will you come?"

She dropped the last of her toast. "Me?" She held her jam-smudged fingers out in front of her, so she wouldn't, I supposed, be in danger of passing the stickiness on to anything.

"Please. You'll like her."

She turned to me, waiting for me to tell her to go or not. I had a brief, strong flash of her at eight years old, looking to me to see if she should take another cookie, to see how she should respond to a comment. I could picture her standing beside my knee, never behind me, but close enough that I knew she really did want to hide. And I could see her face staring up at me, those eyes wide, asking me to tell her what the right thing was. I breathed out slowly, trying to come away from the memory.

"You should come." Then I shook my head and turned to Kin. "She won't be able to ride in the car."

"I can," she protested quickly.

"It's an hour and a half ride each way," Kin told her.

"I'll take the things Riyad gave me. I can do it." She glanced back and forth between us, and I was the big brother all over again, even though she wasn't really pleading this time. She looked like she was daring us to say no. "I want to go."

"We can stop along the way," Kin said. "Let her get out and have a breather." I laughed, because it sounded like what someone might say about taking a little kid on a trip, or a puppy. Kin got the joke and smiled back at me. Saben stared at me, confused, and I laughed again, but then it petered out. Her jaw was set so tight, so stubborn. She wanted to get her way. I was afraid, though. I remembered the last time I'd taken her in a car, years ago. It hadn't ended well. I'd been terrified, and it hadn't exactly been comfortable for her, either.

I looked back and forth between the two of them. They both watched me, a kind of hopefulness on their faces. I figured, at least, if it got too bad, we could just turn around. I sighed. "Fine. But if it's too much, you say, and we'll come home."

Saben tilted her chin up a fraction, which was her way of acquiescing to my conditions. "Fine."

We took Kin's truck. There was no logic behind this. In fact, it was almost ridiculous, because even though none of us could be called anything but slender, stuffing three adults in a truck cab was almost always a bad idea. But there was something about how open it felt that made me consider it a better option than my car. Saben seemed to think the same way. She headed right for it in the driveway. It was like if she could see out all the way around her, the iron wouldn't be so suffocating.

She sat by the window. We rolled them down, and propped open the little triangle windows, too. Sometimes, as we drove, she stuck her head out and breathed. I knew she was hurting. The iron burns when the fey breathe in air that's been floating around it. It stings and makes everything feel raw. If they're around enough of it, it poisons them, just like the fey blood was doing to me. This much iron wasn't anywhere near life-threatening, but it had to be uncomfortable.

I hadn't taken any iron pills before we left. I didn't feel an attack or aches coming on, and I didn't want to be sweating iron around Saben when she was already putting up with the truck. I couldn't smoke, either. Saben couldn't handle the crap in human cigarettes, and Kin's herbs were designed to suppress the fey blood. Instead, we had mixed some of Riyad's anti-iron herbs in tea. Kin had added some different things, too, that he thought might help. I could smell it when Saben opened the cap to sip from it. It was bitter and smoky but soothing.

Kin drove us to the sprites' stream first, so I could take care of their problem, and then we continued on toward Kin's mother's. It was a long drive, like he'd said. Whenever Kin found a stretch of blank highway with a wide enough shoulder, he pulled over, and we got out to walk around. If it had been a long stretch since the last stop, Saben would just stand and take deep breaths, until she was steady again. If it wasn't so bad, she would smile with us while we walked through the grasses just off the edge of the road. Sometimes she picked scrappy yellow flowers, and when we got back in the truck, she'd clutch them in her fist or tuck them behind her ear so that they touched her face. She never complained. She had her little tricks for dealing with the iron. I didn't know how well they worked, but they must have worked some, because I had never seen a fey ride so far in a car. I'd never seen anyone do what she was doing—willfully ignore what her body said it couldn't handle.

We got to Kin's mother's house by early afternoon. When we drove up to the long dirt driveway, I could see Kin tense, just a quick tightening of his neck and shoulder blades. It was like he'd taken a deep breath and held it.

"I always called Catherine when I was coming down," he said when I put my hand on his leg. "She'd meet me at the start of the driveway, and ride up to the house with me. She liked to see me driving. She was the one who taught me."

I squeezed down on his knee.

The house was hidden from view. The first thing we saw was the lake—small, almost more of a pond. It stretched in front of us and off to the side. The water was flat, steel gray and blue, and seemed deep, as if it dropped off into hidden depths just off the rocky, shallow beach.

Brambles and reeds, thick enough that I couldn't always see through them, ringed most of it. They were brown now, dried with the fall weather, but they still had a life about them. Beyond the brambles, tall trees with dark, spreading leaves grew. They circled the lake in a wide swath for as far as I could see, and trailed up each side of the long driveway.

As we rounded one edge of the water, I finally saw the house. It was small, two stories, with worn clapboard siding. The paint was old and peeling, a gray that might once have been bluish, lighter than the color of the lake, but matching it, in a way. The house, too, was hidden in the shade of the trees that surrounded it, the imperfections of it muted by the flickering shadows the leaves cast. A small circle of grass between the house and the driveway was neatly trimmed, and the long, wide porch that spanned the front was swept clean.

Kin parked the truck off to the side, as if to not block another car, even though there were no other vehicles in the yard. I couldn't imagine anyone else driving out here. We weren't that far from the city, but we might as well have been in the middle of nowhere, miles from anyone. In the quiet after the engine died, I could hear birds and the movement of the breeze through the trees, and even a muffled shushing that I thought was the water of the lake hitting the shore. It was a quiet that was full of noise. Kin looked over at us, and I nodded. He got out of the truck, and Saben and I followed.

Saben and I lagged a step behind Kin as we walked up to the house. He didn't knock on the door, just walked in. "She knows we're here, now," he said.

The house opened onto a formal sitting room, with spindly furniture. We passed it and walked through a long galley kitchen, surprisingly wide, then came into a casual dining room. A woman who I assumed was Kin's mother was sitting at a worn, round wooden table off to one side. Windows lined the back wall, and behind the woman, I could see trees and a small garden, with a field of long grasses past it, and then, farther out, more trees, and nothing else. No buildings. No houses. No roads.

My eyes didn't stay on the open space of the yard, though. They went right to Kin's mother. Beside me, Saben was staring too, leaning forward toward the woman.

I'd seen fey who were old. I'd seen fey who were ancient, who were near the end of their very long lives. And I'd seen fey who feigned age, fey with crooked backs and wholly white hair and skin wrinkled all over, fey who pretended age to get things or trick people. I'd never seen a fey who had actually aged, though. I'd never seen a fey who looked like she was wearing her years on her body. Riyad didn't have laugh lines or salt and pepper hair, didn't have joints that creaked from the long wear he'd subjected them to. He never would have any of that. My father would never display how many years he'd passed on his skin or his face or his body, either. Saben—never. I'd thought that Kin would be the same way, never growing old, never showing the signs of his long life in any way but the depth of his eyes. But Kin's mother did.

She was lovely. No one could deny that. She wore a summer dress, cut almost like one of Saben's but longer, and she wore it well. It hung off her in gentle waves, refined and shapely, accenting how long her bones were, how easily she carried herself. When she turned to us, she moved with grace. Everything about her flowed. Her spine was straight, and her eyes, green like Kin's, were bright and very clear. Sharp. But her skin was worn thin. On her hands, her veins stood out in prominent lines, and I could see sun spots. She had wrinkles where her smile lines were, and deep grooves around her eyes. Her hair had obviously been Kin's color once, black so rich it was almost purple. Now, though, it was more gray than dark. She had scales, much like Kin's, although hers seemed even more abundant. They covered her cheekbones and trailed up and down her face, over the bridge of her nose, across the top of her forehead, into her eyebrows. They ran down into the neckline of her dress, and out over her shoulders, down her arms, across her hands, until they wrapped around the edges of her palms. Her colors were pastel to Kin's deep blues and purples. They didn't shine like his, either. They gave off a dull luster, like jade held up to the sun.

She stood when she heard us come into the room. She stepped toward us, and I saw that her feet were bare. Feet are funny things. They always look the same, no matter what age you are. Hers were narrow and her toes were long. The scales there rose in wavering lines from her toes, joining together and wrapping around her ankles.

Those feet moved softly over the floorboards, like she and the floor were used to the feel of each other.

She went to Kin first, and touched his face. He bowed his head so she could reach him, and closed his eyes. I glanced away. After, she stepped to Saben, and held her hand. She smiled and bowed a bit at my sister, like it was a reflex. Saben smiled back tightly, maybe happy, but uncomfortable with the warmth that the woman was radiating. Then his mother stepped in front of me.

She did the bowing thing again. I didn't know how to respond, so I ducked my head at her, the gesture more an acknowledgment of embarrassment than any kind of greeting. She smiled at me, though. Her hands came up and touched my face, like she had with Kin. Her fingers were silk soft.

"*Gomen nasai.*"

I didn't know what it meant, but it sounded almost like some kind of embarrassed apology for touching me. I shook my head.

"He has never brought anyone home before," she said.

I glanced at Kin. His cheeks were flushed, his skin and scales darker than normal.

"I am Midori," she said, bringing my attention back to her. I was shocked. Beside me, Saben flinched. Kin had told me her name, but I didn't know if Midori realized that. To give me her name herself, even if it was only part of her name, was a huge gift. And she was giving it to Saben too.

I ducked my head again. I had a hard time meeting her eyes, her stare was so intense. She seemed to be trying to take all of me in. "I'm Luca," I said. I glanced at Saben, and she nodded, almost imperceptibly. "This is my sister, Saben."

Midori nodded. "Please, come in. Sit down. I will bring refreshments."

"I'll get it, Okaasan," Kin said. He stepped behind me. His hand passed over the small of my back.

Midori ushered us into a room off the kitchen. It was set up like a sitting room, or what I imagined a Japanese sitting room would be like. It was still formal, although there was a feel about it, a comfortableness, that told me this room got more use than the one in the front of the house. A low wooden table, perfectly square and solid looking, sat in the middle. Flat, dark-green cotton cushions were seated around it, like they were the chairs. A cabinet filled with some kind of shrine sat off against one wall. Along the other, there was a couch and two overstuffed chairs, arranged in a half circle. Midori made a gesture, offering us the choice of seats. I glanced at Saben. She looked away, her head turning. I thought maybe it was less a dismissal than a gesture for me to follow her. I did, and sat at the low table with her.

Midori seemed pleased with our choice. She sat opposite me and grinned widely. I smiled back. I didn't know if I'd ever been so uncomfortable in my life.

"Oh," Saben said. She was staring over her shoulder. She turned back to Midori. "May I offer my respects?"

Midori's face smoothed over, but it seemed to soften as well. She nodded.

Saben stood and went to the cabinet against the far wall. She sat in front of it and reached out. I heard a bell ring. Then she clapped and bowed her head over her folded hands.

I turned back to Midori, even more lost. "Should I . . . I'm afraid my sister knows your customs far better than I do."

Midori smiled at me again. This time, it wasn't so overly eager, but gentle. She shook her head. "I think Kin will want to show you. Later."

I nodded. I wished Kin would reappear. I glanced out the windows. The whole back wall was glass. Glass doors would open onto a small back porch. Beyond, rosebushes lined a short gravel path that dissolved into nothing as it reached the meadow. The view of the grasses, nearly at eye level, was breathtaking. It seemed like a simple thing, but I never saw grasses from this angle, like I was part of them, like I could disappear in them.

I looked back at Kin's mother. She had the same nose as he did, I realized.

"He told me about you," she said. "After he met you."

Her English was excellent, but I could tell it wasn't her first language. There was the slightest hint of an accent. Some of her syllables were rounded, like she wanted to add something on to the ends of them.

Asking if he had said good things about me felt too cliché, but it was what I wanted to know.

She seemed to guess it from my expression. Her smile quirked at the side. "He didn't say much. Just mentioned you. So casual. Keeping it light. I knew he thought you were special." She looked happy, so glad to see me there. Like I really was special, like I was something good that had happened to her son.

Saben came and sat back down. I took a breath.

"Do you know what I am?"

"Luca," Saben said, low.

I shook my head at her.

"I know," Midori said. Her smile stayed, but it changed into something sad. "I lived with a human for fifty years. I know what it looks like."

She stared at me again. She stared right into my eyes like Kin did. And I saw it all. I saw how she understood, how she got what it was like to feel different and separate and lonely, never quite in one place or the other. I wanted to look away, and I didn't want to, because it was such a rare thing, to see understanding without pity or fear attached to it.

Kin came back in with a tray of drinks and grapes in a bowl, and Midori and I both used the intrusion to break our gaze. I was comfortable, but at the same time, terribly guilty. When Saben had asked to pay her respects, I hadn't understood. I'd only seen Midori's face go blank. But now I got it. I wondered if I should tell her that I would break her son, some day, in the same way the loss of Catherine had broken her.

I didn't have to say anything more, though. I knew, by the way she'd said the word *human*, by the way she'd given me that look, that Kin had also told her the rest. She was aware, at least to some extent, and she was allowing it. But I should maybe speak up anyway. I should tell her how bad it would be.

Maybe she caught me staring while I wondered how to bring it up, because she smiled at me in a reassuring way. "He told me about you," she said, confirming. "Told me whose son you are."

Saben cocked her head. "Do you know our father?"

Midori shook her head. "I know of him, however. And I knew of Luca's mother." She turned to me. "She did favors. If a yokai needed a human for something, she was there. She didn't care about where we came from. Where any came from. What we were."

"Like you," Kin said to me. "Running favors. I didn't know that."

I held Midori's eyes. I was breaking in half. "Neither did I."

Her face fell. "I have hurt you. I apologize."

I shook my head. I had to take a deep breath. Midori took one too, and it seemed we were still having a conversation, a silent thing passing back and forth between the two of us. "You gave me a gift."

CHAPTER 13

We spent the afternoon there with Midori. It was awkward at first, but after she talked about me and my mother, it was also strangely welcoming. I was safe there, with her quiet words and her eager, gentle smiles, in that house that seemed so far away and removed from everything else in the world. I didn't think Midori knew the details of everything, of me and where I came from and my relationship with Kin, but she knew some of it. She knew the most important, largest parts. There weren't many secrets left, and that made it easier to talk to her, even when it was hard to stand how happy she seemed with me there. She made us laugh. Saben smiled. I was glad we'd come.

Before we left, Kin said he wanted to show me the shrine at the back of the room. Midori stood and offered a hand to Saben.

"I would show you my rose garden," she said, and Saben nodded, gracious. They walked out the sliding door that led to the back porch, and Kin led me to the other side of the room, until we stood in front of the shrine.

"You sit like this," Kin said, demonstrating. He knelt, lined his knees up in front of him and sat on his feet. I knelt beside him.

Inside the shrine, which looked like a regular, tall open cabinet, was a picture in a simple frame. It showed a woman, middle-aged, maybe forty, with light-brown hair that hung to her shoulders. She was laughing and leaning forward, like she was getting ready to say something funny to the person on the other side of the camera.

Kin glanced at me. "This is how the Japanese pay respect to loved ones we've lost," Kin said. He reached up and brushed his finger along the picture. "And this is Catherine."

I nodded. "She looks . . . wonderful."

"Mmm." He busied himself, reaching inside the shrine so, I assumed, he wouldn't have to answer. He picked up a small metal stick.

"You ring the bell," he said, doing so with the stick. "And then you kind of clap your hands together, like this . . ." He slapped his hands together in front of his chest, his fingers pointing toward his chin, and left them there. "And then, um, you can bow your head. You're supposed to pray, kind of, but just, you know, for peace and whatnot." He went to hand me the stick, then hesitated. "If you want. You don't have to."

I shook my head. "I want to." I took the stick and rang the bell and clapped. I didn't believe in praying to any kind of god, but I bowed my head and prayed to the woman in the picture in front of me. It felt right. I thanked her for raising Kin to be who he was. I was tempted to beg her to forgive me.

I opened my eyes. Kin's head was still bowed. He tilted it back after a few more seconds, and turned so we could see each other. I folded my hand over his on the floor between us.

"How did they meet? Your parents?"

He sighed, and he seemed to drift away a bit, like he was going back in his memory. "They met while Catherine was living in Japan, when Midori was still there. They . . . they just fit together, I guess. Catherine wasn't supposed to stay for very long, maybe a year. When it was time for her to go home, they didn't want to be apart. Catherine offered to stay in Japan, to move there permanently, but Midori wanted to leave. She wanted to come here. So Catherine bought this land, and they came."

"Why did she want to leave Japan?"

He shrugged. "She wanted something different. Didn't want to be so confined by the yokai, maybe. Or her family. Maybe she just wanted to be where Catherine had grown up. I think it was a combination, but I don't really know. She doesn't really talk about it."

I turned my attention back to the picture. The woman wasn't beautiful, not like Midori, or even in a traditional human sense. Her cheekbones were too round and her face was plain. There was something about her, though, that shone, even through the picture. A kind of liveliness, playfulness, spilled from her smile.

"So how did you come about?" I wondered out loud, and then I realized what I'd said. I raised a hand quickly. "Sorry, I—"

Kin cut me off. He grinned, but it was too wide. He looked embarrassed, or ashamed. "I don't know. I know they wanted me. My mom always told me that, how much they wanted me. I just don't know how it happened. I don't even know who my father is."

"At all?"

He sucked in a breath. The expression on his face was turning into something tight and hollow. "No. Midori always said I was ningyo, but I don't even know for sure. I could be half elf. Half selkie. Half kappa." He paused. "Half human."

I didn't want to give in to what he was saying, didn't want to acknowledge what he was trying to do. I couldn't help it, though. "Wouldn't you know? If you were half human?"

His fingers reached for the skin of my wrist. "Would you know you were half sidhe if no one had told you? Or would you think you were a sick man who was good at hiding when he needed to?"

I wanted to say that I would know, that there would be something in me that would tell me I was different. But people, humans, fey, do feel different sometimes, just because that's part of being alive, living with other people. If I didn't know what was in my blood, I wasn't sure if I would have been able to convince myself that I was anything other than human.

"I don't care what I am," Kin said, his words quiet and low but harsh. His hand pressed against mine. His head was tipped down so that I couldn't see his eyes. "I don't care what you are."

I brushed my head against his, just enough that our hair tangled, our foreheads touched. "Would you want to be with me if I wasn't fey at all? Just human?" I asked.

I pulled away and stared, kind of horrified at myself for asking so bluntly like that. Kin stared back at me. His eyes were a little too wide, too surprised. I scrambled to find something to say, some way to reverse what I'd said. But my throat had gone tight. I couldn't force any words through, and I didn't know what the right ones would be anyway.

Then Kin smiled at me. It softened his whole face. "Of course I would." He raised a hand and ran his fingers down the side of my neck.

"I've never met anyone quite like you. Anyone so . . ." He laughed, softly. "So tough. So put together on the outside and such a mess on the inside."

I grinned a little. "Thanks."

Kin's smile widened. "I didn't mean it like that."

"You did," I said, but I kept my tone teasing. "You're probably right. But as long as you're okay with that . . ." I let my words trail off.

Kin's face went serious. His hand slipped down, closed tight over my shoulder. His other hand was still around mine, and he squeezed. "I'm okay with it. I am, Luca."

I sighed. "Okay."

He shrugged. "We have time to learn each other. But I like what I know now about you. A lot. And I know how I feel, right now, in this moment."

I huffed out a little laugh. I loved how he could do that. How he just laid things out and made them simple. " I like what I know about you too."

He twisted his hand, threaded his fingers through mine. "Then, good." He ducked his head a little so he could look me in the eyes.

I leaned forward and pressed a quick kiss to his lips. "Good."

We went out and joined Kin's mother and Saben. Midori had offered a tiny rosebush, with bright-red, quarter-sized flowers, to Saben. Saben pulled Kin aside to ask if he would get a pot for her. While they contemplated the best way to dig it up, I stepped closer to Midori.

"Catherine was a beautiful person," I told her.

She smiled and bobbed her head. I marveled at the gesture, the grace of it. It was like a thank-you and an agreement at the same time.

"Midori . . ." She peered up at me, and I knew she knew exactly what I was going to say. Her eyes were so sharp. It was hard for me to force the words out. I didn't think she wanted me to say them, either. "I'm sick. Very sick. I think . . . you know this. I . . ." I swallowed. My throat was catching on itself. "I will hurt him very badly." I wanted her to say something, so I could stop speaking, so I wouldn't actually have to ask, but she just looked at me, waiting. I shook my head. "Why are you happy about my being here, with him, when you know that?"

Midori crossed her arms and cupped her elbows. "He cares very deeply about you."

"I care about him too." I thought my voice sounded like Kin's had when he said he'd want me even if I was all human. Shaky and nervous but certain. And I did care for him, very much. There wasn't any doubt in me about that. We might be together for a long time, or we might find we didn't have much time at all. But it was right now that counted, the times we were together that mattered. I felt this way about him, and I wanted him to know, in case I didn't have much time at all. "This is why I don't understand why you're not trying to stop him."

She wouldn't look away, but her arms pushed inward. It dawned on me that she had them folded not to keep me away, but to keep herself contained, to push against her own core and keep the hurt in. This, all of this, was difficult for her, no matter how much it pleased her.

"Luca," she said. My name didn't come out quite right on her tongue, but she made it sound elegant anyway. "Catherine—I loved her. She was the love of my life. It didn't matter that our relationship was maybe not . . . typical. That I was yokai and she was human. I wanted to be with her. Always." She took a breath. "It hurts," she said, and I saw that it cost her to admit this. "Every day, there's pain. But no regrets. I never regret being with her. Loving. Never."

She glanced over at her son. He was kneeling at the edge of the garden, digging with a trowel, the knees of his jeans getting dirty. Saben stood beside him, watching over his shoulder. Every now and then she would point at something, and he would grin and dig as she'd instructed.

"He loves you, I think," Midori said. I snapped my eyes back to hers. She smiled at me, and it was that grief-stricken thing again, that smile that made me want to turn away. "If you leave now because you're afraid of hurting him, he won't have you, and he won't have memories of love. If . . ." She sucked in a breath, and her hand reached out to touch my chest. "If you stay, and something happens . . . at least he will have the time you spent together. At least he will know it was real." I couldn't keep looking at her. "He might never have this chance again. To love like this. This could be the only time in his life."

Her hand slid down my arm. "What do you want me to do?" I asked her.

"Be with him."

I nodded. I looked at her hand on me. Her fingers were strong, but delicate and graceful. The skin on them was thin and too supple, though, like thick paper. The veins that lined the back of her hand were prominent, a deep blue under that pale skin and scales. Like an older human's hand would be. Not a fey's hand. No fey should age like that, I thought. I wasn't sure about the yokai, the ningyo. But I didn't think it was normal.

"Midori," I said, tentatively. It felt almost wrong to say her name, like I should be calling her "my lady" or something. She had that kind of air about her. But she nodded, to let me know I had her attention. "Kin has . . . offered me something. Something . . . good. And terrible. And I don't know how to answer him."

She nodded and pulled her hand away. "The scales. Kin told me about this."

"He did," I said, voice flat. I shouldn't have been surprised, I supposed. It certainly seemed like Kin was close to his mother, like he'd talk to her about things like this. Things that were worrying him. But somewhere along the line, I'd started thinking of Kin's possible cure as a secret.

She smiled at me. "He didn't want to share your private things. But he asked if I could help. If you said yes. He asked if he could take the scales from me. He thinks I have more magic in me."

I glanced over to where Kin and Saben were still digging around in the garden. They weren't paying us any attention. "Do you think that?"

She shrugged, then shook her head. "No. But I don't know. Not really."

"Do you . . ." I swallowed. "Do you know if it's true? The legend?"

Another shrug from her. She took my elbow and pulled me a little ways away, to the other side of the garden. "I cannot say for sure." She raised her eyes to mine. "I've lived apart from that life, the yokai, for a long time. I don't know. I . . ." She hesitated, and I realized I was asking her to tell secrets. Secrets about her people. Secrets maybe Kin should never have brought up to begin with. "I've never heard of it happening. But that does not mean it's not possible."

I nodded. That was fair. I wasn't sure, even now, what answer I'd been hoping for.

I took a deep breath and let it out. I had to swallow, and swallow again, before I could speak. "I'm bad for him, you know. You should want him to drop me."

Her mouth turned down at the corners. "We've been over this." She sighed. "You think you are the only one who does not know his own life span. What if Kin goes to swim tomorrow and drowns? What if... What if he gets in a car accident and dies?"

"He won't," I said, appalled at how easily she said it.

Her shoulders stiffened, and I realized that hadn't been any easier for her to say than it had been for me to hear. "He could. Anything is possible. He doesn't know his life span. It could be as short as yours. No one knows how long their life will last. Not him. Not me. Not you, either."

She'd hit a switch inside me, thrown light on something I'd been trying to make out the shape of, tucked away in a dark corner. Something about what she said made sense to me. With just a few words, Midori had filled in a hole in me. Like she'd answered something, deep inside me, that I'd been struggling so hard with.

We didn't know. We didn't know how long anything would last. And the thought that followed it, the only thing that seemed to make sense, was that not knowing was what made life worth it. That was what made life worth living.

"And what do you think," I asked, taking another deep breath, feeling like I was about to submerse myself in a deep, cold lake, "about living forever?"

She took her own deep breath. I could see her chest, her shoulders, rise and fall with the force of it. "Sometimes . . ." She shook her head. "I am often grateful that this will not last forever." She tipped her head at me. "Sometimes I want to go. To be with her," she said, her voice so low it was almost a whisper. I leaned forward to hear her. She crushed her free hand to her chest, over her heart. "It aches."

I bit my lip and nodded. It made sense. Complete sense. And it was all I needed to know.

We stayed for a while longer. Kin and Saben came over to us after another few minutes, and somehow, Midori and I managed to make it seem like we hadn't been having the tense, intricate discussion we had. Kin had a huge smile on his face, and Saben glowed a bit, like she'd been in a cage and someone had finally come to let her out. I couldn't remember the last time I'd seen her so free, so happy. But then I remembered how she'd been that morning, when I'd found her sitting on my steps, head tilted back so she could see the sky.

Eventually, we said our good-byes. Kin wanted to get going before the sun went, so we could make it home before it got too late. I wanted to put Saben's rosebush in the truck bed, but she wouldn't let me take it from her. She wanted to hold it. She sat with it on her lap, and her fingers moved through the petals of the baby roses while Kin started the engine and turned the truck around. The pot itself was still dirty from where Kin had rested it in the soil while he moved the plant, but she didn't care. The miniature plant helped with the iron. She held it to her face while we drove, smelling the flowers, touching the leaves, the soil. She made it farther than she had on the drive down before Kin had to pull over to let her out.

Kin and I stayed in the truck while Saben walked a slow circle in the grass and weeds at the side of the road, breathing deeply.

"She did really well," I observed, meaning the ride.

I saw Kin nod out of the corner of my eye. "She's a good kid. She's doing her best."

I turned to him. "I know."

Kin leaned back against his seat. His eyes moved from Saben and focused on me. "My mother wasn't always like that. She didn't always look like that."

I bit my lip. I'd thought as much. But I hadn't been sure. "Do yokai age?"

Kin sighed. "More than . . . Well, differently. You know how some sidhe look like they're in their thirties, but some look like teenagers, even though they're older?" I nodded. "They age as they grow up, and then, at some point, they stop, right? And they don't age anymore. That's how it works for sidhe, right?"

"Yes." When sidhe grew, they never really knew at what "age" they'd stop aging, but it was always young.

"Some yokai stop later than most sidhe."

I nodded again. This wasn't a foreign concept. It was just that I'd never seen a fey actually *aging*.

"But they do stop," I said.

He nodded. "Two years ago, my mother could have passed for my sister. She'd looked young that way my whole life. All the years before. She stopped aging." He shrugged like it was nothing, but his movement was so tight it seemed uncomfortable. "Then she started again."

"Do the—"

He shook his head. "No. I've never heard of it."

"What started it?"

His jaw worked. "I don't know. But I think it's because my mom died. It's like her body decided it didn't want to go on living anymore."

I turned and looked back out the window at Saben. My lungs expanded as I breathed in hard, trying to take as much as I could, until it hurt. It didn't make sense. Yokai and fey didn't start aging again. I wasn't an expert on the fey and all the creatures of the world like them, by any means, but I had never heard of this. It was like a law. Fey didn't age. They died—they weren't immortal. They gained years, sometimes the time caught up with them, like how Riyad had been nearly stripped of his tolerance for iron. Sometimes they retreated inwards. I'd seen fey get thin, like their bones were dissolving or their skin was turning translucent. But they never aged like humans. Even the fey who looked relatively old always had a youthfulness to their bodies, a limberness, a glossiness to their hair. It was how things worked.

I didn't know what to say to Kin. I wanted to question him, but it was his mother we were talking about. He had as good as said that she was failing on purpose, even if it was subconscious. I didn't know what to ask without hurting him or making it sound terrible, because it *was* terrible.

Part of me wanted to tell him, then, what Midori and I had spoken of. How her few sentences had gone so far to help me make up my own mind. How it was like she'd pulled a truth from inside me, and I could feel it growing, hardening, going crystalline. I thought I knew now what my answer would be if Kin asked me again about the cure. It terrified me, but I had the deepest sense that I was right. That the answer was right. That it was the only choice that would ever make sense. The only choice I could live with.

I didn't want to compound Kin's hurt with that, either, though. I didn't want to ruin the beautiful day we'd had. I didn't want to talk about it with Saben there. And part of me was sure that, even now, I wouldn't be able to make the words come out. I wouldn't be able to close that door, give up that hope.

Saben got back into the truck and pulled her rosebush from the floor up onto her lap. She was windblown, her cheeks red, her hair a mess. She smiled at us, and Kin smiled back as he started the truck again.

We dropped Saben off at her apartment. Kin stayed in the truck while I walked her to the building's front door. Just before she opened it, she turned to face me.

"I need you to come by tomorrow and change the rest of my drawer pulls." She sniffed. "I did some, but the iron in the old ones and the screwdriver together is too much for my fingers. It'll be faster if you do it."

I nodded. "All right. I'll be by in the afternoon."

"Also, one of my girls moved in downstairs. I need you to take as much of the iron out of her apartment as possible."

I scrunched up my nose. "Why would she move into a human apartment?"

Saben shrugged. The rosebush in her arms moved up and down. "I don't know. I asked her not to, but she insisted."

"You're setting a bad example. Your followers are too devoted."

She glanced away and then back. "Perhaps. She won't stay long, I don't think."

"Maybe she's in love with you."

"Then she'll be disappointed." She took a deep breath. "I'm not looking for anyone like that. Not even casually."

She said it like it was a big deal. Maybe it was. The fey would think having a thousand casual relationships made more sense than waiting for something serious.

I knew I shouldn't, but the way she stared at me like I'd scold her made me laugh.

"Okay," I said, getting myself under control. "That's fine. It's good."

She nodded tightly. "For taking me with you today . . ." She paused and tipped her face up to the sky, then back down to me. "I was happy."

I looked at her, studied her face. I didn't know her now, not really. She wasn't the person I'd left behind all those years ago. She was someone new. But I thought things were better between us than when she'd gotten one of her girls to ask me for two copper knives in an orchard, not many weeks ago.

"It was good, wasn't it?"

She smiled faintly. "Yes. I enjoyed it."

"Me too."

CHAPTER 14

The next morning, my hands shook so badly I dropped a coffee mug. It smashed all over the kitchen floor, but when I went to reach for the pieces, my knees wouldn't hold me up. Kin found me sitting on the floor, gathering the shards in my hand. I didn't say anything, didn't think to offer an explanation, because it just wasn't necessary, and Kin didn't ask. He took the shards from me and threw them away, then swept up the rest. He swept around my knees and my feet. By the time he was done, the weakness had passed, and I stood up without a problem. A lingering soreness was all that was left.

He sat me down at the kitchen table, after, and looked me over. His fingers flipped my hands, searching for anywhere I might have cut myself on the shards of the mug. He prodded my chest, my legs, checked the reflexes in my knees. I let him, didn't say anything, even though him doing it felt indulgent and relatively useless. When he was done, he made me a strong cup of tea with the herbs he'd brought for me. It tasted as smoky and warm as usual, and I drank it gladly, which seemed to make him, if not happy, at least a bit less tense.

He leaned against the counter, hands braced behind him, and watched me. He stared at me while I sipped my tea, but I just waited. I figured he'd say whatever he wanted to say eventually.

He did. "Be careful." His voice was low and soft. "You could have cut yourself. Just . . . be careful."

I knew he was worried, and he was trying to be kind. But it reminded me of what he'd said the day we went to Riyad's. It reminded me of people my whole life telling me what I could and couldn't do.

"People get cut all the time, Kin." I managed to keep my voice from rising too much, but I definitely didn't sound happy. "What do you want me to do? Sit still? Wear padding? I'm not an eggshell. I'm not that far gone that a fall or a cut is going to be the end of me."

He looked down at the floor. I could hear him breathing, hear the heaviness in him as he dragged in air and tried to calm himself, and I wanted to go to him and take that heaviness away, but I was afraid of what would happen if I did. I was afraid of what we'd say to each other.

"You're right," he said finally. "I'm sorry." He ran his hand over his face. His scales caught the light, flashing iridescent as his hand moved over and away from them. "I'm angry that you're sick. I'm angry with your blood. I take it out on you."

I smiled. "I know."

"I'm sorry."

"Okay." I didn't say it was all right because it wasn't, not completely. I did understand it, though. I understood it enough to let it go.

Kin stayed with me again that night. Once again, neither of us talked about it, about plans or how much time we were spending together. Afternoon slipped into evening and then it was night and he hadn't left, and it just seemed normal. Comfortable.

When I stretched out beside him on the bed that night, and he reached for me and pulled me to him, it felt a little different. Not different in a bad way. Not at all. Different in that I could feel him reaching for me a little too hard, could feel him wanting to hold me against him, or hold me down, like there was something almost desperate in him. I didn't know where it had come from, or what was causing it. Our visit to his mother, him missing Catherine. Or even just that I'd scared him that morning, and that fear was spilling over.

It didn't matter. I wanted to take away whatever was bothering him. I wanted to hold him to me just as hard. He'd been sprawled half over me, one of his legs tangled between mine, but I pushed his shoulder, rolling us the other way, so I rested on my elbows over him. For a second, we stared at each other in the near dark, his green eyes so deep they looked black. Then I lowered my head, kissed his throat, the hollow place just below it. The center of his chest, the place where his heart beat under his ribs, a bird in a cage, the thump of it fast and heavy beneath my lips. I kissed the insides of his elbows, one, then the other, turning his hand in mine so I could press my lips to the soft skin.

I looked up at him when I moved lower, just before I pressed my mouth to the side of his waist. His black hair was spread over the pillow, short strands clinging to his face. His head was tilted back, like he wanted to close his eyes and let go, give himself over to whatever I wanted to do with him. But while I watched, he tipped his face to the side so he could see me, so our eyes met. I smiled at him. He was lovely, all that fine skin, all those sleek muscles. He smiled back at me, almost shy. I knew Kin wasn't shy in bed. He was bold and unrestrained. There was something new between us, though. Like something had changed, sometime between when we'd left with Saben to visit Midori, and when we'd come home. Maybe when we were sitting together in front of the shrine and Kin told me he'd want me no matter what. Whatever it was, maybe it made whatever connection we had a little deeper. It was a good thing, but I thought we were both a bit shy with it, feeling around it, testing it.

I ducked my head and got back to work, dipping my tongue into the space where his thigh met his body. He arched off the bed, a harsh groan escaping him. A second later, before I had time to move my mouth anywhere else, he tapped me on the shoulder. I looked up to see him holding out the little clay pot of lube he'd brought. Something he'd made himself. It smelled like herbs and fresh-cut grass, and it was warm. Fey lube. The thought made me laugh.

"What?" Kin asked, a grin in his voice.

I shook my head and met his smile while I dipped my fingers into the pot and recapped it. I tossed it on the bed, and he reached down, tugging at my shoulders.

"Kin . . ." I gestured, aiming to touch between his legs.

He shook his head. "Come up here. I want to see you."

I crawled up, until we were face-to-face again, breathing the same air. Then I reached down. He bent his legs for me, so it was easy to press fingers inside him. He twisted, his body jerking when I hit the right spot. I did it again, until he arched back, his eyes squeezed shut.

"Now," he said, and it sounded like he was pleading. "Now."

I grabbed a condom from the bedside table and fumbled it on. Then he shifted, moving us together just right. A second later I was inside him. He was so warm around me, his legs coming up to hold me, his hands sliding over my back, then across my neck, into my hair.

He brought one arm around, so he could run his fingers over my jaw, rub his thumb across my cheekbone. He watched me the whole time, his eyes locked on mine.

I moved, slow and easy inside him. I wanted this to last. I wanted to stay with him like this for as long as I could. Looking down at him, seeing him looking back up at me, it was like maybe something was passing between us. I'd heard sex called a conversation before, but I didn't think I'd ever had any that would have amounted to more than a few crude words. But with Kin, it *was* like we were talking. Like we were saying things with our bodies that maybe we couldn't quite have found a way to say out loud. We were connected, like what we were doing for each other, together, mattered.

I rocked up into him and he gasped, grabbing tighter to me, tugging on my hair. "Luca."

"I'm right here," I said, which was completely ridiculous, but he nodded.

"Luca." His hands loosened a little, enough to brush my hair back from my face, to make me pay attention. "I want to be like this all the time."

I laughed. "That might be a bit of a challenge."

He grinned back and shook his head. "Not what I meant."

I smiled, and then I had to duck down and kiss him, because he was so perfect, and I wanted to be like this with him all the time too. I wanted him in my bed and in my house and just here. I wanted to know he was near me.

"I want that too," I said, and he nodded, his face going serious, and I thought my guess about what he'd meant was close enough.

"Maybe some nights I could stay at your place instead?" We were still moving together, and it was a little odd, having a conversation like this while we were doing what we were doing. But on the other hand, I was stripped bare, emotionally as well as literally, and it seemed like the perfect time to suggest things I might not have otherwise. Things that were a little too needy, a little too sappy. "When you have to do your healing?" So we didn't have to be apart quite as much, I thought.

He grinned at my made-up word. But then he nodded. "Yes, please."

"And I can get you a key so you can come walking in without feeling like you're breaking and entering?"

That quick smile again, followed by a gasp and a moan when I rotated my hips. "I don't feel like I'm breaking and entering," he said between panting breaths.

I laughed, a soundless huff of amusement. "You're terrible."

He pressed his heels into my backside, urging me closer, deeper. "Someone has to watch out for you," he said. His eyelids flickered, and then he looked back up at me, right at me, his gaze so direct and so clear. It had been the continuation of a joke. But his expression told me he meant it. That he would watch out for me. That he would care for me and protect me. Maybe whether I wanted it or not. Because he wanted to do it. He wanted to be there for me.

I wanted it.

"I want all that, Luca," Kin said, echoing my thoughts. "The key and the nights together and you. I want it."

I pressed into him, hard, and he cried out. Close. He was close, and so was I. I reached a hand between us, moved my hips a little faster, angling for just the right spot, and he came, shaking and yelling, his feet pressed hard into the mattress, pushing me up into him just a bit further. It was enough to send me over the edge, and I came as well, dropping my head to his shoulder, then collapsing on him, pressing us flat, again, to the bed.

His hand came up and gently pushed the sweaty hair off my forehead. I turned my face and kissed his shoulder.

"I want all that," he repeated, his voice a little hoarse, but still sure and strong.

"You can have it," I promised him. "It's yours. You've got to know that."

I looked up, tilting my head, and he nodded. "All right."

I thought that was enough, for right then. A kind of promise between us. I think Kin thought it was too, truly. But he seemed a little distracted, just slightly, while we cleaned up and switched the light off, and got back into bed together. Like he was tumbling something else over and over in his mind. Maybe the same thing he'd been thinking about when we'd gotten into bed originally, whatever had made him want to hold on to me so badly. Whatever had put that kernel of worry in him.

Just as I started to fall asleep, he turned to me in the dark. I couldn't see his features, just the shape of him, rising over me.

"Luca."

"Mm?" I reached my hands out for him. He lifted them away, his fingers wrapping around mine to keep them still.

"Luca, are you awake?"

I took a breath. "I'm awake."

"I've been thinking. Since we went to see my mother." I heard him take a deep breath. "Before that, actually. Since you fell at Riyad's."

"Oh god, Kin." I tried to roll over, but he wouldn't let me go. He squirmed around until he was sitting in front of me.

"Will you listen? Please? It's important."

I freed a hand and rubbed it over my eyes. Then I pushed myself back against the pillows so I could look his shadowy form in the eye. "All right."

For a long moment, though, he was silent. I could see his silhouette, the black shape of him, the slope of his shoulders, the sharp profile of his face. He was beautiful, even in the dark, even when I couldn't see anything but his outline. Fine and elegant and lovely. I had never expected, I realized, to find anyone. I hadn't wanted to look, because I didn't know what time I had left. I didn't know what I wanted to do with that time. It had seemed like such a selfish thing, to drag someone into my life when it was such a mess. I hadn't dwelled on it, but somewhere in the back of my mind, I think I'd imagined that I would be alone. That there wouldn't be anyone for me. I'd accepted that.

But I was glad Kin was here. I was so happy to have him. To be cared about by him. To be able to care about him in return. Maybe he was a fling—a last, bright thing in my life. I wouldn't have chosen anyone else, though. I wanted him, just him.

His hand reached out, fumbling for mine in the dark and the bed sheets. "I want you to take the cure."

I'd been expecting that. I'd been waiting for him to bring it up again. I hadn't realize he'd put it like that, though. I'd kind of thought he'd ask.

If he'd asked yesterday morning, I might have given him a different answer, or no answer at all. I'd still been so unsure. But the answer was a solid thing inside me now, like a hard gem, lodged in my heart. Steeped in certainty. "No."

His fingers clamped down around mine, an involuntary twitch. Then he let go and reeled back. "What?"

"I can't." I started to reach for him again. I wanted to touch him, to make him understand. To plead with him, maybe. But he'd pulled away, not necessarily physically, but in every other way. I couldn't reach him. "I'm sorry. I . . . Kin. I can't."

"Because it's weird?"

I shook my head. "No." It *was* weird, and pretty disgusting. The whole idea of it creeped me out. But if it would have worked, if it would have cured me without anything else, if it wouldn't have hurt Kin, or his mother, I thought maybe I could have gotten past it. "It's not that. I can't live forever. I don't want to."

"But . . ." I heard him draw in a shaky breath. "It could work. It could cure you."

"It might not, though," I said back, and I did sound like I was pleading now. Like I was begging him to understand, to see it from all the angles.

He moved, leaning to the side, and a second later, the bedside lamp clicked on, making me blink in the light. I looked up at Kin. He seemed broken. His skin was ashy, washed out, and his scales were dull.

"Kin . . ."

"It might work," he repeated, stubborn. His eyes flicked up to my face. "It could make you better. It could save you."

"I can't live with what else it might do," I told him, and when I said it, that certainty was there again. I hadn't known I was going to say that, hadn't even really thought about the words before they'd spilled out. But those words were the truth. They were something I'd known, but hadn't quite realized. "I can't take that risk. Do you know what you're asking me? I can't do it."

His mouth opened and closed, like he couldn't quite believe what he was hearing. "Don't you want to get better?"

My body seized up, my spine going so stiff I wondered if it would break. My jaw was a steel trap, and I marveled that I could still open it far enough to speak. "Don't you dare. Don't you say that to me."

"Then why won't you consider—" Kin started, his voice rising.

"I won't!" I shouted, running over his words.

"I don't want to lose you!" he yelled back, his voice going too high and brittle. "I need you to do this!"

I shook my head hard, my lips pressed together. "I won't. It has nothing to do with wanting to get better. Do you hear me? But I won't do that. It would be wrong."

"Luca!"

I grabbed the sheets in my hands, squeezed until my fingers hurt. "No. Absolutely not. No."

Kin stared and said nothing. I stared back. I wanted him to know that this was my answer. That it was the only answer I was going to give. My heart pounded away in my chest, too fast, too hard. I was afraid, so afraid. I hadn't wanted to answer for so long, because I had never been sure of what would happen between us, what would happen to us, when I did. I still didn't know, and it terrified me.

Kin swallowed. His face was too pale, his jaw set so tight I could see a muscle twitching under his skin. We sat there staring at each other for so long that I almost broke, almost gave in and told him I'd do whatever he wanted, if this would just stop, if he'd just wrap me back up in his arms again.

In a flash of movement, Kin unfolded his body, climbed off the bed. He moved around the room, tugging on his clothes, grabbing his keys from where he'd set them on my bureau. I watched him, stupid. It took me a minute to realize that he was getting ready to leave.

"Kin."

He didn't stop, didn't look at me. He shoved his feet into his shoes, and then he was leaving the room. I leaned forward on the bed so I could see him walk to the front door. I didn't say anything else. I didn't know *what* to say, what would stop him and bring him back. He opened the door, rushed through, and slammed it behind him.

CHAPTER 15

I thought Kin would be back by the next morning, but he wasn't. I'd thought that he'd at least come back to talk. That I'd get up and he'd be on the doorstep, trying to decide whether he should come in or not. But he wasn't. I didn't hear from him, and he didn't come back.

I hadn't been ready for any of this. I hadn't been ready to tell him that I wouldn't try his cure. I hadn't been prepared for what might happen if I did. I'd just wanted to put it off, forget about it for as long as possible. I'd probably known, deep down, for a long time, what my answer would be. I'd just waited until it had grown so big inside of me that I couldn't ignore it. Waited until I could tell myself that there was no way I'd choose the other option. I'd had such a hard time admitting that, even in my own mind. That I'd give something like that up. That there might be a cure, the thing I had spent most of my life searching for, and I wouldn't take it when it was offered to me.

I wished I hadn't said it, though. Not out loud. Not to Kin. I wished I'd gotten to keep him for a little while longer. A few more hours, days. It was so odd. We hadn't even known each other for very long. But his absence was like a physical thing. It was so obvious that he was missing. His lack was like a black spot in my vision. I couldn't ignore it, couldn't help but see it.

I paced the house, restless, not quite sure what to do with myself. I knew I wasn't wrong to refuse. I knew it. As soon as I'd said no, told him I wouldn't do it, the biggest sense of rightness had settled on me. Like it was easy, like that was the only possible path I had, so it was simple to follow it. It hadn't been simple, though. That was the problem. Kin had gone. I'd promised him I'd care for him, I'd made him want things and maybe hope for things, and then I'd taken them away. That was my fault. That wasn't any more right than saying yes to the cure would have been.

I needed to get out of the house, do something else, distract myself. I had a little pile of messages, but they wouldn't keep me busy for too long. I decided to go to Saben's and see if she had any more. And if I got to see her in the process, if she was someone I could talk to, all the better. The thought almost made me laugh. A few weeks ago, I wouldn't have even considered it. But now, she was the person I wanted to turn to.

She knew something was wrong when she answered her door. She looked at my face and flung the door wide, then stepped out of the way. "Aim for the couch, please."

I shook my head. "I'm not passing out." My voice sounded thin even to my own ears.

Apparently this answer wasn't really reassuring. The color leached out of her face. "Can you breathe?"

I nodded, but as I did my breath went short. The skin around my cheekbones tingled. It took me a minute to recognize what the sensation was. I was going to cry.

Saben pulled me inside and shut the door. She shuffled me to the couch and sat beside me. Her hands patted me all over, taking off my jacket, checking for hurts that she wouldn't be able to see.

I slumped back against the couch. "Kin's gone."

Her hands froze. "What?"

"We had a fight. I think he left me."

Saben sat back to face me. Her hands dropped to her knees. "Luca. People fight. People storm out. It's normal." She frowned. "I think," she added, and I wondered briefly if she was going over books she'd read in her mind, searching for romantic fight scenes.

I ran my hand over my face. My fingers were shaky, but I wasn't crying yet. "This was different. This was . . . big."

"How big?"

I knew I probably shouldn't tell her. I knew it. But I had to tell someone. "He thinks he's found a cure. For me."

Her hands twitched. "Excuse me?"

I turned to her, grabbed at her hands. "You can't tell anyone."

She wasn't listening. She batted my hands away, pushing me back. "You told me there wasn't anything you could do. You told me!"

"There isn't. Saben, listen to me!" I reached for her again.

She threw her hands up, palms out, stopping me. "Don't you . . . Don't you touch me. You told me. You told me there wasn't an answer."

I took a deep breath, tried to steady myself. I didn't want this to turn into a shouting match. If Saben was anything at all like she'd been as a child, I would lose. "It's . . . a legend. A legend that says that if I take this thing he's offering me, I will be cured." Her mouth popped open, and I held my own hand up. "The legend says that this stuff causes immortality. So if it actually worked, it would cure me. But if it cures me, it will make me immortal."

"Is it true? Will it . . . will it work?"

I glared at her. "That's kind of beside the point, isn't it?"

Her jaw worked. "Answer."

I shrugged. My hand wandered back up to my jaw. I needed to touch myself to ensure that I was still there. "He didn't sound sure."

"So he thinks that if you take this stuff, you'll get better. And he wants you to do it."

I nodded, trying for patience.

"What is it? What's the stuff?"

"Scales." I swallowed. "From him. Or his mother. He's ningyo." I didn't know if that would mean anything to her. She nodded, but she seemed distracted, more like she was absorbing the information than that what Kin was meant anything to her.

"That's kind of appalling," she said. I nodded. She was quiet for a long minute. Then she said, "I'd want you to do it, if I were him."

I closed my eyes. My head slumped back against the couch cushion. "Saben. Did you miss the part where I said that if it worked, it would make me live forever? I can't do that. I . . ." I opened my eyes, turned my head to face her. "I thought about it. I really did. Part of me wanted to. But I can't. I can't live like that."

Saben sighed heavily through her nose and leaned forward. "You must see where he's coming from, though."

My mouth worked, opening and closing. All my words rushed forward and got stuck. I couldn't think what to say first. "Are you crazy? Can you imagine? All those days, piling up, end over end?"

It would be great at first, I figured. The rush of it. But I'd seen the way Riyad looked sometimes. Worn thin. Tired. Like he had the honest weight of the world on him, because he did. He'd seen too many things. Seen too many things become commonplace and boring. Loved and lost too many people. Like Kin's mother had. I didn't want to be like that. I couldn't. I was already sure, but the more I thought about it, the steadier I was in my choice.

She reached forward, as if she was trying to get me to focus on her, on what she was saying. "I know. It's a lot to think about. I get it. I get that." Her words were low and gentle, but rushed, spilling out while she tried to order her own thoughts. Her hand touched my arm, trying to still the anger inside me. "But . . . Luca. He's desperate."

I shook my head and stood up. "I have to go."

"What?"

"I can't talk to you." I walked over to the counter that separated the room from the kitchen. "I have to go." I was close to passing out, now. I was dizzy and my vision was narrowed, but I thought, I hoped, that was just the anger. And I was probably angry enough to keep myself on my feet.

I pawed around for the messages that were usually on her counter. I didn't want to have to come back for them, see her again, if there were any here. Saben came up behind me. "Stop it." She grabbed my arm. "Listen to me. If I pricked my finger with a needle and told you that a spoonful of my blood would take away your sickness, would you drink it?"

I stared down at her. She was absolutely serious, her face tilted up to me, her body leaning in to pin me against the counter until I answered her. I swallowed hard.

"It would depend."

"On what?"

"On what else your blood would do to me."

Her mouth dropped open. She gulped in air. "Say it would make you well. Say that's all it would do." Her voice was so strained, a whisper that caught in her throat.

"I'd take it."

"But if it did anything else . . . If it changed you . . ." She let her question trail off.

I shook my head. "No."

"Why?" She clutched at my arm, her fingers digging into my sleeve, twisting it. "Why can't you see how Kin's looking at this?"

"It's completely different." I heard my own voice rising, going too loud. "It's nothing like that scenario."

She tilted even farther forward, and her voice climbed, trying to drive me down with its volume. "I know, but you have to—"

"No! It's not the same. He's not offering a cure with nothing else attached. Not something with side effects I could live with. It isn't the same. It would do things to me. It would change me and you know it!" I pushed away from her, pushed her away from me. "This is me!" I slapped my hand against my chest. "I'm sick! I'm always sick! And I hate it. But this is me. I can think and feel and I'm me. I will not become something else to get better. I won't! All you and Kin get is this. This is all I have to give you." A wave of dizziness passed over me. I caught myself against the counter. "Why isn't this enough?"

"Luca . . ." Saben's hands hovered in front of me, unsure, reaching. I thought she wanted to hold on to me for herself more than anything. She had the worst expression on her face. I didn't think I'd ever seen her look so torn apart, so confused and heart sore.

"I know it's not enough time." I was tired. I wanted to lie down and never get back up. "God, Saben, I know that. But this is what I get. I just want to be okay with that. I just want to be myself while I'm still here. Why isn't that all right?"

She shook her head slowly. Her mouth was open like she wanted to say something, but I'd stopped all the words in her. I turned away. "I have to go."

I brushed past her. My jacket was on the couch, and I grabbed it as I passed by. Then I was out the door.

I went back home, to a house that had never really felt empty before. It had always been enough of a home for me, a place where I was safe. But it was like a hollow shell now. I could picture Kin at the table when I walked through the kitchen, could see him in my bed when I passed by the open door in my pacing. In my mind he was rising above me there, the sheets and his hair around us, his hands on my hips. I could feel his fingertips pressing into my muscles, remember him kissing the middle of my chest, the slow burn of his lips on my skin. I could see him holding me, me holding him, and I wondered, not for the first time, what it was that I gave to him, offered him, that made him want to stay with me. He protected me and cared for me and I gave him sickness and sadness in return.

I wasn't sure why I'd gone home. Because I'd been so angry my eyes had gone blind, maybe. Because I hadn't thought I could do anything, drive anywhere, help any of the fey on my list. But I couldn't stay there. I took deep breaths, made myself tea, and then made myself drink it. When I was done, I left again. I put the messages into order by place this time, and then I started with the first request and spent the rest of the afternoon working my way through them. I saw sidhe and spriggans and phouka and some fey who I wasn't even sure I could classify. I didn't care. I hardly noticed doing any of it, seeing any of them. I ran deliveries and mended glamours. I moved iron, patched fences, passed messages. I talked with the fey who wanted to speak to me, and I didn't hear a thing they said. I smiled and nodded and all there was in my ears was a rushing, a distraction turned into sound. My hands moved by themselves, automatically. I couldn't think.

When I was done with requests, I went to see the brownies. Their message was only to come pick up food—no task attached. That was the best stop. Sometimes they wanted to cook and overdid it, and I was the one who got whatever was left over, but there was more to my wanting to see them than that. I liked them, and for some reason, they'd seemed to have taken a shine to me. Poor little half-fey boy, maybe. I didn't care what it was. I just enjoyed being with them. My mind cleared a little in the warmth of their company. They were easy to get along with, and I could pretend, for a minute in front of them, that I was normal. They fussed over me in their gruff way, rough with their affection, but tender. They piled pies and casseroles and salads on me. I wished Kin was there with me to meet them, so they could admire him too. They always asked if I'd found someone. Usually I joked with them, told them I didn't need another person to make me happy, and that was the truth. This time, though, I just shook my head, and it made me hurt all the way through to do it.

When I got home, it was late afternoon, and Saben was sitting on my front step. I got out and stood near the car. I stared at her, and she stared back. All my anger came back to me, boiled up inside of me like poison that I wanted to get rid of. I wanted to throw it at her. I wanted to drown her with it so she could feel how I felt, understand why I'd said the things I had. But she seemed like she was ready for it, like she was steadying herself to take whatever I gave her. And just like that, I didn't want to be angry at her anymore. I let my body go loose, leaning back against the car.

"I'm sorry," she said.

I took in a deep breath. I glanced through the back window of the car. "Come carry some of this."

We carried the food inside. Saben wrestled it into the fridge, even though I told her to wait and let me do it. She was careful and quick, wrapping her hand in her skirt to open the door, and sliding things in with efficient movements. I set a pecan pie on the counter while she did, and cut two slices. The brownies had even given me a container of fresh cream, whipped and sweetened by hand. I had no idea how they did it all. I knew they didn't get their supplies from the people they secretly visited. They always had enough, though, more than enough.

Saben still hadn't said another word. I plopped a spoonful of whipped cream on the pie and handed her one of the plates. We sat at the table across from each other and ate.

"Tastes like brownies made this," she said when she was halfway through her pie slice.

"Meaning it tastes like the best pie you ever had?"

She nodded. "They never make anything for me."

"You don't do them any favors."

She raised her eyebrows at me. Another forkful of pie disappeared into her mouth.

We finished eating. Saben leaned back in her chair. She looked completely inelegant, like she didn't care how she appeared, here in my kitchen, and completely lovely at the same time. It reminded me of the way she'd sprawled with her legs crossed over mine when we were younger, trying to get comfortable while we read together. I looked away.

"I meant it. That I'm sorry."

I shrugged. "All right." I wasn't trying to pout. I just didn't care anymore. I didn't want to argue. I was too tired and too sore and I couldn't do it.

"Luca . . ." she started, and I held up my hand.

"I'm not arguing with you about it."

"But I don't understand," she whispered.

I turned my gaze back on her. "How can you not?"

She swallowed hard enough that I could see her throat move. "What if this is the thing that works?"

I tipped my head back. I wanted to close my eyes and stop this. "What if it is? What if I give up my humanity and I do this thing and it works, and I'm suddenly in possession of a life that will never end?" The idea was so absurd I wanted to laugh. I couldn't imagine it could work. But I didn't laugh, because there was a chance. And I didn't want to take it. "What if I outlive you and Kin and everyone else I know? What if you get old and fade and die and I don't? That's what immortality means. I couldn't take it, Saben. I saw his mother." I swallowed, trying to put into order thoughts that were half formed, fears and truths that had made me tell Kin no, without any hesitation, the night before. "He said he doesn't want to lose me. But if I take the cure, I'll be the one losing him. I'll outlive him and have to watch him die. Watch you die. It's . . . It's an awful thing for him to ask. It isn't fair. And I can't do it. I know that I can't."

Saben's face had gone white while I talked. She clamped her mouth shut and her eyes went too wide, got too dark, and when I stopped talking, she started to cry. Tears tracked down her cheeks in salty white streaks. Her face was perfectly still, though. She didn't make a sound. Nothing except the wetness on her skin gave her away. "You wouldn't be sick."

"What would I do?" I pushed forward even farther, leaning across the table. I'd had this in my mind since Kin had said immortality, a buzzing, a warning, in the back of my thoughts. And it had grown and grown until I couldn't ignore it anymore. Now, it was pouring out of me. "Would I kill myself when you were all gone, when I couldn't take being so alone anymore? Would I be able to? I don't even know what would be worse." I shook my head, resolute. She was still watching me. I stared at her. "Everything dies, Saben. It's the way things are supposed to be. It's part of life. To not die . . . It would be a terrible thing."

And she broke and coughed and cried hard enough that she couldn't pretend it wasn't happening. She slumped over, shoulders hunched. "But Kin loves you. He loves you so much. That's why he wanted this." Her words were choked, forced around the heave of her shoulders and the tightness in her throat.

I closed my hands into fists. My fingernails cut into my palms, and I pressed down harder. "He wants to take away what makes me human. What makes me fey." I floundered, waving my hand angrily through the air. "What makes me . . . me. A being who can love and care and who knows what line is too far to cross."

"He's not thinking any of that." She jerked her chin up. Her hand snapped out and slapped against the table. "He's not thinking. Don't you lose him over this. He's too important." She picked her hand up and pressed it over her eyes.

I stood and got a towel from the kitchen. I ran it under cold water, then went back and tried to press it against Saben's face. She took it and held it over her eyes. I knelt in front of her, like Kin had knelt in front of me the night I'd lost my breath. I didn't touch her.

Her fingers squashed the cloth into her face. I could hear her breathing, could almost see her grasping for control. Her body went still, like she was concentrating. Her shoulders stopped shaking. After another few seconds she sniffed loudly and pulled the cloth away. Her eyes were red, and she hadn't stopped crying, but it was gentler now, a persistence instead of a force trying to work its way out of her.

"Why are you so obsessed with Kin?" I asked, the words coming out before I even knew I was wondering.

She shook her head. "It's not about Kin. It's about you."

I moved my finger in a circle over my knee. "You don't even know me." I'd made sure of that when I went away. She'd made sure of it when I came back.

Saben dropped her hand with the cloth in it. Water was running backward down her wrist, back into the cloth, dripping onto the floor. "I know you. You can't say that the boy I knew isn't still in there somewhere. You can't say that the pieces of me that are all about you are false."

I bit my lip.

"I knew how unhappy you were. I knew. Somewhere in the back of my mind, even when I didn't want to think about it, it was there." She took a deep breath. "I don't know what you were doing while you were gone. I don't know how you felt, or who you were with. But I know I've never seen you like you are when you're with Kin."

She held the cloth out to me like it was my job to take it for her, and I did. She wiped her damp hand against her skirt.

"I told a boy that I was with that I could replace him," she said, her eyes on the table while she spoke. "That he could replace me. That if what we had between us fell apart—and I think then I meant *when*—I would be able to find someone else. I think it was the cruelest thing I ever said to anyone. To tell him that I only loved him as much as I loved anyone else. That he wasn't special to me. And that I wasn't special to him, either, and I knew it." She reached out and let her hand play over the tips of my hair. "Kin's not like that. You can't replace him. He can't replace you. There will never be anyone like you for him. You're it." Her hand slipped down to my jaw. She was looking far away, and I thought she was unaware of what her hand was doing. "Don't you think he'd do anything to keep you here? Can't you understand that?"

I shook my head. "I don't think I mean that much to him, Saben." I wasn't trying to be melodramatic. I just didn't think we'd had enough time. But even while I said it, something clicked into place inside me. Like a truth had settled. "I don't know if he loves me. And I think he probably could replace me."

She gave a watery, stuffy laugh. "You have no idea. You have no idea of how he looks at you. How you look at him." She cocked her head at me. "Do you? Do you know you love him?"

I grinned at her, at the way she put it. So demanding. Always so royal, so self-important. Like she knew she was right, even when she was telling someone who they loved.

She stared down at me, waiting. My smile went softer. Sadder, maybe. Because she was right, after all. "I know I do."

"And you know you can't replace him."

I thought about what Midori had said to me, how she'd reasoned that I might be the only love of Kin's life. It didn't seem fair that he would live so many years and only have me. I wouldn't last long enough. I'd told Saben it was possible that I could get better, and maybe I would. Maybe this thing was running a bad loop right now, and maybe, for a while, it would calm down and I wouldn't be as sick as I was. But eventually, I would get worse again, and die before either of them. It wouldn't matter how much better I got before I went back downhill. The way this would play out was a fact I knew in my bones. And it only seemed fair that, when I was gone, Kin would be able to find someone else.

I wanted Kin to love me, though. I wanted to be the best love he had, the hardest, the most important. I didn't know yet if that would be the case. Like I'd told Saben, I didn't even know if he loved me. But possibility spilled out in front of us. A life that we could have together, maybe. The chance for that. Even though it would be too short. Even though it wouldn't be perfect. The idea of it, the beautiful, nearly but not quite impossible idea of it, was there. I wanted to find out what might come of it. I didn't want to throw that possibility away. Not if there was a chance I could have it. Not if there was a chance Kin might want it.

My life wouldn't amount to much. It had been a mostly quiet thing, even when I'd been traveling. I hadn't ever done anything that seemed very important. The only thing I knew for sure was that when I died, what would be left of me was the people I knew, and how I'd cared for them. I'd never thought it was right to live solely for another person. I didn't think I was doing that with Kin. I'd lived without him. I knew how to make myself happy without another person beside me. But I wondered if loving him and Saben, being loved by them, was the best thing I was doing with my life. Maybe the best thing I'd get to do before I died. It seemed like it, sometimes. Often. If that was the small mark, the only mark, I made on the world, it wasn't a bad one.

And if Kin knew that I had loved him simply because of who he was, maybe I had done something right. I was happy enough with that. It stung that maybe that would be all I got to do. But I could be more than happy with the knowledge that I got to care about him. Love him. Be with him for a little while. It would be enough for me. I just wanted him to know it.

"He's panicking," Saben said. I jerked my attention out of my thoughts and back to her. "He doesn't want to leave you. I can't imagine that he would, Luca. I've seen the way he follows you around a room. That boy is crazy about you."

I took a breath, let it fill my lungs. It burned, but only a little. I was having a good day, for everything I'd put my body through so far. "What are you suggesting?"

She raised her eyebrows at me. "Tell him. Go to him, and tell him what you told me. He's angry. And hurt. And afraid. But he doesn't want to leave, Luca."

I was so proud of her. She was so much more than the little girl, full of potential, that I'd left. She was strong and smart and kind and amazing and I was just . . . so very proud. "How do you know that?"

A tiny smile flickered over her face. "Because I'm angry and hurt and afraid. And I don't want to leave you. I want to be with you for all the time we have left."

CHAPTER 16

I promised her I would find him. That I would tell him. That seemed to be good enough for her. I split half the food the brownies had given me, and I drove her home, helped her put it all in the large cooler, full of ice, she kept in the kitchen, which she was using instead of a fridge. Then I chickened out of going straight to Kin and went back to my place.

I told myself I needed to get my strategy together, but that was bullshit. As much as I wanted to run to Kin, find him and make this better, make this ache inside me go away, I was so scared. I was so afraid that it wouldn't work. I told myself I'd eat dinner, but I wasn't hungry. I made myself drink a cup of coffee instead, heavily laced with cream and sugar. I bounced around the kitchen on the balls of my feet, full of nerves and caffeine, until my breath caught in my lungs. I coughed for a while, then. I went right down to my knees, one hand gripping the counter to keep myself from smacking my head into the floor.

It went on for so long that I started to get bored, but it hurt so badly that it frightened me. When it finally passed, there was a fine spray of blood on the tiles in front of me. I stared at it while I caught my breath. It wasn't too painful anymore, after the coughing had stopped. There was a burn in my chest, and nothing more. The blood was bad, though. There was something broken in me, more than one something. It might get worse. It might get worse, then get better. I didn't know, and it didn't matter. There was nothing, right now, that I could do about it.

It was a good reminder, and sobering enough. I stood and wiped the floor with a damp paper towel, pushing it around with my bare foot. I drank my coffee, slowly, to coax the coughing away. Then I figured I better go. There wasn't anything else left for me to do, any more excuses I could make not to.

I wasn't positive Kin had gone to his little rented house—he could have gone to his mother's—but I decided to try there first. It was close, at least.

I saw Kin's truck parked in the driveway when I pulled up, and my heart did a weird clenching in my chest. I parked next to it, turned the key and listened to the engine still so suddenly that the quiet of the neighborhood didn't even have a chance to sneak up on me. It was just there, in the stillness, wrapping around me, smothering me. And I sat in it and was afraid to move through it.

I had so many things I wanted to say to him. I would never be able to get them out right. I wasn't ready to see him.

I wanted to see him so badly I wanted to fling myself out of the car and right into his house.

I was terrified he wouldn't want to see me at all, that he'd turn me away.

I couldn't picture his reaction. I couldn't imagine, in my mind, what would happen when I knocked on his door, when I stepped into his house. I couldn't see him embracing me or smiling or pushing me out, shaking his head to tell me to leave. It was all black. I couldn't even pretend to imagine what would happen, because it scared me so much. My hands shook where they rested in my lap. My heart was beating so hard I could feel it, rattling against the tightness in my chest. My breath stuttered in and out, and I wondered if I would break, right there in my car, with the fear and the weight of it.

I got out and walked to his door. I raised my hand to knock or ring the doorbell. I was so afraid that he wouldn't answer. So afraid that he'd see me and refuse to open the door, or open it and tell me to go, never give me the chance to say anything at all.

My hand closed over the doorknob. I felt awful and guilty just for thinking about what I was going to do. But Kin had walked into my house the same way. I twisted the knob, and the door opened, easy, silent. Then the guilt of even thinking about walking inside snagged me, and I knocked, hesitantly, on the open door.

"It's open," Kin shouted from a back room, and I realized he probably thought I was one of the fey, come for his services.

I stepped inside and closed it behind me.

The house was still around me. Everything was exactly the same as the last time I'd been there. The plants in the kitchen, the very last of the sunlight streaming in through the living room windows.

"I'll be out in a sec," Kin called.

I didn't answer. I kicked off my shoes at the door, then walked down the hall, my feet making only the smallest sound against the soft carpet. The door I'd seen Kin disappear into that first day was open. I peeked around the doorframe.

It was a bedroom, like I'd thought. There was a dresser and a few bookshelves, a window that looked out onto a side yard. The window was open a crack, the curtains fluttering in the chilly breeze. And there was a double bed, right in the middle, with an iron scrolled headboard, and rumpled blue sheets. And Kin, curled up on it, with his back to me. He was levering himself up on an elbow. He looked stiff, like he'd been lying there for a long time and the act of getting up took concentration.

The sun was slanting in, a deep gold coming across the pine floor. I stepped into that puddle of sun and let its warmth soak into my feet and my ankles and my knees. I followed it to where it touched the edge of the bed. Kin sat up, his back still to me. I stared down at him, his hair all mussed, his shoulders hunched. I followed the curve of his back under his shirt, ran my eyes along his slender waist, down his legs, curled under him, right to the shadows where his ankles bent into his heels. The sight of him, every piece of him so familiar, was a relief. I just wanted to look at him for as long as I could, take him in, know that he was here, right in front of me.

I leaned forward and pressed one knee into the mattress behind him. He jumped when he felt my weight on the bed. His head jerked around. There were those eyes, those sea-glass-green eyes, so wide open and looking right at me, into me.

"Luca." He said my name like he was confirming it, confirming that I was there. Then he was pulling me down to him, grabbing me tight against him, pushing his fingers into my hair. I buried my face in the curve of his neck. My hands twisted into his T-shirt.

Something in my throat caught. "Don't let me go," I pleaded. I yanked on his shirt. "Please don't."

His arms tightened around me. He kissed behind my ear and at the corner of my jaw and then he dipped down and kissed my collarbone where it disappeared into my shirt. I slid my hands around his shoulders. "I'm angry with you," I mumbled into his chest.

"I know." His fingers tugged at the hem of my shirt, slipped beneath to touch my waist. "I'm angry too."

"I know," I said back at him. "I don't want to live forever, Kin. I don't want that."

He froze and drew back enough to see my face. "What?"

"You said—"

He shook his head. "You're not here to tell me you changed your mind?"

I pinched my lips together. "No."

He exhaled through his nose. The closeness we'd had, the relief at just being together again, dissolved in a rush. The sun was still warm on me, the breeze a cold contrast, the curtains flapping a sound that was so comforting, but in that second, we'd created our own little bubble that was uncomfortable and strained. "Right."

I pulled my hands back. "Kin, you've got to understand why I'm so against . . . that."

He tilted his head down so he couldn't see me. "It could save you." His eyes moved up again. "I can't lose you. I can't just sit back and wait for it to happen."

I lowered my own eyes. "I'm not asking you to." But I was. I was asking exactly that.

"It could save you," he repeated.

I glanced back up at him. His hand was on my cheek. I wrapped my own hand around his wrist. "I'm afraid of what it will do to me." I was trying to be gentle. I just wanted him to see what I was seeing. "I *don't* want it."

He stared at me. "How can you not try? What if it works, Luca? What if all of this could be over, and you would never be sick again? What if I never had to worry about you blacking out or coughing till you can't breathe or having a seizure?" His voice rose and shook. "That could all be over!"

"I don't care," I said, flatly. It was true. I took a deep breath. "I want to be able to die, Kin. I don't want it now, or soon. I don't want to go yet. I want to live as long as I can." I almost screamed it. I wanted it so bad. There were so many things I still wanted to do, places I wanted to go, ways I wanted to make and remake myself, and I didn't know if I'd have time. "But when my time's over, I want to be able to die. That's my right. It's what *is* right. Not being able to die . . ." I leaned forward. I wanted to push this into him. "To let life go so long . . . it would wear me down. Something that lasts forever can't be a pleasure for all that time. The pleasure's in the struggle, in the idea that we only get so much time. Whether it's long or short, there's a limit, and we have to just do with it what we can. That's what makes it worth it. That's what makes it important. That it's not infinite. That it ends."

I sucked in a sharp breath, surprised by what was coming out of my mouth, but sure that I wasn't wrong. It was the truth, or my truth, and that was what I needed to hold on to. Across from me, I heard Kin breathe in the same way.

"Can you imagine how sad that would be?" I asked, my voice lower now, pleading for him to understand. "To know that time had left you behind, that you were on the outside of everything? How terrible, to know you'd see everyone you loved die? To know that if you wanted to follow, if you wanted to slip back into nature, you'd need to kill yourself? Would I even be able to do that?" I let my head hang. "I can't fathom it, Kin. I couldn't do it." As I said it, I realized that he was telling me the same thing—that he couldn't stand knowing that I would die before him.

I raised my eyes to him. He sat frozen on the bed. He was like stone, like I had petrified him with my words. "I'm sorry," I told him, and I meant it. I said it fiercely, sincerely. Because I was so very sorry. "I never wanted to hurt you like this. To make you face this. But I can't help it." I took a breath, trying to figure out how to explain this. "You keep saying you don't want to lose me, but that's what you'd be making me do. You'd make me lose you, instead. There's never going to be a balance, Kin. One of us was always going to go first, whether I was sick or not. That's how life works. You can't stop it hurting, for either of us. Not with your cure. Not ever. And I don't want you to."

I was raw with hurt and apology, my back stiff with anger, and I didn't know what to do with it all, where to put it, how to show him what I felt. I breathed in again, tried to remember the feel of that sun on my legs, tried to steady myself with the cool rush of the autumn breeze coming in through the window. It'd be too cold to leave it open in an hour, when it started to get dark, but for now the chill of it made me shiver in a pleasant way, and I could see why Kin had opened it to begin with. I liked the feel of it. It grounded me. "I can't risk your cure. I can't risk that it will work. I will have the death that nature granted me. If getting better comes at the price of losing that, then the price is too high."

He stared and breathed. After a long, tense minute, he asked, "This is all just . . . coming to you now?"

I shook my head. "I think it's been coming for a while. But I wanted it so bad, Kin. I wanted to be able to say yes. I just . . . can't."

He shook his head, once, sharply, but he didn't say anything else. I straightened my shoulders. After a second, his gaze shifted, going to the window, and then down to the patch of sunlight on the floor. His face caught the light, and I saw the wetness on his cheeks.

When he didn't say anything else, I asked, "Will you say anything to me?"

His jaw worked. I could see him grinding his teeth together. He shook his head. He didn't make a sound.

I was splintering into pieces. I was falling apart. That single shake of his head split all the seams and joints that made me complete.

I backed off the bed, stood. I took a shaky breath. I thought I must be crying too. I wiped at my face. My hand came away dry.

"Okay." I didn't know what else to do. Didn't know what to say. I'd done so badly at this. I'd messed it up so much. "Okay. I want you to come back, Kin." I saw his hands curl into tight fists. He wouldn't look at me anymore. He kept looking at the sun on the floor. "I miss you when you're not with me. I more than miss you. More . . . I need you." I breathed hard, trying not to fracture while I did this. I tucked my arms around myself. I was holding my pieces in. "It just has to be this way for me. It's too important. More important than my life."

He dropped his head, letting his hair cover his face. "More important than mine?"

I shook my head. I wanted to say no, to say never. I would do anything for him, if it would save his life. "If it was you who was sick,"

I whispered, "I'd do what you're doing. I get it, Kin. I get it more than anyone." If it had been him in my place, I would have done the same to make him well. I would have given him whatever he wanted. I got that now. "This isn't about your life, though," I told him. "It's about mine. It's my choice, Kin."

He peered up at me. He didn't even look like himself. He wasn't whole. His smile was gone, the warm expression in his eyes that was always there when he saw me was missing. His mouth was a grimace and his skin was damp with tears and stretched too tight over his skin. "Don't say that."

I wanted to reach over and touch him, but I couldn't.

"I'm going home," I told him. His eyes flicked away from mine. I waited a minute longer, but he tilted his head away, and wouldn't look at me. I turned and went to the door.

I didn't want to walk out of that room. Nothing in me wanted to leave. There was a voice in my head repeating *turn around, turn around, turn around* on an endless loop. I wanted to spin on my heels and go to him, hold him against me until his bones pressed into mine, apologize over and over. Tell him I'd do anything if it would make him come back. But I couldn't.

I made my back straight. I told my spine to be iron. I walked out.

I rolled down all the windows, so the wind whipped through the car while I drove home. I was still boxed in, despite how cold and bracing the air was, how good it smelled—not just like grass and sea and leaves, but like gasoline and tarmac and salt. I wanted to be in Kin's truck. I felt less enclosed while I sat next to him in the truck. The windows all around made a difference, but his hands on the wheel did too, the looseness of his wrists as he made a turn, the way he sometimes looked over at me and grinned. I thought of the evening we'd come back with Saben from Midori's. How the sun had gone down around us in slow degrees while we drove. When we'd come to the stretch of road by the sea, the sun had only been a smudge of tangerine orange on the water, the shadows long and blurry. Saben had leaned back in her seat and soaked up the sunset, and I'd known that she could feel it, that she could feel every last bit of the sinking sun on her skin. And Kin and I had looked at each other, just a glance, and smiled, and it was like we'd had a whole private conversation, there with Saben beside us, taking in the last of the light.

I didn't turn on the radio. Driving at dusk always made me feel nostalgic. Tonight, that feeling was compounded by how lost I was, how sure that I'd just left behind the best thing I had. I was afraid that if a song I knew came on, I wouldn't be able to keep it together. I just wanted to get home. I didn't want to cry or think or feel anything else. I'd lost. I'd done what I could and there was nothing else. Now I just wanted to stop.

After I took the exit for my house, though, I steered away from it. I headed down out of the hills, to where it was a little flatter, a little more crowded, a little dirtier. Saben had no car, so I couldn't tell if she was home or not. I walked up to her floor and knocked on her door.

She opened it while I still had my fist raised.

"Did you do it?" she asked.

"Yes and no," I answered.

She swung the door wider and stepped to the side. I walked in and stopped in the weird no-name space at the edge of the living room, just before the kitchen. Behind me, I heard her shutting the door and pulling the chain across it. I turned back to her. I saw her fingers let the chain click into its place. It was covered in cloth so it wouldn't burn her.

"I didn't know what I was doing when I left you."

She raised an eyebrow. Her arms folded across her chest.

I shook my head. "I mean, when I was nineteen. When I left after high school. I didn't know you wanted me to stay."

Her arms dropped to her sides. "How could you not have known?"

"I thought you could make it on your own." I'd needed to go. And I couldn't have taken her. But I hadn't needed to cut her out like I had. I'd cut everyone out, for a little while. I'd been by myself, and I'd wanted it that way. But I hadn't seen the damage I was doing. I hadn't thought it would matter, hadn't thought I'd ever come home. Then I had, and everything had been so messed up.

"I did."

I nodded. "I'm sorry."

She stared at me for a long moment. Then she sighed and flicked her eyes away. She moved around the couch and sat down.

"Where's Kin?"

"At his place." I sat on the other short couch.

"Did you see him?"

"I saw him."

"And?"

I tensed my shoulders. "And he's not here."

She ran her hand over the back of her neck. Her fingers gathered little pieces of hair and tucked them into her messy bun. "Did you tell him what you told me? Did you explain?"

I nodded.

"What did he say?"

"Nothing." I leaned back against the couch. "He wouldn't look at me after I told him." I thought about those few minutes when we'd held each other. It had been so simple, to fit back against him, to mold myself to his body and take in his scent and feel his eyes on me, seeing me. "He wouldn't say anything."

"So that's it?"

"What was I supposed to do?"

She shook her head, slowly, like she was thinking. "No," she said. "You did your best."

It wasn't as reassuring as it should have been.

Her face softened, her lips rising at the corners in a smile that wasn't really meant to make me happy. "He'll come back."

I dropped my head. I just couldn't keep it up anymore.

"Come on." She stood and stepped toward me. "I cooked. Fish. Eat with me."

We ate, and she kept up just enough banter to keep me talking. After dinner, she brought out a bottle of whiskey she'd taken from our father's house.

"Does he know you have that?"

She shrugged and poured it into two glasses. "Water?"

I shook my head. She handed me my glass, and I made the short walk from the kitchen to the couch. Saben mixed her drink with water and came to sit on the floor across from me.

Saben raised her glass to me. "He loves you."

"Kin?"

She smiled and sipped. Her movements were relaxed, almost sloppy, like she knew she'd be drunk soon, and she was eager for it. I wondered if it was still my job to tell her that she shouldn't be drinking, or if that even mattered with the fey. I couldn't remember. And I wanted to lose myself in the whiskey and whatever she had to say anyway, so I let her be.

"Father."

I took a sip of my own drink. The whiskey was good. Too good for us to be drinking in a crappy apartment, feeling depressed. "What are you talking about?"

"He adores you."

I slumped farther back against the couch cushions. "He's not supposed to."

Saben leaned sideways on one hand, her glass in the other. "But he does. I used to be so jealous, all that time you were gone. He looked at me, and I knew he was looking for you."

I closed my eyes. "That's crazy, Saben."

She pushed herself upright. "I'm not saying he loves you best, or anything like that. I just think . . ." Her face lost its playfulness, the little smile disappearing. Her voice went low. "He wanted to be able to love you, to acknowledge you openly, like he does me."

I sat up and leaned forward so our eyes were level. "I know that." I smiled at her, and she smiled too. Her cheeks were flushed, and I knew she hadn't had enough alcohol for that yet.

"You do."

I nodded. I thought about him dragging me to every healer and herbalist and fairy doctor he could come up with. I remembered the way he'd introduced me to people. Always as "my son, Luca." And he had never let a summer go by when I wasn't at his house. I knew he loved me. It was just that I always had to gather that information from those little bits he dropped, and never really from him himself. "If he was a better man, though, maybe he wouldn't have put so much stock in how he was supposed to treat me. Maybe he would have just owned up to what I am."

She kept her eyes on mine as I straightened my spine. "Maybe."

"Look." I took another sip of my drink, a big one, and had to fight not to cough while it burned its way down my throat. "I know what he is. I understand that taking care of the fey, leading them, is his . . . job. I know he likes it, that he's good at it. He protects the fey, and I want him to protect them. I want him to do good for them, and he can. But I'm his son. And I get to begrudge him the attention he didn't spare me. No matter how much I understand."

She slid her eyes away from me. But then she moved them back, to see my face. Such a brave girl, even when it was foolish.

I sighed. "Saben, I'm not drunk enough for this conversation."

Saben set her glass down, resting it close enough to the magicked pitcher on the coffee table that it intruded on the perfect art of it. I noticed that the little rosebush Midori had given her was on the table too. There were plants everywhere, actually. They were probably muting the iron.

She sighed out through her nose. "I'm angry with you," she said, and her voice was lower, softer, than I'd expected. "I'm angry that you gave me hope and then you took it right back."

I closed my eyes, and then I made myself open them again and look at her. "I'm sorry. I didn't want to." None of this was how I'd wanted it to go. "It's not that I don't want to get better, Saben. You have to know that."

She nodded. "I do."

I reached for the whiskey bottle and added another shot to each of our glasses, even though neither of us had finished the first round. Apparently neither of us were very good at drinking. Saben made a face when I handed the glass to her, but she sipped at the now only slightly watered liquor. I sipped at mine again too, rolling it around on my tongue. It tasted hot and smooth and a bit caustic, all at the same time. It was good. Better, probably, than any whiskey I'd ever have again. My father was probably wondering where it had gone to. But I raised the glass to my eyes and stared at the amber color of the liquid. I was always a little disappointed that it didn't taste as spicy and earthy as it looked.

The room went quiet around us. I wanted Kin to be here with us. I wanted to go home and find him there. I wanted to lean myself against him, feel his breath on my cheek, feel his hand on my neck, or the small of my back, anchoring me. I wanted to never have considered that there might actually be a cure out there. Wanted to never have had the hope of it, only to make myself deny it.

I stared into the glass in my hand. Saben had been trying to distract me from thinking about what I'd done, about the last things Kin and I had said to each other. And I'd been trying to go along with her. He wouldn't leave my mind, though. Every time I had a thought that wasn't about my empty house, I was all right, but as soon as it was done, my mind circled back to Kin. It hurt so much, made me so nervous and nauseous, that I wanted to lie down and not wake up.

"He'll come back," Saben said. I glanced up and she smiled that tiny, almost-not-there smile at me that was still so new it took me by surprise every time. She cocked her head to the side. I wondered what had given me away. My silence, or the look on my face, or the fact that she knew me well enough, after all.

"What if he doesn't?"

Her head shook once. "I told you. You can't be replaced. He knows that."

I set the glass down and flopped backward onto the couch. "Maybe it's too hard, Saben. Maybe he realized it would be better to get out now, while he can. Maybe he can't stay with me and watch it all happen."

She laughed. "That time when he could get out without getting hurt is already long gone." She nudged the glass with her hand. "Are you a sad drunk?"

"I don't really know."

"Let's find out," she said. "You probably can't feel any worse, anyway."

CHAPTER 17

The next morning, I stayed at Saben's for as long as I could, sprawled on her couch, nursing a hangover that had more to do with the previous day's events than it did with the amount of alcohol I'd consumed. Saben fed me bread spread thick with peanut butter and made me drink copious amounts of tea, and then she got sick of my depressed state and kicked me out.

"You have to go back at some point," she said, standing in the doorway.

I squinted in the sunlight. "Does it have to be now?"

"Luca." She pushed on my chest.

"I—" I heard someone coming up the stairs behind me. I turned around, expecting to see a person, but it was a very slender fey girl with pale-blue hair and icy-gray eyes. She stopped on the last stair, catching sight of me. She dipped forward into a frantic bow.

"Why are you doing that?" I put my hand to my head, wondering if I was seeing things.

"You're a scary monster," Saben said, her voice dry. She turned to the girl. "You should be grateful to Luca for changing out your iron."

I realized this was probably the fey girl who was living below Saben. She hadn't been in when I'd changed out as much iron in the apartment as I could the other day. I tried to smile at her, but she kept her head down. I leaned closer to Saben.

"Why is she doing that?" I whispered.

Saben stared at me. "All those years, acting so tough around the fey, and you don't get it? Did you even realize you were doing that?" She shook her head. "You're a force, Luca. You scare them."

I sighed. I wasn't up for this right now. I rubbed my hand through my hair and turned back to the girl.

"If you need anything else, let me know." I eased past her, trying to be careful not to touch her. She scooted out of my way, up the last step. I turned to see her and Saben disappearing into the apartment.

The drive home seemed long. Even though it was only just past rush hour, the roads were quiet, almost empty. It was a warm day for the season, and I could hear the buzz of a few lawn mowers, but I didn't see anyone. It made me feel like I was alone, driving through some parallel world, like so many people imagined the fey lived in.

The house was still when I came in. It was as if it had been sealed up for years, not just a day. I stepped in the door and stopped. I could see into the kitchen, could see the sun coming through the back window, lighting up the dust motes that hung there. The bedroom was in front of me, the sheets rumpled, shoved to the end of the bed where I'd left them. I didn't really need to see any of it, though. I could tell Kin wasn't here. I could tell how empty the place was. I pushed the front door closed behind me and rested against it. I didn't know where to go in my own house.

I missed Kin. The lack of him was like a tangible object I was carrying around. It was a weight in my hands, all the time. I wanted him here. I wanted to know that he was in the next room, that I could call out to him and have him answer, or that he could call out to me. It wasn't a new feeling. Even when he was here, I wanted him. When were together, I wanted to be together longer. When we touched, I wanted to touch more, deeper, harder. Sometimes I wondered if I was saving up, saving pieces of him, just in case. Now that he wasn't here, though, it was obvious that all that saving up wasn't enough.

I thought there was a space inside me that missed having the hope, the idea, that there might be a cure too. It seemed like Kin's offer had been the last chance, the last desperate grab at an answer, a lifeline that had come out of nowhere. And I'd declined it. Even though saying no was right, even though it was what I wanted, I missed, deeply, the promise that maybe there really was something that could fix me. I *wanted* to be fixed. But I'd given away what was very likely my last chance.

I didn't want to be here, I realized. I didn't want to sit in my house with all these thoughts tumbling through my brain, telling me over and over again how badly I'd messed up. I changed my clothes quickly, the movements rote, and brushed my teeth. Then I turned right back around, went through the front door, and got into my car again. I drove toward the hills in the north and let my mind wander when I left all the traffic behind. By the time I got into the mess of berry bushes, I was on autopilot.

Riyad stood on his porch, watching the road, like he knew I was coming. I parked haphazardly and pushed the car door open. He came down the steps and caught me. His hands on my shoulders were steady and strong and warm. I wanted to fold myself into him.

He led me inside and sat me on the couch, and made me stay quiet until he'd brought me some fruit and a mug of pulpy orange juice. Then he sat next to me and urged me to eat, and asked me to tell him what was wrong.

I laid the whole thing out while I ate, one bite of apple or pear for every piece of the mess Kin and I were in. He listened without saying anything, without moving a muscle, except to hold the plate up when he thought I should eat more.

When I was done talking, he took the plate from me and set it on the coffee table in front of us.

"Did I do the wrong thing?" I asked him, and I was coming apart. I was a child again with him, my voice cracking, my hands shaking. I hadn't known I was going to ask that, because I'd been so sure I hadn't done the wrong thing. But Kin being gone was like a hole in me, and here, in front of a man who knew me better than almost anyone on the planet, I could admit that I was afraid.

He shook his head. "When I was the age you are now, I would have had a hard time saying no, if that was offered to me."

"Immortality?"

He leaned forward so our faces were close, our shoulders touching. "It would be a heady thing, to have in the palm of your hand. When I was younger... I don't know that I would have been able to walk away from it like you are."

I focused on him, and found he was staring off into space. "And now?"

He closed his eyes and inhaled. "I don't regret living this long, Luca." He opened his eyes and turned to face me. His hand fell, warm, on my shoulder. "I don't regret things I've done, mostly. Don't regret meeting your father, seeing you and your sister grow up. I don't want to go. It's been a good life. Nothing in me is eager for death." His hand fell away from me, and he sat back, letting his spine relax down on itself, a slow collapse, bone by bone, that made him look young and careless and ancient at the same time. "But now. If I was asked to live my life span again, if I was offered that immortal time, I would say no." He blinked at me. "I wouldn't even stop to think. I don't want to stay forever. It's a gift, being able to die. It's a grief, and a lifetime will never feel like enough, no matter how long it is, but the end is a gift too. It's what makes all of this mean anything."

I closed my eyes. Riyad set his hand on my back again. "It's not a right or wrong choice, Luca. It's just what you want. That's all right. It's what should be."

I keeled forward, my hands coming up over my head, pushing into my hair. "Okay. Okay."

Riyad moved forward, circled me with his arms and lay his chest against my back. It occurred to me, for the first time, that he was smaller than me. He was almost insubstantial, wiry and delicate, a body of paper and sand wrapped around me. He was strong, though, his grip tight and fierce, like he would keep me from flying apart with the sheer force of his will. Like he would do his best to protect me from whatever tried to hurt me. He would throw himself in front of it, if he could. I knew that.

I rubbed at my face. "Saben said he'll come back." My voice shook, rising up and down, and I found that I couldn't control the way my words came out. "But what if he doesn't? What if I lose him over this?"

Riyad drew away a bit, but one hand stayed on the back of my neck, gripping hard, holding me. He said nothing, just let his fingers sink into my muscles.

"What if I already did? What if he's already gone?"

Riyad pressed his wrist down against the top of my spine. "I don't know." He leaned forward and kissed my temple. "I don't know."

Riyad kept me at his house. Like Saben, he spent the rest of the day trying to distract me, placing paper and pencils and books and finally gardening tools in my hands, sending me outside to work, making small talk, never letting my mind settle where it wanted to. The sick fear of what I'd done was always there, though. I was nauseous with the idea that I had pushed Kin so far he would never come back, that I had said no to something that could cure me. My skin tingled and my hands twitched and stung and my mind would never focus on anything but the worry of it.

The hardest part was that I knew, for myself, I'd done what I needed to, what was right. Riyad had reassured me of that, in his gentle way. I wanted to take it back anyway. In those hours when it felt like the ache and the agitation of what I'd done would chew its way out of me, I would have agreed to whatever Kin wanted if I knew it would make that hole that had opened up in me go away.

We didn't discuss it, and I didn't ask, but when evening came, he made dinner, and when we had finished eating, he wondered out loud whether I'd like an extra blanket on my bed in his spare room. I was happy to take the blanket and the bed, both. The last thing I wanted to do was go back to my own place and sleep in a bed that would feel strangely empty, even though it had only been occupied by two bodies for a matter of days.

In the morning, Riyad had breakfast ready for me when I got up. And then, like Saben, he told me I should go home.

"I'd like you to stay as long as you want," he said. He held up a glass milk jug, and I nodded, letting him pour it over the oatmeal he'd made. "I like having you here. And I understand why you don't want to go home. So if you want to stay, you should."

"But?" I took a bite of the oatmeal. Riyad had sprinkled it liberally with dried berries and honey, and it tasted sweet and dense and real.

"What if he comes to see you and you're not there?"

I plopped my spoon back into the bowl. I watched it sink down slowly, getting buried by the fruit and the oats. "What if he doesn't?"

Riyad leaned forward, his hands braced against the edge of the counter. "If it gets to be too much there, come back here. Anytime. All the time. But . . . just go for now. In case."

I took a deep breath and picked the spoon back up. "All right."

CHAPTER 18

found myself standing in my living room again, the keys clenched in my hand. I went into the kitchen and set them on the counter, took off my jacket, and slung it over my chair at the table. I pushed the chair in until it couldn't go any farther. I tried to make my hands steady, even though my movements were awkward and unnecessary. Tried to be methodical, to just do things as they came, so I wouldn't have to think. My boots were still on, so I went back to the front door to shuck them and drop them on the floor, then wandered into the kitchen again. The whole routine had taken maybe five minutes. It had been a lot of work.

I was underwater. A cough bubbled up from inside my lungs, and I bent forward, hacking into my hand. I refused to sit down. I was afraid if I sat I would sit there all day, not moving, but thinking, sinking deeper and deeper into the hole that my thoughts were. So I coughed standing up, locking my knees and leaning against the counter, hoping it wouldn't get any worse.

It wasn't a bad spell, and when it was done, I was almost disappointed. It had given me a focus, for those few minutes.

I needed something to do with my hands. I wasn't hungry, but my head ached. I pulled the coffee carafe from its place and held it under the sink, filling it. I had some vague idea that I would make coffee and drink it, and enough time would have passed, when I was done doing that, that I could retreat back to Riyad and his orchards and his quiet solidness. I let myself measure out the coffee grounds by muscle memory, watching the dark grain pile on top of the filter. Just keep moving, I told myself. I couldn't let myself think past that. Everything had gone wrong, so fast, so suddenly, and I had caused it. This stillness in my house, this persistent ache in my chest, I had caused. If I let myself think about it, I would never stop.

I pushed the Start button on the coffee machine, and at the same time, I heard a car pull into the driveway. My brain was blank while I moved to the door. I know I didn't think a single thing. I didn't even ask my feet to move. They just did it on their own.

I opened the door and saw Kin's truck parked in the space that I'd started thinking of as his. He saw me while he was sitting in the cab, his face turning toward me just enough to catch sight of me. He'd been moving around, rolling up the window, tucking away his keys, but he stopped when our eyes met. He froze and stared at me.

I wanted to do so many things at once, I couldn't do anything. I stood as still as Kin. I was torn in each direction. I wanted to run to the truck and grab him and demand that he stay. I wanted to retreat inside, close the door behind me, give my mind some time to catch up, even though this was the only thing I'd been hoping for. A tiny part of me even wanted him to go away, because I couldn't deal with it if he was here to try to convince me again. I wanted to yell at him. I wanted to cry. I thought the most likely option was that I'd end up falling down. My knees were already going out from under me, and I wondered if it was my illness, picking the perfect time to attack, or if anyone would have felt like this, unsteady, unsure, in this moment. I grabbed for the doorframe, but I couldn't take my eyes off Kin, and my hand missed. One knee hit the concrete in front of me, and I finally looked away, looked at the ground so I could get my hand in front of me and keep myself from falling on my face.

Kin's hands came around my arms and held me up. I raised my head and saw him, half-kneeling in front of me, supporting me. His arms went around me, and we sank a little further toward the ground anyway.

"I don't understand." I clutched at him, pulling him to me, shoving my fingers into his ponytail, scratching his neck.

"You told me to come home." I almost couldn't hear him, his mouth was so buried in the curve of my shoulder.

"I know, but . . ." I hadn't thought he would. Saben had said he would, and Riyad too, but I hadn't really believed it was a possibility anymore. "You were so angry." I pressed closer. I was holding him too tight. I could feel him, solid in my arms, could feel my bones pressing into his skin.

He moved his arms lower, wrapping them around my waist, and hauled us to our feet. I wouldn't let go of him. I knew I should, so we could go in the house, but I couldn't make my hands obey me. Kin let me stay as I was. He aimed us toward the door and we did an awkward stumble inside.

"Where are we going?" he asked after he shut the door behind us.

I laughed. "I don't know. Right here." I tugged him the few steps into the kitchen. I pointed him at a chair and he sat. I went to move toward the seat next to him, but his hand on my wrist stopped me. He pulled me forward until I stood between his knees and he could rest his forehead on my chest.

"I wanted to go after you. As soon as you left the room."

I held him against me. "Why didn't you?"

He rocked his head. "I couldn't." I heard him draw in a breath, breathing me in. "I wanted you to change your mind."

"I won't," I said, but softly, and I held him to me harder as I said it.

His arms tightened around me. "I know. I just . . . I don't want to do this, Luca. I don't want to be afraid anymore. I wanted this to be the answer."

My lungs contracted. "Kin." I tried to make it a warning, a sign that arguing about this wouldn't go any differently than before, but I didn't know if I was strong enough to go through it all again, and I probably just sounded afraid. Afraid I'd give in. Afraid he'd let me loose again.

Kin inched away from me enough to see my face. He brought his hands up and ran his thumbs over my cheeks. "I know."

"It's not the answer."

He tried to smile at me, but he looked like he was going to disintegrate. His mouth twisted into something that was sad and sorry and regretful, and he stared up at me, his eyes moving around my face, taking me in. "I know."

He took a breath and let it out slowly. I tried to step closer, but I couldn't, so he scooted forward in the chair. Our legs bumped. We were so crunched together he had to lean his head back to see me. "When you left . . . I just wanted to be with you. It was all I could think about. Being with you again. That was all that mattered. Whether you were sick or not, I wanted to be next to you."

I pulled his hands down and tucked them in mine between us. "You took a long time getting here."

"I had to think." He dropped his head. "I still wanted you to do it. I was still angry. I tried to pretend that it was better that I wasn't going back, because I couldn't not ask you to let me try. But I kept hearing your voice, telling me how much you didn't want it. *Why* you didn't want it. How you'd rather . . ." He trailed off. He opened his hands, freeing them from mine, and pushed his fingers into my hips. "It sunk in, why you didn't want it." He looked up at me. "I hadn't considered it, Luca. I didn't think it through. I didn't think about how much it would hurt you. I just wanted you better."

I stared down at him. Even now, part of me wanted to give in, say yes. I didn't want to hurt him. But it was a small part, and one that I knew would never get bigger, or louder. I was so certain about this. It had taken me a long while, too long, maybe, to come to this point, but now I was here and there was nothing that would make me change my mind. Not even Kin.

"I won't ask you again," he said, agreeing with what I was thinking. "Can you do that? Can you let it go?"

He turned away, so that I saw only his profile. Then he looked back at me. He seemed like he was in pain. "I wish it could have worked," he whispered.

I leaned forward, put my arms around him and held him to me. "I know. I do too. I wish I wasn't sick for you, Kin."

"It's not about being sick with me. It's about you being sick at all."

I started to say something, but he squeezed his hands around me.

"I wouldn't want it either," he mumbled into my collarbone. "To live forever . . . I wouldn't want it. You sounded so frightened, and I didn't even really stop to think about why." He took a breath, and his lips brushed the skin of my neck. "I didn't know what I was asking of you, Luca. I didn't even consider how . . ." He swallowed. "How bad it would be. But I see it now. I get it."

A tremor ran through me, a shaking that was relief and nervousness and just that emptying of adrenaline that happens when the worry you've been holding on to for so long finally leaves. I was still scared.

I knew that this thing wouldn't have left his mind yet, because as bad as the cure was, and as much as he recognized that, it could have been an answer. But I was so happy to hear him say those things. The release of it made me weak, drained, but in the best way. It was awful, that this cure had been in reach and I'd pushed it away. But Kin was back. That was the thing I'd wanted, needed, most. And his return meant that maybe not everything was quite so wrong after all. Like maybe I could live with the rest of it.

I pressed my hands to his shoulder blades. "Kin. I don't think it would have worked, anyway."

He looked up at me. "Are you trying to make me feel better?"

I was. I definitely was. But I kind of believed it too. I couldn't take the risk, couldn't chance that there was a slim possibility that a legend that no one had ever heard of coming true, actually was true. But I didn't really believe it. "Kind of," I admitted. "But I think it was . . . so unlikely. No one's immortal. We've never heard of anyone like that, not in the fey world, not with the yokai." I waited, and he nodded. "And . . . Kin, your mother is fading. Her magic is going. And what's in your veins . . ." I shrugged. "It's a mystery. So even if I had taken her scales, or yours . . ." I shook my head and watched him, waiting.

"You don't think it would have worked at all. For one reason or another."

I pushed my fingers into his hair, pulling out his hair tie and spreading the black strands over his shoulders. "I don't know. I still wouldn't want to try. But I think maybe not."

He stared up at me. "Would you have come and told me that to make me come back?" His words were slow, measured.

I bit my lip, then shook my head. "I needed you to allow me the choice. I needed you to come to me and tell me it was all right for me to choose." Even when I'd been desperate, even when I would have done anything, something in me had stopped me, kept me from racing right back to his house. And I knew it was this. I needed to know that he would let me determine what happened in my own life.

He pushed his face against me. "It was your choice. And my choice to come back or not."

"You came back."

His squeezed his hands down on my hip bones. "I just want you near me, no matter how long it is. I wish it could be long."

I rubbed my thumb over his cheek.

"I wish it could. But that's what I want. I wasn't going to ask again. If this was going to take you away from me faster, I don't want it either. And it was. Wasn't it?"

"I walked away."

He nodded. "That was hard, Luca." He swallowed. "That was . . . Don't do that again."

I pulled him against me. "I'm sorry." I meant it, with everything in me. And he held me tight to him, like he knew it and believed me.

For a while we just stayed there like that, me standing, him sitting, arms around each other. I didn't want to let go. I thought about what Saben had said, how she'd practically bullied me into admitting what I felt for Kin. I didn't want him to have to pry it out of me like that. I wanted him to know, even if it was too fast, even if it was too soon. I just wanted to tell him. In case. Just in case.

"Saben told me something interesting," I said hesitantly, not really sure, even now, how to say this.

"Mm?" His voice was muffled by my shirt. I could feel the heat of his breath.

I moved my hands, pushing them through his hair, brushing his bangs back from his face. "She told me that I was in love with you. And that you were in love with me."

He turned his head, just a little, just enough that he could kiss the inside of my wrist. "I am."

It was that easy, after all. That simple. "Me too."

That night, I nestled against Kin in bed, my head on his chest. He was running his fingers over my head, patting me like I was a cat.

"Where did you get this hair?" he asked, his voice sleepy.

"Hmm?"

"It's soft." He flexed his fingers. "I want my hands in it all the time."

I laughed. "It can't decide what color it wants to be. Too light. Too dark. It doesn't look like anything but a mess."

I heard his head move on the pillow. "I like it, Luca. I always have."

I closed my eyes. I spread my fingers farther across his stomach, trying to touch as much of him as I could. Every time I breathed in, I could smell the saltiness of his skin. I opened my eyes and watched my hand, studied the movement as I curled it into a loose fist and dragged it across the tops of his hips.

"Stop it." His hand came down and caught my wrist. "I'll want you again."

I flattened my palm against him. "So want me."

He rolled in one motion, so he hovered over me, his face a few inches from mine. His body pressed into me. He leaned down the rest of the way and kissed me, long and slow, like he wanted to know all the ways our lips went together. His hands slipped around my shoulders, tugging me closer. I slid my palms down the back of his neck, down the center line of his shoulders, and he arched against me. Our hands moved slowly over each other, reacquainting, like after our short absence from each other we were remembering the lines of bones and the curves of waists, how it felt to run a finger down the smooth plane of his shoulder or my neck.

When he drew back, I gathered his hair in my hands and moved it behind him so I could see his face. "Is this okay?"

He looked down at me and brushed his knuckles across my cheek. "I said it was. I promised."

"But..."

"Stop trying to talk me out of it, Luca." He smiled a little to show he knew why I needed to keep asking. I wanted to dig until I couldn't anymore. I wanted to turn the problem over and over until it was smooth, all the sharp edges gone, and I could hold it without it hurting, without fear that it would come back and stab me. "I saw the look on your face when you were standing there telling me you didn't want it." He bent and kissed my throat, then straightened again. "I've never seen you look like that. Never. I knew it right then, how wrong it was. It just took me a while to realize that I knew it. I just wanted you to give in and let me try to make you better." His palms smoothed over my shoulders. "But I know why you won't. It isn't right. It would be more wrong than ..." He stilled, suddenly, his whole body going tight. He took a deep breath and closed his eyes. I ran my hand over the side of his face. His lips twitched in something like a grimace but he didn't say anything. I moved so our foreheads touched. I could feel him shaking.

"Than letting you go," he finished, the words not much more than a breath.

I closed my own eyes and breathed out. I was relieved and hurt at the same time. Kin's hands tightened against my back.

"I'm not leaving."

He nodded. I let him rest against me. Let him gather himself. I hated myself for making him feel this. For doing this to him. But I knew, too, that it wasn't my fault.

He rolled onto his side, taking me with him, keeping me close. He opened his eyes. "I'm sorry."

I shook my head. We stared at each other. Our gaze held and held. I'd never experienced anything more intense in my life. I could feel him breathing against me, feel the rise and fall of him. I moved my hand down, ran it along the length of his body. I shrugged my shoulder, just a twitch, a question. He nodded.

He pulled me closer, until our skin met everywhere it could. We kissed, and then we let our lips touch while we breathed, my breath pooling in him, and his in me. His fingertips smoothed over my body, ran hot and sure down my sides and my legs and my arms and my chest and my face. I could feel the blood rushing in my heart, flooding through all the tiny veins in my body in response to his touch and his presence and the idea that he was here for me, wanting me. I knew Kin could feel it too, could tell what he did to me, in the slightly desperate way I reached for him, could see it in the flush spreading down my neck, across my chest, could feel it in the heat of my skin under his palms. In return, I saw the same things in him. The bright, rich color of his scales and his skin, saturated with his own want. The darkness of his eyes, pupils blown wide, steady on me. The way his fingers skittered across my ribs. The same desperation to be closer, to be together. The same desire. It was all right there, obvious, in him and in me.

And I felt so alive.

Dear Reader,

Thank you for reading Eli Lang's *Half*!

We know your time is precious and you have many, many entertainment options, so it means a lot that you've chosen to spend your time reading. We really hope you enjoyed it.

We'd be honored if you'd consider posting a review—good or bad—on sites like **Amazon, Barnes & Noble, Kobo, Goodreads, Twitter, Facebook, Tumblr,** and your blog or website. We'd also be honored if you told your friends and family about this book. Word of mouth is a book's lifeblood!

For more information on upcoming releases, author interviews, blog tours, contests, giveaways, and more, please sign up for our weekly, spam-free newsletter and visit us around the web:

Newsletter: tinyurl.com/RiptideSignup
Twitter: twitter.com/RiptideBooks
Facebook: facebook.com/RiptidePublishing
Goodreads: tinyurl.com/RiptideOnGoodreads
Tumblr: riptidepublishing.tumblr.com

Thank you so much for Reading the Rainbow!

RiptidePublishing.com

ACKNOWLEDGMENTS

A thousand thank-yous to my parents. I'd get mushy about it, but then we'd all be embarrassed. Many heartfelt thanks to Alexis Hall—without your immense help, support, and encouragement, this book would never have seen the light of day. Lots of thanks also to Sarah Lyons and everyone at Riptide for being wonderful. And Ryan—thank you for keeping my mind steady, even when you didn't know you were doing that. Tons of thanks to the Blanketeers, for hand-holding, support, advice, assistance, and overall awesomeness. I adore all of you. And thank you to my friends, especially everyone in Group—I'm so lucky to have gotten to know you.

ABOUT THE AUTHOR

Eli Lang is a writer and drummer. She's played in rock bands, worked on horse farms, and had jobs in libraries, where she spent most of her time reading every book she could get her hands on. She can fold a nearly perfect paper crane and knows how to tune a snare drum. She still buys stuffed animals because she feels bad if they're left alone in the store, believes cinnamon buns should always be eaten warm, can tell you more than you ever wanted to know about the tardigrade, and has a book collection that's reaching frightening proportions. She lives in Arizona with far too many pets.

Website: leftoversushi.com
Facebook: facebook.com/EliLangAuthor
Twitter: twitter.com/eli__lang
Goodreads: goodreads.com/eli_lang

Enjoy more stories like
Half
at RiptidePublishing.com!

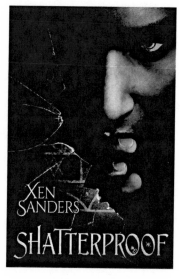

Rogue Magic
ISBN: 978-1-62649-528-9

Shatterproof
ISBN: 978-1-62649-460-2

Earn Bonus Bucks!
Earn 1 Bonus Buck for each dollar you spend. Find out how at
RiptidePublishing.com/news/bonus-bucks.

Win Free Ebooks for a Year!
Pre-order coming soon titles directly through our site and you'll
receive one entry into a drawing for a chance to win free books for
a year! Get the details at RiptidePublishing.com/contests.

CPSIA information can be obtained
at www.ICGtesting.com
Printed in the USA
LVOW11s1046290117
522510LV00003B/584/P